'Yes,' Rose said. 'I
strong, and it is Scottis

'Some day I will tell y
in me. But it seems alw
having an interesting
Where is it you must go in the Lawnmarket?'

'To Brodie's Close. To the house of Deacon Brodie.'

Why was it that the night became a little darker, a little colder, and the noisy bustle of the town seemed to recede into a strange hush? There was a distant chill in the atmosphere now, both outside the carriage and within it.

'To the house of Deacon Brodie,' Cameron Kyle repeated slowly and heavily.

'Yes, to Miss Jean Brodie. I am to be her companion.'

The silence went on so long that Rose trembled with excitement and fear.

'Is there anything wrong?'

'No, there is nothing wrong, Rose.' Cameron smiled immediately, too immediately to convince her. He had been debating something in his mind, she was sure of it, before he shook his head like that and answered her so quickly. 'Of course not. I was thinking of my sister. When she hears how I have spent the afternoon, she will insist on calling upon you.'

But that was not what he had been thinking at all . . .

Inga Dunbar was educated in Dumfriesshire, at the Academy and then at Edinburgh University and College of Education. She became a Head Teacher, living and working extensively throughout Scotland, from Edinburgh in the east to Ayrshire in the west, from Gretna in the south to the Shetland Isles in the far north. She now lives in Aberdeen. Upon her retirement in 1983 she turned to her life-long ambition—to write stories. *Rose Royale* is her second Masquerade Historical Romance.

ROSE ROYALE

INGA DUNBAR

MILLS & BOON LIMITED
15–16 BROOK'S MEWS
LONDON W1A 1DR

First published in Great Britain 1986 by Mills & Boon Limited

© Inga Dunbar 1986

Australian copyright 1986 Philippine copyright 1986 This edition 1986

ISBN 0 263 75373 5

For Charlie, my husband

Set in 10 on 10½ pt Linotron Times 04–0486–77,100

Photoset by Rowland Phototypesetting Limited Bury St Edmunds, Suffolk Made and printed in Great Britain by Cox & Wyman Limited, Reading

AUTHOR'S
NOTE

THE HEART of historic Edinburgh lies in the Royal Mile. Walk its length some sunny afternoon, put out a hand to touch the walls so little changed over the centuries and you are back to the flickering darkness of a winter's evening in 1788. Then Deacon Brodie was out upon his 'night business', his eyes glittering behind his mask, with his dark-lantern in one hand, his bunch of keys in the other, and his gang of thieves and adventurers at his side.

But by day he was once again the respected businessman, Deacon of Wrights and Town Councillor everyone knew: the grandson of Brodie, Laird of Milntown, who became the capital's oldest Writer to the Signet; son of Francis, a prosperous cabinetmaker under the guidance of William Adam, the architect, who in 1740 had married Cecil, the daughter of another Edinburgh lawyer who had come from the north-east of Scotland.

The story of Deacon Brodie's life—shocking, tragic and yet thrillingly exciting—has been the inspiration of many writers, not least Robert Louis Stevenson, who was fascinated by the Deacon's disintegration of personality, and in *The Strange Case of Dr Jekyll and Mr Hyde* took as its theme the retribution that follows hypocrisy.

Retribution followed swiftly for Deacon Brodie when Mr Williamson, the King's Messenger for Scotland, dragged him back in chains to Edinburgh on 17 July 1788, to be tried in August and condemned to hang on 1 October on the very gallows he had himself designed. Even when from his castle in the north-east of Scotland Brodie of Brodie appealed to the Secretary of State that his kinsman's sentence be Botany Bay rather than the gallows, there was no reprieve.

To tell the tale again is another opportunity to see and hear the people who really lived it—young Walter Scott, who became Sir Walter Scott; Mr Creech in his bookshop; Lunardi floating overhead in his hot air balloon; Miss Jean Brodie and her sister Jacobina, married to Matthew Sheriffs; Brown and Ainslie, the accomplices who went free; Smith, who hung alongside the Deacon —and Lord Braxfield, who had the last word (in broad Scots) at another famous trial over which he presided, that of the reformer Gerald:

Mr Gerald—'My lord, all great men have been reformers. Even our Saviour was one.'
Lord Braxfield—'Muckle he made of that! He was hingit!'

And yet, did the great 'Braxie' have the very last word of all at Deacon Brodie's trial? Henry Raeburn never painted William Brodie. There is no memorial to him in Princes Street Gardens or the Royal Mile of Edinburgh. But when his friends cut him down from the gallows and rushed his body to Michael Henderson and the French doctor in the Grassmarket, and afterwards buried him quietly in the churchyard near George's Square, his coffin was suspiciously light.

CHAPTER
ONE

ROSE CAME out upon the top step of the little forestair still lost in thought, her kerchief in her hand. What was it doing in her hand, and not round her shoulders, she wondered vaguely? She must put it on, for without it she was not properly dressed . . . But still she stood there staring at it, her mind a thousand miles away, and not in Longcakes Lane at all.

'Hey there, Rose! Rose Barbour! Come down here and give us a kiss!'

'Go on, Rosie, show a leg! Go on . . .'

She smiled faintly as a large hand seized the two apprentice bakers by the scruffs of their necks, knocked their heads together and dragged them back in through the bakehouse window.

She was not in the mood for their catcalls and their banter, not today. Knotting the kerchief absently round her shoulders, she tucked its points into the low square neckline of her dress. Her hands were trembling. But then, they had been trembling ever since she had got out of bed. She could not seem to stop them.

The shock of it all was forcing her mind to function on two levels. On the one hand she saw that everything in Longcakes Lane was just the same as it always was. Down in the courtyard the grassy weeds were even greyer, more flour-choked than ever, since the bakers had to work twice as hard on Saturdays to bake enough bread for Sundays too.

And this was a Saturday. Saturday, the seventh day of September, 1787, to be exact, and the clock on the tower of the old Newhaven Kirk was chiming seven, although neither Rose nor anyone else living in the upstairs

houses of the Lane needed any reminding of the time of
day.

For two hours now there had been the ceaseless clatter
of heavy oven doors opening and closing from the bake-
houses on the ground floors below, and the thudding
of iron trays on the long deal tables as the loaves were
set to cool under open floury windows. Dusty billows
of steam pervaded everything, obscuring even the sky,
along with the tantalising smell of fresh-baked bread.

Rose saw it all, smelled it all, and yet none of it
registered, for on the other hand, on the other level of
her consciousness, she was still in her bedchamber
where the accident had happened less than an hour ago.
Less than an hour ago? How could she believe it? For if
she faced the truth, the small incident was really the
climax of burying her head in the sand for years, of
refusing to sort out the reality of her memories from the
dreams of her past.

She was too quick. Aunt Bea had always said so. It
must be true, for as she had dashed out of bed, throwing
back the covers, there had been that soft sickening crash
on the bare wooden floor.

'Oh, *no!*' Rose said. 'Not you, Poo Pay!'

To any other girl of seventeen, soon to be eighteen, a
broken doll might not have been such a tragedy. But to
Rose, as she knelt by the side of her bed with the tiny
spotted dress crumbling into dust in her hands, and the
bleached china face smashed into smithereens, it was
worse even than that, for it severed the last link with her
mother and her early childhood—whatever, wherever
that had been . . . The pathetic little pile of pink threads
and sawdust became suddenly blurred as she thought of
Mama, and then tried her best not to think of Mama, as
she had been trying not to think of her for the last ten
years.

But in spite of herself the tears spilled over and ran
down her cheeks for a long time before she squared her

shoulders, got up from her knees, and in a determined fashion splashed her face with cold water. Then she donned first her white lace-trimmed under-petticoat, then her ankle-length red and white striped outer flannel petticoat, and last of all her overdress of pale green muslin, looped up round her hips with a string in the hem. It was only when she turned to leave her room that her eyes caught a little gleam in the rubble on the floor.

She bent over the remains of her doll again, touched the glinting metal, and drew out a chain of gold. A little bauble like a tiny birdcage dangled from it. That was just like Mama, Rose thought despairingly—a fleeting picture of a lady in pale blue silk, her fair hair piled up elaborately, before her mind's eye—when from behind the chain a golden coin rolled out, teetered on the wooden floorboard for a few seconds, and then fell over on its side and lay still and glittering, and brand new.

She could not bear to look at it. She thrust it deep into the pocket of her flannel petticoat, and her fingers closed over the other coin already there, Aunt Bea's small silver shilling.

Yesterday evening, sitting before the fire, Mistress Barbour had got quite excited as she read the *Caledonian Mercury*, four pages of closely printed news.

'You know, my dear, that tomorrow marks the start of the Leith Races?'

Rose smiled. Aunt Bea could not resist her little flutters on the horses.

'And there is a horse here, in the Novices' Race, called The Moroccan. Oh, Rose, do listen to this,' and she read out, '"No dark horse this, although as black as the Ace of Spades. He runs like an arrow shot straight from a bow." What do you think of *that*, dear?'

'That the gentlemen who write the newspapers are very clever, Aunt Bea.'

'Just you tell Uncle George tomorrow morning that this whole shilling is on The Moroccan's nose. You will run over to the Turf Inn for me, won't you, dear?' Mistress Barbour said anxiously.

'You know I will. Don't I always?' Rose smiled fondly at the small plump figure opposite. 'But what if your horse does not come in first? You will lose your shilling.'

'Oh, George Abercromby will cover me, don't you fret. He will have studied the form as well,' her aunt said grandly. 'I think you should go early in the morning, dear, and get my bet in first.'

'It will be in first, never fear,' Rose assured her, smiling at the old familiar gleam in Aunt Bea's eyes, always there when she scented a winner.

It was the same every Friday evening, Rose thought, trying to subdue the laughter sparkling in her brown eyes, wide and clear under her red-gold hair. Aunt Bea did what she called her 'studying form', which consisted of reading down the lists of horses and picking out a name she felt she had some connection with, however far-fetched. Only by the purest chance did she ever win, but at least she always got her shilling back, for when George Abercromby came to supper, as he did every Sunday, he regularly made up some excuse to see that she did.

'Then let us drink one last glass of lemonade before we go to bed,' her aunt said, stretching her toes comfortably upon the footstool in front of the dying embers. 'And let us hope that no poor soul will need my help tonight.'

Rose smiled across at the most popular and most respected nurse in the whole of Edinburgh and for miles around it, even if she *was* English, and raised her glass.

'To The Moroccan, then. What else made you choose him, Aunt Bea, apart from finding his name in the news-sheet?'

'Oh, it is such a lucky name, dearie! I just feel it!' Mistress Barbour said enthusiastically. 'That last child I brought into the world the other day was in Morocco's Land in the Royal Mile of Edinburgh. And, by a strange coincidence, it was to Morocco that my poor Herbert made one of his last, and his luckiest, trips as a sea-captain. He made a great deal of money in Morocco.'

Dear Aunt Bea, Rose thought now as she ran down the thirteen stone steps of the forestair. She hoped for her sake that The Moroccan could only win. Not that her aunt needed the money.

'It is not the money,' she would tell Rose. 'You must never worry about money in this house. Herbert left me quite comfortably off, and on top of that I am well paid for my services—too well paid, many a time, I am afraid. But many people insist on it, when they see their nearest and dearest recover from serious illnesses.'

Herbert Barbour had met and married her in Newcastle, and brought her back to live in Newhaven, where twenty years later he had left her well provided for when he was lost at sea, more than able to move away even into Edinburgh, into the most fashionable part of the town, had she chosen.

But Mistress Beattie Barbour did not choose to do anything of the sort. She salted away her money and stayed where she was among the friends that were hers for life, now, among the fisherfolk, happy and healthy in the clean sea air with the child she had adopted as her own. Besides, there was George Abercromby to con-sider . . . Mistress Barbour considered him minutely and very tenderly. She had been doing so for years.

No, Rose thought, it was just that Aunt Bea loved the excitement of the horse races, and she, in common with every other one who had ever had cause to be grateful to her—and they were many—vowed that in whatever way she could she would repay her some day.

Because, of course, it could not last much longer, this happy childhood in Longcakes Lane. Rose bit her lip thoughtfully as she considered her future. She should be starting to earn some money now, at least for her keep, although never had such a suggestion been made to her.

The question was, how?

Aunt Bea had never brought her up to do any work except around the house. She had not even let her do too much of that. She had insisted that she was a lady, and herself taught her to read and write and count, and impressed on her that she should not speak too much about it in Newhaven, nor about the fine dresses and underwear in her closets.

'When in Rome it is wise to do as the Romans do,' she said, and she and Rose dressed every weekday in the colourful and picturesque dress of the Newhaven fisherwomen, although Rose seriously doubted if Aunt Bea would know one end of a fish from the other, and it was just as well that Pansy Paris came every day to cook and to clean.

Rose sped out through the narrow archway at the top of the Lane and out on to the wider path of the Main Street, its cobblestones glistening with the dampness of early morning mixed with the salt from the sea-breezes of the Firth of Forth, and now the day burst upon her in a blue and white glory of sky and sea.

With a lift of her heart she looked out over the familiar semicircle of Newhaven's little harbour, where a few boats were already tied up alongside, and further out to where the gulls swooped and screeched raucously as they escorted more fishing boats in with their catches.

The fisherwomen, thirty or forty of them, were busy on the quay in various stages of welcoming their men and throwing the herring off the boats and into their creels. The Newhaven coach was rumbling away with the first women loaded up on its journey to Edinburgh, to the Tron Kirk in the Royal Mile, where, within half an hour they would be selling their wares and shouting, 'Caller herrin', Caller herrin',' and then all the ladies would send out their servants to buy the fresh fish.

Nobody paid any attention to Rose as she passed by, as familiar a figure to the fisherfolk as one of their own daughters, with her gilt curls bouncing off her back as she ran. She headed east until the road dwindled into a track through the dunes, and she was forced to slow down.

Inchkeith sparkled blackly in the blue waters as she began to climb steadily, her feet sinking a little in the yielding sand. She kept her eyes fixed on the Rock, as if seeking its unchanging solidity, now that the very foundations of her own life seemed to have crumbled away along with her doll.

She must have been very young when she got it, only an infant. And yet she could still remember that day, when Mama had given her it and told her it was called 'Poo Pay'. In another brief flash she could even remember the carpet she had sat on to play with the new doll and her little dog with its long golden hair. It was a blue carpet, with pretty pink patterns on it and pale green flowers, and a man lay on a couch under some furs, with a very pale face. She thought it was her Papa, but she was too excited about the doll to remember clearly. All she could recall after that was climbing aboard a big ship with Mama and her doll, and then no more until the ride in the coach.

Perhaps she would never have remembered any of that terrible journey at all, had it not been so long and so tedious and so cold, and if Mama had not looked so sad. The sun had gone down, and still they were bumping along in the coach, when she had been wakened out of her sleep with a tremendous bang and a searing pain in her leg. She knew it was bleeding, even in the dark, but she could not find Mama, and could not stand up to go and look for her. She just had to lie still on the road among the debris of the coach.

It seemed to Rose, looking back now, that they had always lived with the gipsies who picked her and Mama up and nursed them back to health. At first they were happy, happy days, roaming the byways and the hedgerows of country lanes in the leisurely caravans, and playing with the other children and their lurcher dogs and piebald ponies.

Best of all Rose loved Grandmam Maddy and Granfer Nathan. They told her stories every night around the fire, while they ate hedgehogs baked in clay and little potato cakes. Under the stars, Nathan told her about animals, horses especially, and Maddy taught her the secrets of the wild herbs and plants, and how they could cure so many illnesses.

They were the King and the Queen of the tribe, and Rose knew she was very lucky to live with them in their *vardo*. It was the biggest *vardo* and the best, the most gaily painted and the most glittering. It was called a Churchey, because it was rounded over the door like a church.

Nathan kept patching up the woodwork of it, and Maddy went behind him with her paint-pots, touching up the red cloverleaves and the pink roses, and the castle on the door. Then she would polish the three brass rims on the black enamel chimney, which Rose knew was made out of three old tins.

And inside it was like a palace, with frilly curtains and pictures and ornamented dishes—even books. Neither Nathan nor Maddy could read, but Mama could, and every day while they were recovering she would read out stories from them.

But Mama had not stayed long in the royal *vardo*. Before she was even fully restored to health, she went to live in the next caravan with Uncle Leon, who was not a real uncle at all, but the elder son of Grandmam Maddy and Granfer Nathan, who did not approve of the move in the least, although Rose did not understand why. Leon was very bold and very handsome, with black curly hair and a flashing smile.

Rose liked Uncle Benny better. He took time to talk to her, and whittle little wooden dolls for her, and his wife Albina was so jolly, always laughing, and she made the best honey-balls in the whole encampment. Rose felt sorry for the *gorgio* children, shut up in houses, and never knowing what freedom was.

It had all gone on in this fashion for several years, until one terrible night. The gipsies were having a party round the large fire within the circle of all the caravans, because the Lee tribe had come to visit them for a few days.

Rose could remember every single detail of that night. She only wished she could forget. The music had wakened her, and she had got out of her bed to sit on the top step of the *vardo* with her doll to watch the dancing. And oh, how they danced! The music throbbed and swelled, and the fire blazed up in a shower of orange sparks. They were reflected in Rose's eyes as she searched for Mama, and finally caught sight of her in the middle of a crowd of gipsy women.

It was always easy to pick out Mama with her long yellow hair, which once was dressed in golden ringlets, and now hung carelessly in wild ripples down her back. Poor Mama, whose slim body had become so thick round her middle! Why did she not take better care of herself? And why did Leon go less and less often to her caravan recently? The dance ended in a burst of stamping, and clapping in a wild staccato and another rain of sparks from the fire, and she almost lost sight of Mama. Then, through the smoke, she saw that all the women were gathered round her mother as if to protect her, as if to shield her from something they did not want her to see.

From her vantage-point on the top step of the *vardo*, Rose saw Leon as he stole away behind the ring of caravans into the woods, hand in hand with Katina, the beautiful one—as beautiful with her apricot skin and her pomegranate lips as Leon was magnificent in his dark swarthiness—and somehow knew even at seven years old that this should not be happening. Not to Mama . . . And it would lead to terrible trouble.

How long was it after that? Days or weeks? In Rose's

childish mind she did not understand any of it, except that Mama cried so much, and kissed her so much with the tears running down her face, until the day came when she was icy calm and said that they must leave the camp that night, and join the stage-coach travelling north from London.

Mama took her doll away and stitched and sewed her, when there was not a hole to be seen in her, not in her rag body or even in her pink spotted dress.

'Look after pretty Poo Pay, cherry. She is all you may have, now,' she kept saying. Mama often called her 'cherry'. It was a funny pet-name.

After that there was the long ride in the stage-coach, the nightmare bumping and churning through the darkness once again, with the even more terrifying moaning of Mama, until all of a sudden she had screamed up to the driver,

'*Mon Dieu! Mon Dieu!* Where is this place? Where are we?'

'Edinburgh,' was the reply.

'Then make haste to a midwife, for God's sake,' Mama sobbed.

The next thing Rose remembered was Mama lying on white sheets, while she cowered in a corner, and a cheerful plump lady ran back and forth to the fire where large black kettles steamed and hissed. In some part of the room there must have been a bed with curtains to pull round it, and she must have slept in it, for the plump lady woke her up. There was complete silence now in the small empty kitchen, and the lady's cheeks were pale, and her face drawn with crying. She lifted Rose up in her strong arms. 'Oh, my poor little lassie, all alone now in this terrible world,' she said sadly, and took her away to another room, to a warm bed, and oblivion.

It was years later, when Rose was growing up and understood these things, that she spoke to her aunt about it.

'Did Mama come to you to be delivered of a child, Aunt Bea?'

'I delivered a child,' Mistress Barbour said sadly, 'but he was already dead. Your Mama was such a delicate little thing, and the boy was so big, that the struggle was too much for them both. Poor mite, he had a shock of black hair on his head, I remember.'

'Yes. I thought so . . .'

'Your Papa, Rose—I have never liked to question you too closely, dear. I have not wanted to upset you. Was he black-haired too?'

'I think it was my Papa who died when I was little more than a baby. Mama closed the curtains. It was in a big house, and the curtains were very long and blue, like the walls, and all along the edges of them were flowers with three petals, like feathers. Then Mama took me on a journey. The coach crashed, and some gipsies took us to live with them. Mama lived with Leon. He had black hair.'

Mistress Barbour looked sad. 'Where were you going on your journey, Rose?'

'I never knew. Mama did not tell me.'

'Well, it was the driver of the London to Edinburgh coach who brought you here, since I was the only midwife he knew. It put another two miles on his journey to come out here to Newhaven with you, for his finishing stage was in the White Horse Close near the foot of the Royal Mile, but your poor Mama was so very ill he could not have the heart to leave her. The poor lady was so frail and so pretty, and you are so like her, Rose—in the face, I mean. Thank God you have grown up to be taller and stronger, although, like her, far too slender for my liking.'

'Oh, Aunt Bea!' Rose laughed. 'You would rather have me like a barrel?'

'Have you been happy, living here with me, Rose? That is the main thing, next to your health. After all, I was a complete stranger to you, although you called me Aunt from the first.'

'How can you think you must ask me that?' Rose cried, flinging her arms round Mistress Barbour's stout little frame. 'Of course I am happy! I love you, and Uncle George, too. You are the two best friends I have in the world.'

'Ah yes, George,' her aunt sighed. 'He had been here that first night you arrived in this house, he and two other friends, and we had been playing whist all evening as you see us doing still, from time to time, But in those days he always brought a tappit hen with him, and set it in the middle of the table before we began, and we all drank a glass or two while we played.'

'A tappit hen? What on earth is a tappit hen, Aunt Bea?'

'It is a two-quart ale-pot with a small measure, out of which the company help themselves. Your uncle uses them in the Turf Inn, and the customers make up their own bill with chalk upon the table, although, of course, he did not expect our friends to do that here.'

There was a pause, and then to Rose's consternation, her aunt burst into tears.

'Oh, Rose, I had drunk a glass of ale that evening! I have wondered ever since if that was why I could not help your Mama as much as I might have done! At any rate, I have not touched strong drink from that day to this, and that is the reason why I do not allow it in this house.'

'One glass of ale would not have had such a serious effect, Aunt Bea. You have not been worrying all these years since about that?'

But her aunt continued to sob.

'Your Mama did manage to speak, you know, Rose. She did tell me your name and hers, but she spoke so low that I could not catch them. It is a dreadful thing that you are going through your life without even knowing your real name, Rosie. I feel it is all my fault . . .'

Rose made up her mind that she would never bring up this painful subject again.

'I am afraid that my Mama brought all her troubles on herself. But what is wrong with Rose Barbour?' she asked gently. 'The name you gave me is very pretty.'

'Perhaps those gipsies would know,' Aunt Bea said. 'Do you remember what tribe it was?'

'No,' Rose admitted. 'But I would know it if I heard it, I feel sure.'

'Then all we can do is pray that we hear of them, I suppose,' Aunt Bea sighed.

By this time Rose had reached the top of the long slow incline, and there over the other side lay Leith, its sands stretching flatly for miles. A damp little sea-breeze tugged at her hair, and she unknotted the kerchief from round her shoulders and tied it over her head.

She would never allow her hair to become the tangled mass Mama's had become. Long ago she had asked Aunt Bea to brush it into ringlets, and she had worn it like that ever since, tied high with a ribbon at the crown, and smooth and neat around her face. It was not easy to achieve, and it was her only vanity.

The path left the dunes now, and wound through yellow gorse bushes and tough short grass. In the distance she could see the Turf Inn. But first she would have to pass a carriage, drawn off to the side. Not far from it stood a gentleman leaning on the wall bordering the Swifts, the long rough stretches of grass beyond. He must be watching the horses on their early morning gallop.

As she drew nearer, Rose could not help but admire the elegant proportions of his figure, from the crispness of his hair, which no amount of tying it back like that in a severe little tail could hide its fair crinkles, to the breadth of his shoulders and right down the lean long lines of him. It all suggested power, subtly restrained, and her feelings of admiration became charged with a tinge of exhilaration at such a thought.

Had he been wearing rags, they could not have disguised the grace and strength of his spare frame. But as it was, in his donkey brown cutaway coat in the height of fashion, smoothed to perfection over his broad shoulders, and his buckskin breeches fitted so tightly to his legs under brown leather riding-boots, polished like a chestnut, he was nothing short of imposing.

Still, he did not turn round when she approached, and she wondered if perhaps he had not heard her step on the grass for the thunder of horses' hooves. Her eyes followed his, and immediately fastened on the light bay with the blond mane and tail. It was not very tall; in fact it was small-boned, but infinitely graceful in every movement of its body and delicate legs. And it could run! How it could run! Rose could not take her eyes off it.

'Oh, what a beautiful horse he is!' she burst out involuntarily.

The man did not jump in surprise at the sound of her voice at his side. He did not even glance down at her. Suddenly she realised he had seen her coming all along. He was not a man to be easily taken by surprise.

'Which horse?'

'Oh, the bay. He is beautiful, is he not?'

'*She* is beautiful,' he agreed.

She looked up into his face. 'She?' she repeated. 'Do you know her name?' and was immediately arrested by the startling blueness of his eyes. It took her so much by surprise that she seemed rooted to the spot, while she watched different expressions coming and going in their vivid depths—appraisal, a faint shock, the flare of admiration even, before it was swiftly hidden—and to her amazement a little frown, the merest line, formed between his resolute eyebrows.

Rose was not accustomed to even the slightest suggestion of disapproval. If it came to that, she was not accustomed to strangers, either. As this thought struck her, she recognised how disgracefully she was behaving, actually to address a strange man at all.

What on earth would Aunt Bea say, after all her careful training, if she only knew? But mercifully her aunt was not here, and what her eye had not seen her heart would not grieve, Rose decided, with crimsoning cheeks and tightened lips. She could actually feel the sparks fly off her red hair and smoulder under her kerchief, and her sherry brown eyes took on a dangerous gleam. She had only asked the name of a horse! How dare this man suggest, even by a look, that she was accosting him?

'Pray excuse me, sir,' she said icily, her cheeks burning with indignation.

At that he glanced down at her briefly, then started; after a long, lingering look, the ghost of a smile touched his lips.

'What for?' he asked coolly. 'You asked me the name of the bay filly. That should be enough, surely, to prove to any man that it would take a young lady of some breeding to recognise another?'

What was he saying? Was he, by any chance, endeavouring to pacify her? Or was this some further insult? Rose preferred the latter diagnosis, even when she raised her eyes and saw that he was smiling now, a broad smile which showed off his attractively uneven white teeth. She suspected that she was being honoured, that he did not often smile.

But it was too late, now. He had thrown down the gauntlet, had he not?

'You must forgive me, sir,' she repeated, and turned to walk away.

'Wait!' He touched her arm. 'Don't go! Do you not want to know the name of the horse? It is Rose Royale.'

'Thank you,' she said, shaking off his hand. 'Good day to you.'

'Cameron!' drawled a feminine voice, and Rose saw that two ladies had descended from the carriage and were coming towards them, blocking her path. 'We thought we must get out and take a closer look at a fishwife, since we have so little opportunity. The servants usually deal with them.'

It was the smaller of the two ladies who spoke. She was short and slim, with carefully arranged black curls under a wonderful concoction of feathers, and her dress was of a heavy red brocade. She was like a bird of paradise.

Rose regarded her steadily out of angry, unblinking eyes. Her colour had heightened a little. She had no idea of the impact she made in her colourful clothes, with the rebellious golden-red fronds of hair escaping from the kerchief and curling round her cheeks.

'Oh,' said the second lady—tall, fair, and more plainly dressed—'how appropriate your Newhaven costume is, my dear, against this background of blue and white sea! It is we who are quite out of place, Cornelia. Do you live in Newhaven, or here in Leith?'

The tall fair lady had spoken kindly, and her blue eyes were so like those of the gentleman that Rose could not mistake that she must be related to him. But she was not to be appeased, and certainly not after two insults, now.

'I live in Newhaven,' she said tautly.

'Then what is she doing in Leith, looking at horses?' Cornelia laughed carelessly. 'What can a fishwife know about horses? That is very fishy, is it not?' She laughed again at her own play on words.

It dawned upon Rose that this lady did not want her in this company, and in particular, not engaged in conversation with the young man. In fact, that was why she had taken the trouble to get out of the carriage.

'Oh, Cornelia!' the tall lady protested.

'On the contrary, my dear Cornelia,' said the gentleman quietly. 'She can certainly pick out a horse.'

Rose fixed her eyes on Cornelia's feathers, sadly

drooped now in the damp sea air, and struggled for composure.

'Fishy?' she said. 'But does that not imply dishonesty? There is the world of difference, madam, between the honest fisherwomen, the ladies of Newhaven, and the fishwives I understand are to be found in all classes of society.'

'*Touché!*' the young man laughed, while Cornelia had the grace to look a little abashed. 'I like a lady of spirit, on two legs or on four!' His eyes were frankly admiring, now, when Rose curtsied shortly to them all.

'Pray excuse me,' she said coldly, and walked away.

'But where are you going?' he called after her. 'We can take you in the carriage!'

But Rose pretended she did not hear, and broke into a run. It was not often that she had had the occasion to speak to people of Edinburgh society, unless to her minister in the Kirk on Sundays or when he came to visit his parishioners, but if Miss Cornelia whatever her name was, was a sample of them, she would be in no hurry to speak to any more.

Of course, the thought struck her, she may be Mistress Cornelia. She may be the young man's wife.

She had to admit, as she ran on, that the tall lady and her brother had tried to be pleasant, but in her present outraged state she found even that to be unacceptably condescending. She resented it bitterly. They would be more condescending still, she thought unhappily, if they had known she had no real name, and could not even tell where she had come from. Worse still, that she had once lived with the gipsies.

Well, that was the end of them, anyway. She would never see any of them again.

She arrived calmer but panting at the Turf Inn, with the sun shining and the damp breeze burned away in its rays, and taking the kerchief off her head, tried to smooth her hair before she opened the door.

'Ah, Rose! Rosie!' went up the familiar shout from the gentlemen already seated there, for she was a weekly visitor at the Inn.

'That will be enough, gentlemen!' George Abercromby silenced them with one glare from his stern grey eyes under darkly bristling eyebrows. He was a big stout man with grizzling hair and a fierce expression. Rose believed he could be very fierce if he had to be, but she knew him privately as kind and soft-hearted, and as putty in Aunt Bea's hands. 'What will it be today, Rosie?' he asked her when she got up to the counter.

She laid down the shilling. 'The Moroccan,' she said.

'Oh, ho, The Moroccan, is it?' he boomed. 'Well, I always said Beattie Barbour might pick out a winner some day. That's a good horse.'

'Will you place her bet at three o'clock, Uncle George?'

'I will that, lassie. And now, a dish of tea?' He beckoned to the small round table behind him in the corner, reserved for his special friends.

'Oh, how I should love a cup of tea!' Rose sighed, for truth to tell, the adventures of the morning so far had left her quite exhausted.

'Sit still, then,' George Abercromby said. 'I will bring it directly. The pot is fresh brewed.'

Rose smiled. Uncle George drank such great quantities of tea that Aunt Bea called him an old Tea Jenny. But then, he could afford it, with tea at a pound a pound, for he was wealthy. The Turf Inn prospered.

The door opened again, and remained open so long that her eyes were drawn, to it, to see the reason why. It revealed a carriage outside, a carriage which she found suspiciously familiar, and a party was descending from it and coming in to the Inn for some refreshments. To her horror, Rose saw from her table almost hidden by the corner of the bar counter that it was composed of the same people she had encountered minutes ago on the Swifts.

George Abercromby came through from the back room to welcome the newcomers, laying down the cup of tea before Rose on his way.

'Ah, Mr Kyle, sir,' he said warmly. 'It is a pleasure to see you here again in the Turf Inn. How may I serve you?'

'The ladies require coffee, George.'

At the sound of Mr Kyle's voice, Rose withdrew even further into her corner.

'Coffee it shall be, sir.' George Abercromby lowered his voice. 'And since it is not opening time yet, strictly speaking, I shall make yours a little stronger.' He waved the barman away to prepare it. 'And what of the horses, Mr Kyle? Do you have any racing today?'

'None today, George. I might have had, but it is the same old story: lack of premises near here in which to breed them. So I have managed to train only one for the races this week. A filly, and I am saving her for next Saturday.'

'*Next* Saturday? Do you mean for the Caledonian Hunt Cup?'

Mr Kyle laughed. 'A little ambitious, do you think, George? Ah, but she is a runner. Not only a runner, but a jumper, too.'

'There will be a lot of competitioin, sir,' George Abercromby said doubtfully. 'Ah, here is your order, now. Shall I take it over to your table?'

'Take the ladies'. I will drink mine here.'

Rose wondered in the interval while Uncle George was serving the ladies if she could possibly manage to slip unseen into the back room, but before she could make up her mind, he had returned. She avoided his eyes, in the sincere hope that this made her invisible.

'Yes, George,' Mr Kyle said, continuing where he had left off. 'I have a total outsider on my hands. Nobody knows anything about her, except me—and one other. A lady I met this morning on the Swifts.'

'Hm . . . Then the odds will be long, sir,' George Abercromby said, in a speculative manner, and to Rose's acute embarrassment turned round to ask her, 'More tea, my dear?'

Mr Cameron Kyle's eyes were drawn to her at last, sitting so quietly in the corner. 'But there she is! That is the lady I met this morning! Who is she?'

'Would you like me to introduce you to her?' Uncle George asked, and to her dismay brought the gentleman over to her table. 'Rose, my dear, may I present Mr Cameron Kyle to you? This is Miss Rose Barbour, sir. I have known her since she was seven years old.

'Well, now we have been properly introduced, Miss Barbour,' he said, taking her hand in his. 'So you have no more excuse to run away.'

'How do you do, sir,' Rose said coldly, and would have pulled her hand free. But he still held it in a firm grasp, and his blue eyes were as insistent as his hand. 'You should never cover hair as beautiful as yours.'

'Thank you, sir,' she said, and to her annoyance felt the flush rising again in her cheeks. 'But it is as I said: I should not have spoken to you without being intro-duced. That is not the way I have been brought up.'

She could not bring herself to raise her eyes from Mr Kyle's embroidered cream silk waistcoat. She had an uncomfortable feeling that those blue eyes would be laughing at her again. She managed to slip her hand from his grasp.

'How did you come to be speaking to Mr Kyle, Rose?' George Abercromby asked, sternly surprised. 'It is true that her aunt does not permit any indiscretion. What have you been up to now, Rose?'

'I could not help remarking on the bay filly, on the Swifts. That was all.'

'Well, I shall not tell your aunt,' Mr Kyle said, 'if you will not. And I am sure Mr Abercromby will not, if I ask him. Will that do?'

'Of course, sir,' she said, struggling between the desire to laugh and the desire to cry. 'But then, you are never likely to meet my aunt.'

The words darted out of nowhere. Rose could scarcely believe she had uttered them. What did it possibly matter whether he ever met Aunt Bea or not? The man had a knack of making her say the most outrageous things. Twice in one morning.

'Stranger things have happened before, Miss Rose Barbour. Out of all the world I have met you, have I not?'

This time there was no mistaking the sincerity in his voice, and when at last she dared to look up into his face she found no hint of amusement now, but a strange look in his eyes, half appreciative, half challenging, a flood of blueness that seemed to hypnotise her. Rose stared back, aware of feelings she had not experienced before, of how much she wanted to memorise every line of his features. He was so very handsome . . . With a little shake of her head she recollected herself, how just one tiny frown between those eyes had made her feel so insulted, and so hurt. She bobbed the very merest curtsy which good manners would allow.

'I have been pleased to make your acquaintance, Mr Kyle,' she said, unsmiling.

He regarded her steadily for a moment, then inclined his head with a wry little smile. 'Oh, yes, we *shall* meet again, Miss Barbour, for I have been very much more than just pleased, to make yours.'

The set of his broad back as he turned away spoke volumes. He was angry with her, and no doubt offended. Then she had certainly made her point, Rose thought, on this second encounter. But, strangely, it was a victory which was beginning to feel a little hollow already, if not evaporating altogether, as she watched the tall handsome man who marched off to his table, collected the two ladies, and ushered them out of the Inn.

CHAPTER
TWO

'Now THEN, Rosie, what was all that?' Mr Abercromby asked in amazement.

'Come into the back room with me, Uncle George,' Rose sighed. 'I have something that I must speak to you about.'

'What is it, then?' he asked, when they were seated before the fire.

'That horse of his—Nobody who saw her could have helped remarking!'

'Is that all? But Mr Kyle and I have agreed to forget it, Rose. The trouble is that you have not had to deal with many strangers so far in your life. You will not make the same mistake again, child.'

How kind he was, just like a father. How kind he had always been to her. The tears gathered behind her eyes at the contrast between his gentle words and Cornelia's spiteful attack. She had not recovered from it, even yet.

'No, Uncle George. But that is not what I wanted to speak about. It is this,' and she took the gold coin out of her pocket and laid it in his hand.

'Where did you get this?' he asked slowly. 'Nobody gave you it, I hope?'

'I think perhaps someone did. Perhaps Mama. It rolled out of my doll this morning when she fell off my bed and broke. It must have been inside her for years.'

'Out of your doll? A sovereign?'

'There was a necklace as well. Perhaps they were all she had left to give me.'

'But it is not a sovereign, Rose,' he said, looking at it closely. 'It is a *louis d'or,* a French coin of the same value.'

'Oh,' she said, crestfallen. 'And I had made up my

mind to put it on a horse.'

'Rose!' George Abercromby was scandalised. 'You know you must not even think of such a thing! Ladies do not gamble! Although it must seem so to you,' he sighed.

'Do you think I do not understand about Aunt Bea? It is always the same shilling that I carry back and forth, is it not? I know it is only a little game you play.'

'Well, then.'

'Perhaps this is also different, Uncle George. A special case, since it was Mama's. That is what I feel, that it is a special coin, and I would like to use it in a way I shall never do again, and perhaps will never have the chance to do again. Will you keep the secret with me? And will you put the money on a horse for me? On the outsider?'

'Do you mean Mr Kyle's horse? But he did not tell me her name!'

'I know her name. It is Rose Royale. Do you not think that is lucky?'

George Abercromby looked at the flushed, vital little face before him, and knew he could refuse Rose nothing, any more than Beattie could. By a strange paradox, she had been the duty as Mistress Barbour saw it, which had prevented her from marrying him all these years, while at the same time she had become the daughter to them they might have had together.

'You are beginning to sound like Beattie Barbour,' he laughed. 'Lucky, did you say, when the odds will probably be 100 to 1 against her! All right. I will do it. But we cannot tell your aunt.'

'Oh, thank you, dearest Uncle George! How I wish it was today that Rose Royale was racing!'

'But then, according to you and Mr Kyle, she would outstrip The Moroccan, would she not? And that would never do!'

'No,' Rose smiled. 'That would never do. Who is this Mr Kyle, Uncle?'

'The grandson of Lady Susanna Kyle, who died

recently. The tall young lady is his sister, Alison.'

'And the other lady?' Rose longed to ask, but for once kept her counsel. 'Well, I had better be going back,' she said instead. 'Aunt Bea will be wondering what has happened.'

'Tell her I will be to see you tomorrow as usual then, my dear.'

It was as she had predicted when she arrived back in Longcakes Lane. Mistress Barbour was in a fine state of agitation.

'Rose!' she exclaimed. 'Where have you been? And look at you! Did you not remember about the procession? It started at ten o'clock from Edinburgh. It will be in Leith by eleven, and we shall lose our places if we do not hurry.'

'I need only to wash my face and hands, and attend to my hair, Aunt Bea.'

Ten minutes later they set off to watch the procession going down Leith Walk behind The Purse. Every year it was the same. The Town Guard, their uniforms and themselves well washed and brushed for the occasion, marched down behind a city officer bearing a pole from which dangled a gaily ornamented purse to the beats of the drums, and as they marched the people fell in behind them until everyone arrived at the Sands. When The Purse got there, the first race could begin, in a whole week of racing.

'What is The Purse?' Rose asked her aunt as they hurried along to the foot of Leith Walk.

'It is full of gold, for the owner of the winning horse today,' she said. 'The owner of The Moroccan, I'll be bound. Here is a place to stand, dear. It cannot be long now before we see them!'

By twelve o'clock Rose would not have believed so many people could gather on the Sands, more than ever this year. They were in their hundreds, walking and in carriages, and every one in boisterous spirits.

For a while she and her aunt wandered watching the games and the side-shows, held their ears against the shrill voices of the ale-wives, and then found a patch of grass to sit on and eat a picnic lunch of small mutton pies, hot and delicious from the meat stall, and held in their hands with papers round them. Aunt Bea had taken the precaution of bringing a bottle of her own lemonade with her, to wash them down.

'I declare, they never taste the same, eaten indoors,' she said to Rose, who agreed. 'It must be nearly one o'clock,' she added, and as she spoke they heard the first shot fired to start the races, and the clamour of the crowd as they roared for their favourites. Long before three o'clock they had battled their way to the railings, to lean on them and wait for The Moroccan to be paraded.

'Only look at him, Rose,' Aunt Bea said, her eyes shining. 'He is as black as the Ace of Spades, indeed!'

'He looks a big strong horse,' Rose reassured her, gazing at The Moroccan. 'He looks as though he could win.'

'Oh, he will, he will!'

The excitement rose to fever-pitch in the crowd, for this was the race for The Purse, until at last the gun was fired to start.

'They're off!' went up the shout, and the horses with their riders flashed past in a blaze of colours as everyone waited to see who would turn first at the bottom of the long oval course.

The horses were still in a bunch as they rounded the first bend of the oval. At the second, they started to spread out to come up the home straight.

'Who is it? Who is it?' Aunt Bea clutched Rose's arm. 'I can't see.'

'It's Tally-Ho coming up first,' said a shifty-eyed man beside them. Rose had not liked the look of him from the first. 'I know their colours. And then two black horses.

One of them is The Sweep. And the other is The Moroccan.'

The horses thundered towards them, sending up sprays of sand in clouds at either side.

'Look! It's The Moroccan!' shouted the man, and suddenly the race was over.

'You've won! You've won!' Rose hugged her aunt.

'And your winnings?' the man asked. 'I can pick them up for you, if you will wait here. I know where to go.'

'That is very kind of you, sir, but it is being taken care of,' Mistress Barbour said in freezing tones. 'By Mr Abercromby.'

'George Abercromby of The Turf?'

'The same.'

'Oh,' said the man, and melted suddenly into the crowd.

'He did not mean to come back with your money, Aunt Bea.'

'Of course he did not, dear. But do you know, Rose, I am almost glad that happened? It will serve as an illustration to you of the lesson I have tried to teach you so often! It simply does not do to speak to strangers, especially strange men, my dear. Some of them can be so plausible, as you can see.'

'Yes, Aunt Bea,' Rose said, with a savage pang of conscience.

'And there are pickpockets and thieves at every race-course, anywhere that money changes hands. No, no, George Abercromby will bring the money tomorrow when he comes. He would never permit me to carry it around here.'

'Why have you never married him?' Rose asked suddenly.

'Married him?' Aunt Bea laughed. 'Well, it has not been for the want of him asking! Perhaps I shall, some day.'

They walked home through the crowds and past all the

carriages. But look as she may, Rose did not see the tall elegant figure she was searching for, the ash-blond head and the lean amused face of Mr Cameron Kyle.

She was surprised to find, when she went to bed that night with the gold chain and its tiny birdcage pendant in her hand, that she was a little disappointed. She did not understand herself at all.

'Today is the last day of the Leith Races,' Rose reminded her aunt, one whole long week later, as they sat at their breakfast of fresh hot baps and butter. How she had contained herself so long without speaking of it she did not know.

'Yes, dear,' Mistress Barbour said calmly. 'It is the big race today, the Caledonian Cup.'

'And you are not going to watch it, Aunt Bea?'

'No, I had not thought of it. There is no point in going, unless to watch your horse, and I have placed no bet for today.'

'I wondered that you did not speak of it last night, as usual. Why not? I could have run over with it this morning again.'

'Two reasons, I suppose, dear. I was so lucky last Saturday, and I do not like to tempt providence twice in a row. And then I do not care to bet, except on a sure thing, Rose.'

Basking in the glory of her success of last week, Aunt Bea had become very knowledgeable of all things pertaining to the Turf, even to adopting its terminology.

'Besides,' she added, 'it is a hurdles race. The horses often fall.'

Rose experienced a sinking feeling in the pit of her stomach. She had never thought of that. What if Rose Royale fell, with all that money on her?

'No, dear,' Mistress Barbour went on. 'I had thought we would stay at home today, and take time to clean the house thoroughly with Pansy Paris. A lick and a promise was all it got last Saturday, after all that rushing about we had when we came home from the Sands, to get ready for Uncle George's visit the next day. There is always so much food to prepare on a Saturday, as well.'

Rose listened with one ear. That meant she would have to wait another day, until George Abercromby came, to hear the fate of Rose Royale. She did not know how she was going to manage it. Would Aunt Bea allow her to go and watch the race herself, she wondered? As fast as such a wild dream floated through her head, it floated out again. Aunt Bea would have a seizure at the very idea, and Rose supposed ruefully that she had done enough damage in Leith already without adding any more to it.

'. . . what we are going to eat tomorrow, dear?' Rose caught the tail end of her aunt's last remark. 'You know we dare not lift a hand the whole day, tomorrow.'

Oh no, not on a Sunday, Rose shuddered. No work of any kind must be done on a Sunday, not even the preparation of food. In the morning they would go to the Kirk and listen to the long, dreary sermonising of the minister. Then they would come home for a bite of something cold before they went back again in the afternoon.

'Here is Pansy now,' Aunt Bea said when the door opened and a middle-aged woman came in and took off her shawl. 'How are you today, my dear?'

'No' bad, Mistress Beattie. Just a wee touch of the rheumatics. It'll rain today. I can always tell.'

'There's not much help for the rheumatics, Pansy, I fear.'

'Ay. Auld age doesnae come itsel', Mistress Beattie,' Pansy sighed. 'So what will it be today?'

'We were wondering about the supper tomorrow. What shall we prepare? What did we have last Sunday?' Aunt Bea asked vaguely.

'Cock-a-leekie soup, a nice leg o' lamb, and an apple pie,' Pansy said crisply.

'Yes. Always the apple pie! Could we not make a little change? A butterscotch tart, perhaps? What do you think, Rose, dear?'

'You could, Aunt Bea. But Uncle George will not like it.'

'Nevertheless, I shall set about one. There is a mutton-bone there for the Scotch broth, Pansy. And would you make your collops? Nobody makes collops like you, and I think I have still a jar of rowan jelly to accompany them. Rose will run out for the meat, won't you, dear?'

And, having set her small household about their first tasks, Mistress Barbour directed her attention to her pastry.

On Sunday they came home from the second service and threw off their bonnets and gloves thankfully. They had survived the tedium of the day by looking forward to George Abercromby's visit. He always came late in the afternoon, for the Turf Inn was closed on Sundays, and stayed to supper.

'Is the fire still alive?' Aunt Bea asked anxiously.

'There is still a little glow.'

'Well, then, dearie, put on just a few lumps of coal to begin with. It would not do for a lot of smoke to come belching out of our chimney. When the fire has got a hold we will add another few lumps. There is no use in inviting trouble to our door.'

No, indeed, Rose thought while she nursed the fire. There were men who went around on Sundays, the Kirk Spies, watching out for any breach of the strict rules laid down by the Kirk Session. Children were not even allowed to play with their toys, and the only relaxation permitted was the reading of the Holy Bible.

Soon the fire was a bright orange glow behind the bars of the narrow grate, and Mistress Barbour looked out the pan of Scotch broth and the bowl of collops.

'Here he is! I hear his foot on the stair, Aunt Bea,'

Rose said, running to open the door to Mr Abercromby.

'Come away in, Geordie,' Aunt Bea smiled at him.
'We have been waiting for you. And,' she added
warningly, 'thinking a great deal about the pudding.'

'Then you have been wasting your time, Beattie.
There is only one pudding for a Sunday. And that is
apple pie.'

'Oh, George Abercromby! Let us have a change! I
made such a nice butterscotch tart.'

'Butterscotch tarts are just the thing for Mondays, my
dear. It will keep.'

Rose looked from one to the other as they argued
amiably together. They were just like an old married
couple, she thought, just as comfortable.

'Besides, I have no apples in the house,' Aunt Bea
said triumphantly.

'Then it is as well I brought one with me, although I
had the devil of a job to conceal it under my coat.' Mr
Abercromby ended the little argument, drawing out a
dish covered with a white napkin, knotted at the top, 'for
I have noticed a strange reluctance for apple pies on
Sundays in this house lately, Beattie.'

'Oh,' she said, laughing, 'you men are creatures of
habit, to be sure! Well, none of the meal will take long to
heat up. Half an hour.'

'Long enough, then, for Rose and me to take a little
promenade. Round the harbour and back again, my
dear?' he said with a wink.

'Put on your cloak, Rose. It is always cold out there,
exposed to the sea and the elements. Half an hour, then.
No longer!'

Once out of Longcakes Lane, Rose slipped her hand
under Mr Abercromby's arm. 'I swear I will burst, Uncle
George, if you do not tell me at once! How did Rose
Royale run yesterday?'

'You must prepare yourself for a shock, my dear.'

'Oh,' said Rose, her heart sinking to the soles of her

dainty Sunday slippers, sapphire blue to match her gown. 'She lost, then?'

'She won, Rose, and the odds against her were truly 100 to 1, which means that instead of one pound, you get back a hundred pounds, plus the *louis d'or* you put on her to begin with.'

Rose gripped Mr Abercromby's arm, and sat down suddenly on the harbour wall. She scarcely noticed the wind whipping open her cloak and tearing at the silk of her gown.

'Oh, Uncle George, that is a great deal of money! What am I to do with it?'

'Well, my dear,' Mr Abercromby drew her up to walk on. 'You will have to think very carefully about that. There are so many things you could do with a hundred pounds. It could change your life. Yes, perhaps Rose Royale has changed your life! At any rate, here it all is, in sovereigns, in this little bag. Put it inside your cloak, and think well over it.'

For the rest of the way back they were silent until Mr Abercromby dipped his head again to pass through the little archway into Longcakes Lane.

'Uncle George,' Rose said, and stopped.

'Yes, my dear?'

'Will you leave me to tell Aunt Bea about this in my own way?'

'I was hoping you would,' he smiled. 'But after the apple pie.'

The dishes were all washed and put back along the racks of the large oak dresser which occupied most of one wall in the small kitchen, when they sat down before the fire. As a rule, Rose loved these Sunday evening conversations when Uncle George told them of his experiences in the boxing booths, and Aunt Bea related tales from far away which her husband had told her, and tales from Edinburgh, and the people who lived there. But tonight she was very quiet.

'Are you well enough, lassie? You were very thoughtful all through supper. And you scarcely ate a bite.'

'Yes, I am well,' Rose assured her aunt. 'I have been
thinking, that is all.'

'Hm. Worrying, more like. There has been a definite
crease between your eyebrows. If you worry much
more, it will become a line, and stay there for ever. What
are you worrying about?'

'I have always heard it said that too much money can
be a serious worry and a heavy responsibility, and now I
believe it,' Rose sighed, 'after the weight it has been on
me for the last hour and a half, when I became the owner
of too much money. Look at this!'

She fetched the little black bag from the inside pocket
of her cloak, and emptied its contents on to Mistress
Barbour's shiny silk lap.

'Landsakes! Oh my! Oh, Geordie!' she shrieked.

'Now, now, Beattie! Now, now.'

'Oh, Aunt Bea, I did not mean to give you such a
shock,' Rose said, gazing in alarm at the rosy cheeks
turned quite pale, and grasping her aunt's hand in hers.

Calmly and deliberately, George Abercromby related
the tale of the *louis d'or*. By the end of it Mistress
Barbour was beginning to recover. Her colour was
returning, and with it a spark in her eye.

'Rose Barbour!' she gasped. 'How could you? Have I
not brought you up to know better than that? A young
lady, *gambling* . . . ! What are you both laughing at? Oh
my, it is a great deal of money, to be sure . . . *How* much
did you say is here?'

'A hundred and one pounds, and it is all yours, Aunt
Bea. And even so, a mere drop in the ocean compared to
the fortune it has cost you to raise me all these years. But
you do not need to tell me that gold could never repay
you for all that. Only take it, dearest Aunt Bea, for a
present.'

'I could never take money from you, Rose! Besides, it is luck money, and it would be unlucky to give it away. Of course I will keep it safe for you,' her aunt said, looking suddenly sad and tired, 'until we decide what must be done with it. It will be just one more thing to be considered now, for I have been thinking a great deal myself, lately, and worrying too.'

'We both have,' George Abercromby said.

'What about?'

'Your future, dear. Next month you will be eighteen, a very critical age for a young lady. You must give me time to think about it. I shall talk it over again with Uncle George. He always comes to such sensible decisions.'

But it was not until the twentieth of October that the subject was discussed again in the house in Longcakes Lane, with another Sunday come and almost gone, and Rose had almost forgotten about the little bag of sovereigns.

Supper was long past. At the end of it, Rose had wished a wish and sliced the plum cake Pansy Paris had baked and covered with sugar frosting, and Uncle George had gone back to the Turf Inn. The wag-on-the-wa' ticked noisily in the silence that followed his departure, and the coals seemed to make a loud crash when they fell down in the ashes, only to burst into flame again for their last flickering dance of the evening.

'And so now you are eighteen, and have come of age, my little Rose,' Aunt Bea said sadly and quietly, and so differently from the happy, bantering way she and George Abercromby had spoken and laughed with her all through her birthday. 'Ten years, and they have passed so fast!'

Suddenly Rose felt a little lurch of her heart. Aunt Bea did not usually speak so seriously, even mournfully, to her. What was coming next?

'Your Uncle George and I have talked about it, and talked about it, up hill and down dale, ever since the night of the Caledonian Cup when you won all that money, my dear. We have considered it in the light of your future, and what best to do. Best for you, Rose.'

Rose said nothing. She was remembering the morning her doll broke, and all this began, along with her presentiment.

'Although I would keep you here with me always, and indeed perhaps have held on to you too long already,' her aunt went on, 'I have come to see that it is not right for your sake that I should do so. Newhaven may be too small a world in which to cage you, Rose.'

'But I have always been happy here, Aunt Bea. I have not found it too restricted.'

'Perhaps not, dear. You do not know anything else. That is what I am trying to say. The day is coming that I have dreaded for so long, when I must allow you to spread your wings.'

'Oh, no! I do not want to leave Newhaven, and you!'

'I know, lassie, I know . . . It will be hard on us both. But,' she straightened her back against her chair, and spoke more briskly, 'it must be done. You must have your chance in life, the best chance I can give you. I have tried to be a mother to you from the first. And now I cannot shrink from my duty to do what any mother would for her daughter, in the end.'

The flames of the fire were flickering their last now, and in their glow Rose saw that her aunt was quite determined. And once set upon her course, Rose realised with a sinking heart, nothing could dissuade Mistress Beattie Barbour. Nothing ever had, once her mind was made up.

'Well, then, and what have you decided?' she asked, smiling, and quite unprepared for the shock of the answer.

'I have friends in Edinburgh, as you know. What I have never told you is that many of them are in high places, those I have done a service to, in the course of my profession; for high or low, Rose dear, we are all mortal, and illness can strike at any time.'

'Yes, Aunt Bea.'

'One of my friends is Mistress Margaret Scott, wife of the great lawyer, Walter Scott, Writer to the Signet, whose son I helped to nurse through a severe illness which almost paralysed him. Happily, young Master Walter pulled through with no more than a limp. I have arranged with her that you shall go to her house next Saturday, by which time she will have secured a good position for you. There are few to whom I would have entrusted such an undertaking, but Mistress Scott is to be trusted absolutely. She is a pillar of society.'

'What sort of a position? I am trained for nothing!'

'Oh, but you are, Rose. In my own way I have been training you for the last ten years. Of course you had the breeding to start with, as anyone can tell from your appearance. You can read and write and count to a high degree. You can sew and you can paint. You did not go into Mistress MacPherson's Academy of Music all those Saturday mornings without learning to sing and to know the dancing steps. And you have the elements of hygiene and nursing, which is more than most girls of your age can boast. But most of all you have been, quite naturally, a most pleasant and endearing companion. It is as a companion to some lady that Mistress Scott will secure a position for you. It will be your entry into Society.'

'What lady?'

'You will not know that until next Saturday, when you go to see Mistress Scott.'

'But will you not be coming with me, Aunt Bea?'

'Of course I should be coming with you. It is a matter of the gravest concern and disappointment to me that I shall not be in a position to introduce you myself. But it is six months now since I promised Mistress Balfour of Pilrig to attend her, and her time will come on Saturday or Sunday. I cannot let her down, or the baby either.'

'No,' said Rose despondently.

'But is it not exciting, my dear?' her aunt said with some of her usual sparkle returning. 'To be standing on the threshold of your life, so to speak, and to have a little flutter, and see how you come out?'

Mistress Barbour smiled at her niece, the same old little gleam back in her eyes.

'You are incorrigible, Aunt Bea!' Rose laughed, infected by her change of mood. 'And you have placed a bet on me with Uncle George, I shouldn't wonder! But when you put it like that, I suppose I must go, and as you say take my chance.'

'It is all a matter of chance, Rose, in this life. You will come to see that you must take every one that comes your way. I do not want you to grow old and regret those that passed you by.'

'A matter of chance it certainly was when my doll broke, Aunt Bea. I keep thinking that but for that accident I should still be staying here with you.'

'That is exactly what I mean. That was an accident. It happened by chance. You took a chance with the *louis d'or* then, and came out the winner. Every cloud has a silver lining, if you look for it,' Mistress Barbour said. She was a great one for her proverbs. 'But you are not quite right in your assumption. You would have been going in any case, as I have explained to you. And about your doll, child? It is the end of her . . . The end of her little life, but the end of so much more, is that it?'

Rose nodded, amazed that her aunt understood so well how she had been feeling.

'I remember, when you were only eight years old, that I asked you why you would not call her by some more suitable name. Dolly perhaps, or even Jinty, but you would not. It had to be Poo Pay and nothing else.'

'It was silly and childish to persist with it. But I was only a child, and trying to cling on to the things I had known. That was the name Mama called her.'

They shivered involuntarily both at the same time, and the coals shifted yet again into the cinders, and now there were no more flames, hardly even a glow. Mistress Barbour rose to light the night candles. They fluttered into their uncertain flames in the candlesticks, and Rose saw her aunt's sad expression.

'I understand about your doll, my Rosie. I hope I have always understood you. You must not think of yourself as all alone in the world, now that the past is dead and gone. George and I, we will not fail you.'

'I know you will not, Aunt Bea.'

Her aunt grasped Rose's hands in hers. 'Oh, there is the future to look forward to, Rose! Oh, how I wish I were eighteen all over again! Young and fresh and pretty, and only starting out! Although, of course, my dear, do not make any mistake about it, we are all still only eighteen at heart, as any older person will tell you. That is why some of us do such foolish things, such as contemplating marriage again at nearly fifty,' Mistress Barbour roared with laughter.

'Do you never take life seriously, Aunt Bea?'

'You know I do. Very seriously, Rose. How can I do otherwise, when I have lived so long with births and deaths and the illnesses in between? But sooner or later I see the funny side of it, and thank God for that, and then I do not take it seriously for too long. In this life you must laugh, or you must cry. Which is it to be for you, Rose?'

'So long as I always have you to come back to, I shall be laughing.'

'That is a great relief to me, that you know this is your home, always, no matter what happens. So we have a week to get you ready. And we shall be happy together for another whole week, Rose? No tears, and no good-byes, dear. Now, about the money.'

'I shall leave it here with you.'

'I had thought of that, too,' Mistress Barbour admitted. 'But there are two things against it. First, I am out of the house a great deal, and you will no longer be in it, to watch over it, in case of thieves. Second, when you are in Edinburgh you may need a new gown, or slippers, at any time, especially if you are invited out a lot, and I think you may be. You must have money to spend. So you will take it with you, and put it in the Bank of Scotland in Old Bank Close. That is the most sensible thing to do with it.'

In the days that followed, Pansy Paris dragged down Herbert Barbour's old sea-trunk from the loft of the house, and bubbles of soap and water ruled the days in Longcakes Lane. But in the end, no part or particle of Rose's belongings were left untouched. They were washed, cleaned, and ironed to perfection.

'Now,' said Aunt Bea on the Friday evening, 'it is the tin bath. The water is hot, all four kettles of it. Every inch of your skin must be clean before you step out.'

Rose smiled, and wondered what her aunt would do when there was nobody left in the house for her to look after.

By the time she had bathed and they had thrown the bathful of hot soapy water down the steps of the little forestair, Rose and Mistress Barbour were quite exhausted. They drank their small glasses of lemonade by nine o'clock and went to bed. But Rose was too excited to sleep.

Where might she be tomorrow night at this same time? Somewhere in Edinburgh—but with whom? She calmed her troubled thoughts with the reassurance that it would be with some great lady. Aunt Bea had said so, and with that thought she eventually fell asleep.

In the morning, not quite refreshed, she dressed in the sapphire blue silk, her Sunday best. The skirt of her gown came right down to her slippers. She had always found that irksome, after the freedom of every other day of the week in her Newhaven costume. It was in these moments, while she was dressing, that Rose began to think that living in high places might have serious drawbacks.

By two o'clock in the afternoon all the rushing about and the packing of the trunk was over, and they sat down to a cup of tea.

'Now, Rose dear, here is your bag of sovereigns.'

Rose eyed the little black velvet pouch doubtfully.

'Put it right in the bottom of your reticule. And here is a letter for Mistress Scott to put on top of it. I have not mentioned the money to her. It is nobody's business but yours. Do not open your reticule again until you are safely arrived in her house, dear.'

By half-past two they were ready and waiting for the caddies when they came up the forestair to carry the trunk over to the Newhaven coach.

'We shall be along in ten minutes to see that the trunk is delivered,' Aunt Bea told the messengers, handing them a coin as they staggered down the steps.

'And here are some small coins for you, Rose, to put in the pocket of your cloak, and to save you opening your reticule.'

A quarter of an hour later they found themselves the only ones to arrive for the stage-coach for Edinburgh, with the trunk safely strapped on. They got in together to wait for the hour of departure.

'The afternoon coaches do not go to the Tron,' Aunt Bea told Rose. 'They stop at the foot of the Royal Mile, in the White Horse Close. You must not worry about getting to Mistress Scott's house from there, because you will see the chair-men in their dozens waiting for passengers, and two of them will convey you and your trunk in a sedan. Now you have plenty of coins in your pocket to pay them, and your coach fare is paid already.'

'You have thought of everything, Aunt Bea,' Rose sighed, for now she was feeling quite apprehensive.

'I have tried to, dear. But I shall not rest until I hear from you. You will write me a note, at the first opportunity? Ugh! This coach reeks of fish!'

Mistress Barbour pulled down the window and they heard three striking on the tower of the Old Kirk. She descended the steps to the ground and slammed the coach door shut from the outside.

'You will be covered with scales by the time you get there!' she said, still lamenting when the coach began to move off.

'Goodbye, Aunt Bea,' Rose said, with her head out of the window, and waving her handkerchief. She watched the gallant little figure of her aunt growing smaller and smaller, and finally disappearing altogether as the coach rounded the corner at the end of the Main Street, and a tear trickled down her face. They had never been parted, not for a day or a night, since Rose was eight years old.

She sat back in her corner by the open window, glad that nobody else was travelling in the three o'clock coach today, with her head resting on the leather upholstery, and gazing out unseeing at the passing scene. There was yet half an hour alone with her thoughts before her new life began, and it came to her suddenly how strange it was that each new chapter of her life always began with a coach journey. The thought was chilling, and she shivered violently, and stood up to pull the window back up again.

But still the chill persisted, although the day was soft and balmy for October, a blue and gold day in a lazy Indian summer, and it reminded her of something Grandmam Maddy used to say, long ago, when she got these attacks of the shivers. 'It is the goose, walking over my grave again,' and then Grandfer Nathan would look serious, and a little sad, and keep everyone away from her while he sat with her silently and held her hand. Always after that she would tell him of something she had 'seen' when the shivers went away.

It was unusual to have the gipsies so much in her mind as recently, Rose thought. There had been that first journey from the ship in her early childhood, to end with the coach crash, and the beginning of the years with the gipsies; the second from the gipsy camp to Newhaven, to end with the death of her mother, and the beginning of her life with Aunt Bea. Now, with the third coach ride, what lay ahead?

She would never go back to live in Newhaven again.

Rose sat bolt upright in the shock of this forewarning, her face drained of every vestige of colour, her hands trembling, and with fear clutching her heart. There was trouble ahead, without doubt. It was part of the pattern, she saw with dreadful clarity. It had happened like this twice before in her eighteen years, and it would happen again for the third time. Where would it come from? How would it strike?'

With a tremendous effort she forced herself to be calm, and to try to think logically. If it did indeed all follow a pattern, then whatever trouble was coming would be overcome, as it had been overcome the first time with the help of the gipsies, and the second time with the help of her aunt. Somehow, and from somewhere, she would receive help again.

But the threatening shadows did not begin to melt away, and Rose did not come to herself again until the Carlton Hill came in sight out of the right side of the coach, and she realised she could not be far away from her destination. There to the left lay Holyrood Palace behind its walls and gates, and soon they would be entering the Royal Mile.

With a rumble of wheels the coach rolled into the historic street. Rose looked out of the windows at it, from down here where it was called the Canongate, further up to where it changed its name to the High Street, further up still to where it became the Lawnmarket, and right to the top, to the Castlehill where Edinburgh Castle crouched like a lion on the Castle Rock, and once again felt the old familiar thrill of just being there, and a lift of her spirits.

She remembered Uncle George's words when he had taught her about Edinburgh a long time ago. 'Think of a herring, Rose, and you will understand the Royal Mile. The long street is like the thick backbone, one mile long, and the little closes running down from it, on either side, are the fine bones.'

The coach was turning into one of the closes now, edging slowly through the opening barely wide enough for it, to the little square beyond where it came to a halt. Facing them was the White Horse Inn at the back of the square, and tall buildings pressed close together all around. It seemed to Rose that hundreds of people were running about, rushing here and there.

She waited until the coach driver opened the door for her and set down the little steps, and as she descended them there was a concerted rush of men towards her, all waving and shouting at the same time. The coachman heaved down her trunk onto the cobbles of the courtyard and left her standing beside it, alone in the centre of the crowd. These must be the chair-men, she thought despairingly, and she did not like the look of any of them. In fact they were terrifying, dressed in ragged tartan, and she could not understand a single word they said.

Rose pulled the hood of her cloak off her head and gazed at them dumbly, little knowing that a shaft of sunlight had somehow filtered down through a chink between the rooftops, to set her hair ablaze, and throw her into sharp relief as would the footlights on a stage. Frightened and confused, she searched the sea of faces for a gentler one among them to tell him where she wanted to go. But her throat was dry and the words would not come out.

Then there was the sound of a man's voice above the mob, a voice like a whiplash, and the chair-men fell back to make a path for someone coming towards her from the stables under the White Horse Inn.

'I told you I would see you again!' Cameron Kyle smiled into her terrified eyes, and once again she was overpowered by their blueness.

She smiled at him tremulously, thankful to hear a voice that she could understand. He turned round abruptly, and with a few words dismissed the chair-men.

'You need not be afraid of them,' he told her. 'They may look dirty and ragged, but they are proud and honest to a man, disbanded from the Highland regiments. They speak in the Gaelic tongue and know very little English. Next time you require a chair, point to one of them and say where you are going, and the rest will go away.'

'Thank you, Mr Kyle,' Rose said with quivering lips. 'Then I had best call for one of them now.'

'You will not call for them today, for I have told them that my carriage is at your disposal. I shall take you wherever you are going, Miss Barbour.'

'I could not dream of troubling you, sir,' Rose said, with a proud lift of her head, and turning her eyes away. 'But it is very kind of you to offer.'

He put out his hand and pulled her back round to face him. 'I insist upon it. And in any case, Rose Barbour, you have been troubling me for the last six weeks,' he said grimly. 'My horses are not yet out of the shafts. We are ready to go. Where is it you wish to be taken?'

Her eyes fell beneath his stern and unsmiling gaze. With the Newhaven coach come and gone, and the chair-men all straggling out into the Canongate again to look for other fares, she had no alternative now but to accept his offer. She must get to Mistress Scott's house before any more time was lost.

'To No. 25, George Square, sir.'

'To the Scotts'?' His eyes flared briefly, she thought in surprise. 'Wait here, then, and I will have the carriage brought out again.'

He signalled to his driver, and the carriage bowled out

into the little square, and while his man was loading on the trunk he gave him his instructions before he turned back again to hand Rose inside. She sat down, and he handed her the reticule.

'What do you keep in there?' he asked. 'It is very heavy.'

'Yes, it is heavy,' Rose agreed, grasping it nervously. She had not remembered it was so heavy.

'Put this rug over your knees,' he said, dropping it on her lap. 'You may find it cold in this open carriage. We were just about to change over to the closed carriage for the winter when I saw you.'

'Oh,' she said. 'I am afraid that I have detained you.'

'I would not have recognised you, if it had not been for your hair. Not in that dress,' he smiled. 'I had got used to thinking of you in your Newhaven costume, against that background.'

She glanced up at him, sitting there beside her so calmly, at his fair hair, his stern profile, reminding her every minute of their first disastrous meeting, and bitterly regretted that she had not known about the chairmen before. If she had, she would not be here now, while he confessed his thoughts to her, which more properly should have been concentrated on his wife.

'Then you are both the same, you and your wife,' she flashed at him before she could stop herself. 'You take people at face value.'

'And what do you mean by that, Miss Barbour?'

Rose glared at the Tron Kirk indignantly. They were turning left off the High Street now, the carriage bowling merrily away from the hubbub of the city, its horses and carts, the caddies and the chair-men, the bustle of the Royal Mile.

'I mean, sir, that you took me for a fishwife, just as she did. But now that you see me in a different dress, that puts a different complexion on it altogether. It is a case of clothes maketh the man, in your opinion.

Or the woman.'

'Ah . . .' He smiled down maddeningly at her, a lazy smile which made her heart turn over. 'So you are passionate, to match the colour of your hair, Rose Barbour! That is more intriguing than ever! And I must remember in future that when you are angry you mis-quote, to suit your argument. It is "Manners make the man".'

'Oh,' said Rose. 'Well, it was near enough.'

'And, in any case, I am not married. Not yet.'

'Oh,' said Rose again feebly. Who was Cornelia, then? And why must she always say the wrong things in this man's company? She did not want to say them. She did not usually say them. 'I beg your pardon, Mr Kyle. I have been very rude. Again,' she sighed.

'You could not be rude,' he said. 'You are too polished.'

'Now you are laughing at me again. Polished?'

'No, I am not laughing. And yes, polished. Your hair is polished. Your appearance is polished. Even your speech is polished. It is not the speech of the Newhaven fisherfolk, no matter what your dress. But I did not need to hear you speak either, to know you were a lady, and a very beautiful one at that.'

Rose gazed at him, speechless.

'Too beautiful and too innocent to be let loose on the Swifts at seven o'clock in the morning, unescorted,' he added, severely.

So that had been the reason why he had frowned at her! Her anger vanished like the mist before the sun, and she smiled up at him for the first time in their acquaintance.

At the sight of so much radiance Mr Kyle drew in his breath sharply. 'That's better,' he said. 'Now, perhaps, we may begin again. Do you not think you owe me some explanation? I understood you lived in Newhaven.'

'I do—I did,' Rose stuttered. 'I did until today.'

'And today?'

'Today I have come to live in Edinburgh . . . I think,' she answered truthfully.

'With Mistress Scott?' he asked, after a pause during which he appeared to be trying to digest her last statement.

'No. But Mistress Scott will tell me where I must go from there. She has secured a position for me, as a lady's companion.'

'So you do not know yet which lady?' he frowned.

'No, sir,' Rose then fell silent, beginning to feel very apprehensive.

'Well,' he said, 'it will not be long till we get there. I know George Square, you see. I lived in it myself until recently. The horses know it, too. I believe they could find the way there themselves.'

Rose smiled wanly. He was trying to calm her and cheer her, she realised. He was saying things she could not possibly absorb in her present state of nervousness.

'Now we turn right at this opening. Along here is No. 25.'

The carriage came to a halt, and the driver climbed down and unstrapped the trunk from the back step. Mr Kyle jumped out and held open the door for her, and lifted her down beside him, and for a moment of complete dizziness his blue eyes were very near her own.

As they ascended the steps of the house together, she read a gleaming brass plate which read 'Walter Scott, W.S.', and then he pulled the bell beneath it. Rose held out her hand, and when he took it she could feel the warmth of his even through her glove, oddly comforting in this strange place.

'Goodbye, Mr Kyle,' she said. 'You have been very kind.'

'Not goodbye, Miss Barbour. Now I know how to find you again,' he replied, in no hurry to leave, and as he spoke the door opened, and a maidservant looked from one to the other.

'Mr Kyle, sir!' she said, and then, 'Miss Barbour?'

'Yes, Agnes,' Mr Kyle said easily. 'Mistress Scott is expecting her.'

At the sound of their voices, a lady came into the hall, dressed in brown silk with a cascade of ivory bows from the bodice down to the hem of her dress, and with her hair drawn up under a cap of ivory lace, beaded with pearls. She looked strict, full of common sense, and every inch a lady.

'Rose!' she said. 'Beattie Barbour has told me so much about you. Welcome, my dear—and you, Cameron! This is an unexpected pleasure.'

'I happened to be in the White Horse Close when the Newhaven coach came in,' he said. 'Just in time to rescue her from the tender mercies of the chair-men.'

'So you two know each other?'

'Indeed, yes.' He smiled amiably at their hostess, while somehow contriving to glance warningly at Rose. 'For some time now, although our meeting today was quite a coincidence. But I do not mean to intrude, Mistress Margaret. I have delivered Miss Rose to you, and now I shall take my leave.'

'You will do nothing of the sort, Cameron Kyle,' Mistress Scott said flatly. 'That is, unless you have business to attend to?'

'None that is too pressing,' Mr Kyle admitted.

'Then you will stay for tea. We see far too little of you as it is, and of Alison too. How is she?'

'Thank you. She is recovering well, I am happy to tell you. But, I wonder—would you excuse me for a moment while I have a word with my driver? The poor fellow is still waiting down there.'

'Of course you may, my dear.'

Mistress Scott turned to Rose, as they stood there in the hall, with the front door open. 'Such a very personable young man, and with delightful manners! How did you come to know him, my dear?'

'Through my aunt and Mr Abercromby, Mistress

Scott,' Rose answered carefully, 'in Newhaven.'

'Very proper, I am sure.'

Rose resolved that she would mention Mr Kyle in her first letter to Aunt Bea. She would have to, now.

'I have instructed him to come back in an hour,' Mr Kyle said as he came back up the steps and closed the front door.

'Come into the drawing-room, then, Cameron,' Mistress Scott said, throwing open one of the doors in the hall and ushering him in. 'There is so much news to catch up with, but in the meantime I will send Walter to entertain you, while I attend to a little matter with Rose in the back sitting-room. We will not be long.'

'I am in no hurry, Mistress Margaret,' Rose heard his deep voice assuring their hostess from behind the drawing-door, 'and it will be a great pleasure to see young Walter again.'

Mistress Scott closed the door of her drawing-room behind her, clearly charmed by the diplomacy of Mr Kyle's last remark. 'Agnes,' she said to her maid who still stood with Rose in the hall, 'send Master Walter to the drawing-room at once. Tell him who has arrived. And we will all take tea there in twenty minutes.'

As Rose felt herself gently but very firmly propelled towards the door of the back sitting-room and an entirely unknown future, she could only feel relieved that at least she had not been thrown into the den of the lions entirely alone.

Of course, it was not the way she had visualised arriving at No. 25, George Square, not at all. Especially not with a man with whom she had only the very slightest acquaintance, and not the long-standing relationship of friendship he had claimed, although she could understand that Mistress Scott would be very strait-laced about the conventions. Nevertheless, she could not help feeling that with Mr Cameron Kyle at her side there was still one tenuous and very unexpected link between her old life and the new, and from that she took heart.

CHAPTER
THREE

'THIS IS a smaller room, my dear, less formal than the drawing-room. I thought you may find it easier to talk in here. Large rooms can be a little overpowering, can they not?'

The back sitting-room was indeed very small, with a small fire burning in the grate, a small window in front of which an oval table was drawn up with books and papers on it, and small portraits so old that they had all faded now to a uniform shade of sepia. But it had a homely, cosy air, as though it might have been the room in which a mother gently chastised her children.

'Please take a seat,' Mistress Scott said.

There were two armchairs, one at either side of the fire. Rose ignored them and chose instead one with a wooden back directly opposite the window. She sat down, remembering to keep her spine as straight as the back of the chair, and tucked her crossed ankles demurely out of sight.

Mistress Scott moved across to a chair behind the oval table and sat down facing her. There was a shade of slight approval on her face. It was a face which would not seem so plain if it was not so severe, Rose thought, thankful that she must have made a fairly good impression, so far.

'I hope I find you well, Rose?'

'Very well, thank you, madam.'

'And dear Beattie Barbour?'

'She is well also, Mistress Scott,' Rose said, opening her reticule. 'And she sends you this letter.'

She stood up to put it on the table, and retreated again, into her upright position.

'Yes,' Mistress Scott said, when she had read the letter, 'she was always very thoughtful, as well as a person of exceptional ability—and capable of a great deal of fun.' As she said this, a smile lit up her stern features, and Rose saw that she was not plain at all, but a woman of considerable charm. 'It has clearly distressed dear Beattie that she could not accompany you here herself today.'

Rose smiled back, a little sadly.

'But she says she will come to Edinburgh as soon as Mistress Balfour is safely delivered of her child, to see us. She would not let anyone down.'

'No. I know that, Mistress Scott.'

'Of course I do not need to tell you anything about your aunt, child—your adopted aunt, that is. She has told me so much about you too, over the years. My association with her goes back over nearly seventeen years, when my son was struck down with infantile paralysis. He responded better to Nurse Beattie than to anyone else. She told him stories, so many of them about you, of your playmates, of your games, and made him laugh so much that I was often quite frightened for him. The first half of his life was dogged with illness, you see.'

'She knows how to deal with children, although she had none of her own,' Rose agreed. 'I have been very fortunate.'

'But then, so has she, she says. Parting with you has been a very painful wrench for her. In my view only the best is good enough for Beattie Barbour, for I am convinced that without her great nursing talent my dearest Walter would not be here today.' A burning light of mother-love suffused Mistress Scott's brown eyes. 'And so it must be only the best for you, my dear, as a token of my esteem. Many ladies have applied to me for your company, once I let it be known that it might become available. But I have chosen the lady with the most impeccable credentials.'

'Yes, Mistress Scott?'

'She is Miss Jean Brodie, the sister of our admirable Deacon Brodie, who is held in such high esteem in this town. She keeps house for him, for they have never married, although he must be now forty-five or forty-six years old, and Jean, I suppose, in her late twenties. She said that there were almost twenty years between them, I remember.'

'Oh! Then Miss Brodie is quite young?' Rose said, visibly brightening.

'Y-Yes. Yes, of course, my dear. Yes, she is quite young.'

Rose wondered why there had been that slight hesitation. 'Where do they live, Mistress Scott?'

'That is a very good question! The answer to it will prove the high position and circumstances of the family. To begin with, their grandfathers were both very important lawyers. Then their father was a substantial wright and cabinetmaker in the Lawnmarket, and he was made first a Burgess, then a Guild Brother, and later elected a member of the Town Council as Deacon of the Incorporation of Wrights, important enough to have the close he lived in called by his name. It is Brodie's Close, Rose.'

'I have seen it, Mistress Scott, when in the Royal Mile.'

'The present Deacon has followed in his father's footsteps. The family house is very beautiful, as would befit the home of a long tradition of cabinetmakers. I feel sure that you will be happy in it.'

Rose saw that their conversation was drawing to a close.

'I can only thank you, Mistress Scott, for your efforts on my behalf.'

'Miss Jean expects you some time this evening. I think you will like her when you get to know her. She is so—so very lively.'

There it was again, that little shadow of doubt.

'But remember, my dear, that you are free to consult me at any time, should you experience the slightest difficulty, although I anticipate none.'

'You are very kind,' Rose said as she was swept graciously out of the back sitting-room and into the drawing-room, feeling quite elevated as the result of the little interview, and only slightly puzzled at the small hesitations here and there. Or perhaps Mistress Scott had been merely catching her breath.

'You have not met my son,' she was saying now. 'This is Master Walter.'

He looked so young, perhaps only fourteen or fifteen, with his round boyish face, and he was no taller than she was herself. She shook his hand, and then the teacups arrived, and the silver cakestands.

Mr Kyle had been lounging, his long legs outstretched on the velvet carpet, on one of the damson brocade sofas when they entered. Now he drew himself upright and slipped into conversation very decorously, even a little guardedly, perhaps. As she sipped her tea from the delicate teacup, and nibbled at an even more delicate ratafia biscuit, Rose wondered why.

Her gaze fell upon Master Walter, so pleasant and so frank, with a grace of manner so far removed from that of the young apprentices and fisherboys of her acquaintance that she felt compelled to study him more closely. It was his eyes which gave him away, she decided. An extraordinary intelligence shone out of them. He was older than she had at first realised. His mother had said 'nearly seventeen years ago' and he might have been one or so then. With a little shock, Rose calculated that Walter Scott must be around the same age as she was herself.

She was glad that his mother drew her only fleetingly into the ensuing conversation. It gave her time to look around the graceful room, at its high ceiling and large windows draped in damson brocade to match the furniture, while she listened idly. The longer they talked, the more spirited Mistress Scott and Walter became. They were very amusing, but then so was Mr Kyle, who was more than able to hold his own in the discussion of the moralities of the times, or rather, the lack of them. Mistress Scott waxed eloquent in her condemnation of the general deterioration of manners, not to say the depravity all around, and Mr Kyle proved adept at side-stepping neatly any subject which might be too controversial.

He was forever edging the talk away from the subject of their meeting, she realised suddenly, and sat to attention. Thank goodness she had picked up his cue at the outset. Edinburgh Society, especially its ladies, would not permit anything so casual as that had been. She felt herself becoming pink all over at the thought of Mistress Scott's reaction if she only knew of her brief encounters with the gentleman who was turning the conversation so adroitly now to the latest scandals.

'It is inconceivable,' Mistress Scott said, 'that we are forced to read every night in the *Edinburgh Evening Courant* of yet another burglary. I do not know what this town is coming to. We are hardly safe to sleep in our beds.'

'Oh, come, Mama,' her son laughed, 'the burglars would not come out here to George Square. They are most interested in the shops and premises of the Royal Mile. That is where the money is. It is money they are after.'

Mistress Scott recollected her other visitor. 'Do not listen to him, Rose,' she advised. 'Master Walter loves to make up stories. It is his greatest weakness.'

'Perhaps there is a gang,' he said, 'with a master burglar at the head of it. Perhaps they all meet in the dead of night to plot out their next job.'

'What did I tell you? His head is forever in the clouds,

imagining blood and thunder, when it would be more properly employed buried in his books, if he is ever to become a lawyer.'

The longcase clock in the hall boomed the half-hour, echoed by the sparkling tinkle of the little clock on the mantelpiece, so pretty between its daintily painted nymphs and shepherds, when the rumble of carriage wheels was heard outside the windows, carriage wheels that came to a halt.

'Time is up, I fear, Mistress Margaret.' Mr Kyle got to his feet. He reminded Rose of a coiled spring suddenly released.

'You will be going back through the town, perhaps, Cameron?'

'And I will take Miss Rose to her destination. Her trunk is still aboard my carriage.'

'Oh, well then! How convenient that is! How very fortunate that you happened to see her at all this afternoon, Cameron dear! Otherwise I should not have heard all the news of Alison, and we should not have had this delightful chat.'

'Very fortunate,' Mr Kyle said, smiling into Rose's eyes.

'Now then, Rose, do you have all your belongings? Your gloves? Your reticule? You must tell Miss Jean that I shall call on you next week.'

'Thank you, Mistress Scott. I shall deliver your message.'

By the time they had said their farewells and taken their departure it was quite dark, and the night was fine and mild. Mr Kyle settled her into her seat again, with the rug tucked round her, and expelled a long breath.

'The fresh air is very pleasant,' he observed.

'Very pleasant,' Rose agreed, turning her hot cheeks to the cool air.

'You acquitted yourself rather well, I thought.'

'Not half so well as you did, Mr Kyle. I must thank you for putting me on the right track to begin with.' Rose thought again painfully of her first encounter with him on the Swifts. No wonder he had frowned. She had learned a lot since leaving Newhaven, already. 'I was very taken with Master Walter.'

'Yes. He would be about your own age,' he smiled.

Something teasing in his tone stung her.

'Of course,' she said, 'I prefer older gentlemen.'

There, she had said it again. Something quite ridiculous. This man brought out the very worst in her, certainly the most indiscreet.

'That is a very refreshing confession. So you like older men, Miss Rose? How old?'

'How old are you, Mr Kyle?'

'I have never met a lady so direct as you!' he laughed. 'Near thirty. Is that about right?'

'Oh, no,' Rose said, thinking of Uncle George. 'Much older than that. I have observed that the older they get, the gentler and kinder gentlemen seem to become. The younger they are, the crueller, and the more they tease.'

'Oh, dear! But I am heading in the right direction, would you say?'

Rose regarded him out of clear brown eyes. 'You have showed me kindness, sir,' she agreed.

'Then, in return, will you call me Cameron? And permit me to call you Rose?'

She glanced up at his lean face, quite taken aback. Perhaps she had not known him long enough to permit such familiarity. In the light from the dim street lamps she saw the lines etched from his nose to the corners of his mouth.

Thirty really was quite old, it seemed, with cares and worries. It was an age of responsibility. Had he not made himself responsible for her all afternoon? He need not have bothered, she thought, and in her present state of anxiety sudden tears of gratitude filled her eyes as the carriage turned left at the Tron Kirk again, to go up to the Lawnmarket.

'Yes,' she said. 'I like Cameron for a name. It is strong, and it is Scottish.'

'Some day I will tell you the feelings your name evokes in me. But it seems always to be the same. Just as we are having an interesting conversation, we are cut off. Where is it you must go in the Lawnmarket?'

'To Brodie's Close. To the house of Deacon Brodie.'

Why was it that the night became a little darker, a little colder, and the noisy bustle of the town seem to recede into a strange hush? There was a distinct chill in the atmosphere now, both outside the carriage and within it.

'To the house of Deacon Brodie,' Cameron Kyle repeated slowly and heavily.

'Yes, to Miss Jean Brodie. I am to be her companion.'

The silence went on so long, while the carriage stopped gently, the driver got down to unstrap her trunk again, and they descended the little steps soberly, that Rose trembled with excitement and fear.

'Is there anything wrong?'

'No, there is nothing wrong, Rose.' Cameron smiled immediately, too immediately to convince her. He had been debating something in his mind, she was sure of it, before he shook his head like that and answered her so quickly. 'Of course not. I was thinking of Alison, just for a second. When she hears how I have spent the afternoon, she will insist on calling upon you.'

That was not what he had been thinking at all, her strung nerves told her as they walked into the Close.

'Then you must tell her that she will be welcome,' she said automatically. 'Is this the stair?'

'Yes, this is the stair. But I will come with you to the door, for I don't suppose you know how to tirl the risp?'

They had gone up the turnpike stair and were now standing before a massive oak door, remarkable for its curious and elaborate workmanship. Rose stared at it. It did not seem to have a bell-pull or a knocker. Then she saw that a small serrated bar of iron was screwed perpendicularly to the door jamb.

Cameron grasped the little ring which hung down from it and pulled it smartly up and down several times. It produced a harsh and grating sound.

'The young bloods come out of the ale-houses at night looking for some sport,' he said, 'and the Royal Mile has many ale-houses. One of their pranks is to steal the knockers off the doors.'

The driver came up the twisting stair behind them and laid down the trunk at Rose's feet. From inside the house they heard the sound of faint movements.

'Someone is coming now to open the door. So I will say good night, Rose.'

The movements grew nearer and nearer until she could make out the sound of low voices behind the door. Rose watched as Cameron Kyle went back down the turnpike stair, waved his hand to her from the bottom, and disappeared under the arch into the darkness. Waves of homesickness broke over her with his going. As long as he had been at her side, she had not felt so much a stranger, so much alone.

Someone was turning the key in the lock from the inside, first one way and then the other, and back again. Rose heard the sound of heavy bolts rattling back, top and bottom, and then at last the door opened and she was dazzled in the light of a night lantern held high in somebody's hand.

'Miss Barbour?' said a girl who was holding open the heavy door.

'Yes. Does Miss Brodie expect me?'

'You are to come in, miss. Stand back, Jessie, and take that light out of her eyes. Come away in, Miss Barbour. Is that your trunk?'

'It is,' Rose smiled, for now she saw that these were two young maidservants, dressed in their close-fitting frocks, shawled around the shoulders, and their mob-caps on their heads, and with shoes upon their feet. She was surprised at that, for she had expected them to go barefoot. The Brodies must be very rich.

'Stand guard over the trunk with the lantern, Jessie, then, until I come back to help you to carry it inside. It is this way, Miss Barbour, through this door.'

The maidservant opened the door of a room which made Rose gasp. 'If I might take your cloak, miss? I will announce that you have arrived.'

Left alone, Rose felt dwarfed under the high ceiling of the room and crept a little nearer to the fireplace where a log fire burned brightly, its flames lighting up the wood panelling of the walls. Candles burning in the silver candelabra, one at each end of the mantelpiece, drew Rose's eyes to the chimney-breast itself, where a large picture of the 'Adoration of the Magi' had been painted directly on to the centre panel.

At the two furthest corners of the room, behind the projecting chimney-breast, she saw the first steps of little staircases spiralling to the floor above. The whole room would have been like a hall, had it not been for the polished rectangular table with its matching chairs which occupied so much space in it.

The maidservant's feet came pattering back on the parquet floor glowing honey in the light of the fire and the soft light from the candles.

'Miss Jean is ready to see you now, Miss Barbour.'

She led Rose along a passage with a closed door at the end of it, and paused with her hand upon the handle. 'Do not worry, miss,' she whispered encouragingly. 'Miss Jean is a nice wee soul, when you get to know her.' Then she flung open the parlour door, and ushered her inside.

As soon as she set eyes upon Miss Jean Brodie, Rose knew that here was a sight she was unlikely ever to forget, ever as long as she lived. A tiny doll-like figure rose up at their entrance, and after a pause during which her eyes inspected her visitor from head to toe and then all the way back again, she began to toddle towards them.

She wore a satin brocade ball-gown in a most violent shade of purple, its huge skirt tucked and ruched ornately, and so widespread that she must have been wearing paniers to support it. Her overskirt, tucked up at the sides, was of scarlet, although her little slippers peeped out bright green from under her swaying skirts.

Ribbon rosettes adorned her sleeves from shoulder to elbow in random colours, and gauze and feathers floated round her neck as she walked. Her hair was piled up over a wire frame, greased and heavily powdered under more feathers, and in her hand she carried a large feathered fan.

Rose stared at her dumbly, stricken with dismay. Everything the little creature wore was much too big and much too slack for her, and the overall effect of her incongruous appearance was more that of a wizened little old lady, rather wandered in her wits, than that of a young woman not yet thirty years old.

'Miss Rose Barbour!' She took Rose's hands in hers and peered up into her face. 'I am so happy to see you at last! You may leave us now, Ellie,' she added to the maidservant, 'and close the door on your way out.'

'Thank you, Miss Brodie,' Rose said gently. 'I am pleased to be here.'

'No, dear. You must call me Miss Jean. And I shall call you Rose. What a very delightful dress! Do turn round and let me look at it.'

Rose turned round slowly, and felt the tiny hands stroking the blue silk of her gown, feeling it and making little stabs at it, like little fluttering birds.

'But you wear no decorations? Except for that golden necklace? What is that dangling from it?'

'I have often wondered, Miss Jean. I am afraid I do not know. It was left to me by my Mama.'

The little face, which reminded Rose so much of a

cat's face, wider than it was long, crumpled suddenly.

'I have lost my dear Mama too, Rose. I know how you must feel, and it is very lonely. Now that she is gone, and my brother out so much about his business, I have been very lonely.' She tried to control herself. She made a tremendous effort and smiled again, patting her hair in place in a pathetic little gesture. 'But now it will be different, will it not? We shall have so much to talk about. And I shall teach you all I know of the art of dressing, for as I am sure you can see for yourself, I am a great expert on fashion.'

Rose suppressed a wild desire to laugh. 'Yes, I can see that, Miss Jean,' she managed to say quite soberly, and sat back in her chair while Miss Brodie explained to her the finer points of her attire. Surely she did not dress like that every evening? To sit alone? But as she prattled on, Rose realised that indeed Miss Jean must. And if this was how she adorned herself at home, how must she look when she went out in the town? As Mistress Scott had said in her superb understatement, she must look very lively.

There was a footfall outside the door, and with a sinking heart Rose realised that there was still another occupant of the house to meet. But perhaps, being so much older, Miss Brodie's brother would be more restrained.

It was a forlorn hope, immediately dispelled, dashed to death when the door opened and Deacon Brodie stepped into the parlour, resplendent in a suit of clothes so white that they were positively dazzling. His silk breeches were white, his long tail-coat was white, his shirt, his cravat, his very hose were white. Even his hair, of whatever original colour, was so heavily powdered that it, too, was white. Only his little shoes were black, for like Miss Brodie he was small, small-boned, only skin and bone, and undersized.

Perhaps he must wish to be a foil for his flamboyant

sister, that where she was so gaudy, he would be the opposite, to produce just as vivid an effect. Rose had never seen, or ever known such an importance placed upon dress before. And to make matters worse, neither Deacon Brodie nor his sister succeeded in anything more than to make themselves look very foolish.

'Then you must be Miss Barbour,' he cried, 'since you both seem to be struck dumb! I am Deacon Brodie, child, the master of this house, but in reality a very jolly fellow, when you get to know me. You must not be put off by the whitewash of my dress.'

He smiled at her out of his similarly cat-like face set upon narrow shoulders from which there seemed to be no neck, out of eyes of the same indeterminate colour as his sister's. Yet there was a sparkle in them that hers lacked, a merry brilliance infinitely disturbing, infinitely out of place.

Rose tried to define it when they went into the dining-hall and sat down at eight o'clock, three of them at one end of the long table in the beautiful room. More candles had been placed upon the table, where they flickered and glowed and softened even Miss Jean's garishness.

But she could not define it, any more than she could decide why he had used such a strange word as 'whitewash' to describe his own appearance. She frowned, thinking that surely whitewash implied some sort of cover or disguise? Some sham or form of concealment? False colours, like the colours of windows whited so that no one could see into them?

The mussel brose was delicious, yet she could not drink much of the soup, and when Ellie brought in the roasted chicken and Deacon Brodie carved it with a flourish, she tasted only a few morsels. It was the same with the lemon syllabub, which as a rule was one of her favourite desserts.

'You are not eating, Rose,' Miss Jean observed.

'It is only the excitement of the day,' Rose smiled.

'The food is excellent. Who has cooked it?'

'Our dear old Mattie,' Deacon Brodie replied. 'She was here in our mother's time, and although she is getting on in years now, my sister will not part with her. She cooks this one meal in the day, and the other servants cook the others, because we insist on it. Other than that, Mattie acts as Miss Jean's personal maid.'

He emanated an atmosphere all round him of confidence, cheerfulness and great good humour spiked with an elusive mischief, as he laughed and jested his way through the meal with the two ladies.

At the end of it Rose was forced to confess herself uplifted, flattered and cheered, and considerably happier than she had been for a whole week. Outrageous they might be, but the Brodies were so very amusing with it, so kindly and so stimulating. They had ideas she had never even dreamed of. At any rate, they had succeeded in making her want to see more of them, to find out how it was their minds worked. She had never met any people like them before.

'You must be tired now, Rose,' Miss Brodie said when the Deacon excused himself and left the room. 'You have had a long day, and come into a strange new world compared to Newhaven. I will ring for Ellie, to show you to your bedchamber. She will bring you hot water, should you desire it, and see you into bed.'

She shook her silver bell, and within minutes the young maidservant was at the door. 'Attend to Miss Rose, Ellie. See that she is comfortable for the night. And send old Mattie to me, for I am tired now, and I think I shall retire.'

Ellie curtsied. 'Mattie will be along directly, Miss Jean. I will go and fetch the candles.'

'And Deacon Brodie?' Rose asked, when she had departed. 'Does he, too, go to bed at ten o'clock?'

'Very rarely, if ever,' Miss Brodie replied with a sigh. 'So often he has business only starting at this hour. So many places to go, so many people to see, and so many of them tradespeople requiring maintenance or repairs of their premises, which they have not had time to discuss until the day's work is done, and the evening meal is over! Sometimes he gets back home again only in the early hours. I am so glad you spoke of this, Rose.'

'Yes, Miss Jean?'

'Because I may have neglected to warn you, without such a reminder, that you may hear doors opening and closing, footsteps in the middle of the night, and become frightened. It is nothing more than my brother returning from his night business. I do not even notice it now.'

'Then I shall say good night, Miss Jean,' Rose said when Ellie reappeared with a candlestick in her hand, and an old woman close behind her.

'We have not had much chance to talk, dear,' said Miss Brodie, 'but it will be different tomorrow. That is, if you like it here? You will stay, won't you?'

Rose smiled into the anxious little face. 'Yes, I will stay, Miss Jean.'

'I hope you sleep well, then. Good night, Rose.'

Ellie led Rose back through the dining-hall again, and up one of the little staircases at the rear. She saw by the flickering flame of the candle that it was wood-panelled too.

'Hold on to the hand-rail, Miss Rose,' Ellie advised her. 'These stairs are steep.'

Rose marvelled at the hand-rail, how it curved with the wall. No tree trunk ever grew in such a curve, and yet as she slid her fingers along it with every step, she could not feel a single joint. They walked along the dim landing at the top, past two doors on either side—guest-rooms, she imagined, for she did not think the Brodies slept up here. There was dust on the floor, and this upper flat seemed to be disused. Then they came to another door and Ellie turned the handle; Rose saw that this was her room, for her trunk lay on the floor.

The maid lit more candles from the flame cupped in her hand, and the room sprang into life, large and well furnished with an unusual arched window under which an upholstered seat was fitted.

'I chose this room for you, Miss Rose, when Miss Jean gave me orders to prepare one. Do you like the window? It looks down on the Lawnmarket. I thought it would interest you, and before long you would grow used to the noises from the street. They do not go on much after eleven, and the rooms to the back of the house have no windows at all, only skylights.'

'It is a lovely room, Ellie. And you have cleaned it.'

'I cleaned it and aired the bed. The warming-pan is still in it. And I took the liberty of laying out your nightgown, since it was on the top of your trunk along with your brush and comb. But I did not unpack any of the rest of your things, for there will be plenty of time for that tomorrow. Now, would you like some hot water to wash in?'

'Oh, yes, please,' Rose said, a little surprised that it was not already there. 'Of course, Ellie.'

'The Deacon and his sister do not require hot water at night, you see, Miss Rose. They do not wash before they go to bed. But I took one look at you, and heated the kettles.'

She had better not relay that little piece of information when she wrote to Aunt Bea, Rose decided. Her aunt would not think much of that at all. While she waited for the maid to come back, she went across to the window and looked down on the scene below. To her right the massive shape of the Tolbooth loomed before St Giles Cathedral, a few lights shining out of small barred windows on the ground floor. There must be prisoners inside tonight. She shuddered and looked away to the street directly below, and watched the people passing by.

Her attention became drawn to a small figure who had

darted out on to the pavement. If he had been dressed all in white, she could have sworn it was Deacon Brodie, but this man was dressed in black. And besides, his hair was dark, what she could see of it, under his tricorn hat. A tap on the door announced the arrival of Ellie with the hot water.

'I shall help you to undress first, Miss Rose.'

'Are you trained as a lady's maid, then, Ellie?'

'Lord bless you, no! Although that is my ambition. No, this is the first time I have been taken into service, and Miss Jean does not spend time in training her servants. But old Mattie did teach me how to wait at table.'

'Well, you must have picked that up very easily. I thought you did well.'

'Thank you, Miss Rose,' Ellie smiled, rubbing the back of Rose's neck gently with the flannel and then patting it dry.

'I was looking out of the window while I was waiting for you, and I thought I saw Deacon Brodie. But of course I was mistaken, for the man was dressed in dark clothes.'

'Oh, it would be him, all right,' Ellie said with a sniff. 'He always changes into a black suit when he goes out upon his night business.'

'Isn't that a little strange?'

'Now shall I brush out your hair? I have always longed to brush out a lady's long hair, and yours is so very beautiful.'

'Yes,' said Rose, laughing. 'You may practice on me, Ellie.'

They had moved over to the dressing-table now, and Rose sat down on the stool in front of it and looked in the mirror. Now she could see the girl's face reflected in it, and she liked what she saw as Ellie talked and brushed her hair at the same time in long, easy strokes.

Ellie was a big girl, fresh faced and spotlessly clean.

Her dark blue eyes were sharp and full of fun, and her black hair was short and curly.

'You do not wear your hair long yourself, Ellie?'

'Oh no, miss. My mother had eleven of us, and she cut all our hair short. It is easier to go through short hair with a fine-tooth comb, and my mother is very particular for a poor working woman.

'And your father?'

'He died three years ago, when I was fourteen. It took my mother another year to find this work for me. I must do well in it, for she needs the money . . . But yes, it is strange, as you say, for the Deacon to change his clothes at this time of night. It is not as if it would matter if he got dirty. He has three or four more white suits, after all, and they are for ever in the wash. But then, there are plenty of servants here to attend to all that.'

'Why? How many are there?'

'Five maidservants, who live in. Besides old Mattie and little Jessie—that was Jessie with the lantern at the door—there are another three girls, counting me. We sleep in the attics up above here. But we have to use the staircase from the kitchen.'

'Do two people really need all those servants?'

Ellie laughed. 'Besides us five, there are two seam-stresses who come in two or three times a week.'

'Ah. So they make Miss Jean's dresses?'

Ellie nodded at her in the mirror, and a little dimple appeared in her cheek, but she did not comment. Then she could be discreet, Rose thought, although she was such a chatterbox.

'That is done,' the girl said instead, admiring her handiwork. 'Your hair is like a shower of copper down your back.'

Rose shivered, a sudden picture of Mama before her eyes.

'But you are cold, and very likely tired now. Will you go to bed, Mis Rose? Before you do, bolt the door. Oh yes, it has a key, but bolt it all the same, and then the noises in the night will not matter.'

'Yes, I know about the noises,' Rose said, wondering at Ellie's insistence.

'Then good night, Miss Rose.' The maidservant took the warming-pan out of the bed, and with the candlestick in her other hand repeated, 'Bolt the door, and I will waken you in the morning.'

The bed was warm and cosy when Rose tucked herself up in it. But she could not sleep. A thousand impressions drifted through her mind, and she could not believe that it was only this afternoon that she had left Newhaven, and Aunt Bea, and a life which seemed a hundred miles away instead of the three that lay between.

And there were so many questions. One question-mark lay opposite Deacon Brodie's name. Rose did not understand him at all, so far. He was not what she had expected. She had thought he would be taller, more solid, since he was so highly respected, perhaps with a look of severity, of solemnity under the weight of his many arduous commitments. She found it hard to reconcile his impression on her with all of that. But still, she thought with a sigh as she turned restlessly in her bed, she had seen him with her own eyes, still so industrious so late at night.

She would have to wait until tomorrow to see how her mistress, poor little Miss Brodie, went on. For one who was so interested in the fashions, how could she be so ludicrously far removed? But there was something more than just her disastrous choice of colour schemes. It was as though she were determined to hold on to the old fashions, as if she wanted to retreat into the past, to be someone she was not. Rose puzzled over it for a long time.

The Lawnmarket was hushed now, and the silence was unnerving. Ellie had been wrong to imagine that the street noises would disturb her. She had not minded them; they had kept her company. This quivering silence was much louder. It pressed in on her, heavy with little rustlings and whisperings she could not quite hear, and perhaps only imagined.

She remembered that she was all alone up here: that if the door of her bedchamber were somehow opened, no one would know, and if she screamed out, no one would hear, and her flesh crawled in the black night, in this strange and lonely place.

But the key was on the little table beside the bed, and the bolts had been stout when she pulled them across. She was being silly and fanciful. Perhaps it was because the people of Newhaven did not live like this, in fear and trembling. If they bolted their doors at all, it was against the savage nor'easterly gales to stop them crashing open, and not against the burglars.

The burglars! Her reticule! But when she put out her arm her fingers found it under the bed where she had laid it down. It was still safe. Tomorrow she must take the sovereigns and put them in the bank.

Walter Scott had laughed and joked with his mother about the burglars. He said they met in the middle of the night to plot their evil deeds. They could be prowling up and down the Lawnmarket or the High Street at this very minute, or smashing in a window to get into someone's house.

Rose lay very still and strained her ears far into the night, but there was no sound of tinkling glass, no footsteps creaking up the staircase, no whispered voices and no hand upon the handle of her door, and at last she grew drowsy.

It was then that the last question, the most important one of all, brought her wide awake again, in the shape of a tall fair-haired man with vividly blue eyes. He had suggested that his sister might come to see her. But Cameron Kyle had not promised as much, himself. Why should he?

She could not move in the same circle of Society as he did—or Alison, come to that. He had said it only out of politeness. Or perhaps to let her down more lightly in a final farewell. Or had he meant that his sister would be interested to see what had become of the little fishergirl she had seen on the Swifts? Rose did not believe that either. Alison would have forgotten her long ago.

Rose forced herself to face the facts. To judge from what little she knew of Cameron Kyle, except that he was a gentleman, and quite clearly very rich, the fact that he had devoted one afternoon out of his life to her was more than a mere lady's companion could reasonably expect.

She would never see him again. How could she ever see him again, unless by chance as today's meeting had been? All she really knew was that he owned a horse called Rose Royale, that he had a sister called Alison. That, worst of all, he seemed to be on intimate terms with a lady called Miss Cornelia. She did not even know where he lived. But she *had* hoped . . . She had hoped he would be her friend.

It was a long time before Rose fell asleep at last, with the teardrops still wet upon her eyelashes.

CHAPTER
FOUR

THE SUDDEN barking of dogs, a man shouting and doors flung back awakened her. It must be very early, not five o'clock yet, for it was only the first light of dawn. But the Town was waking up.

Rose lay still and listened to the voices of the early caddies and the chair-men calling to each other as they slithered and cursed through the night-rubbish on their way up to the Lawnmarket to meet the Glasgow coach and the carriers from Inverness.

The light was still thin when the scavengers arrived next, trundling their barrows and grumbling at their work. She could hear their shovels grating against the cobbles. This upper part of the Royal Mile was kept respectably clean at least, for it was from here that travellers and visitors caught their first glimpse of Auld Reekie.

Now she could open her window and let in the fresh air and the sounds floating up from below. Even that, she thought sadly, would keep her company. And then the whistling and the tramping feet began down in Brodie's Close. She leaned out to watch the cheerful workmen going down to the timber-yard at the far end of it, and soon she could hear the saws in the workshops and smell the sweet clean scent of the sawdust from the wood.

When they had all gone in, she went back to bed and lay propped up on her pillows. She was wide awake now, and still the questions of the night before persisted in her tired brain. As the daylight grew stronger she could see the interior of the room more clearly. Her aware, unhappy eyes roved from one piece of meticulously crafted furniture to the next, from the huge carved wardrobe, the marble-topped washstand, the bow-fronted chest of drawers, the exquisite writing-desk right round to the dressing-table, mahogany faced, the wood perfectly matched and elegantly glazed, its fretwork as delicate as lace.

The spent candle, its grease thickly rivuleted upon its plate, lay on the little cabinet beside her bed, and in the middle of the floor the small round mahogany breakfast table waited with its four chairs tucked underneath. Close by it lay her trunk with its lid upraised as though it had paused in mid-flight. It had an air of being here only briefly, only for a moment on its way to somewhere else.

Rose gazed at it with a sudden spark of hope. It seemed to be telling her that it did not have to stay here. She did not have to stay here, either. It would be the easiest thing in the world to rise out of this bed, dress, pack up again and go back in the coach to Newhaven, to her own haven of safety and happiness in Longcakes Lane. The more she thought about it, the more enticing and then the more imperative it became.

She had one foot out over the edge of the bed when a knock came to the door.

'It's only me, Miss Rose. Ellie.'

With a deep sigh, Rose got up and unbolted the door. The maid was standing outside, clean and shining, with a large jug of steaming water in her hands.

'You have not slept,' she accused Rose at once.

'No. I suppose it was all too strange, Ellie.'

'Too strange, and just as I said it would be, far too lonely,' Ellie said with triumphant asperity as she bustled around exuding energy and a brimming indignation. 'But we'll soon see about *that*. Never mind, Miss Rose. You will feel much better when you are washed and dressed and with some breakfast inside you.'

'Perhaps,' Rose sighed doubtfully, eyeing her trunk again.

Ellie caught her glance, and her eyes took on the

sparkle of a woman with her mind made up. There was a purposeful bounce to the short black curls under her mob-cap as she set light to the fire in the grate and turned to go.

'I'm away to fetch your breakfast,' she said briskly, 'and I may be half an hour in the fetching of it. That will give you time to wash and dress up to your petticoats, Miss Rose, and by the time you have put on your dressing-robe I'll be back and that fire should be burning bright. It's a fine sunny day, but a wee bit nippy now in the mornings.'

Ellie's footsteps echoed away hollowly along the passage and down the wooden staircase, and silence descended again in the room like a depressing grey fog. In spite of the city sounds outside, the gleam of the sun through the window and the small sparks and spits of the fire as it crackled up, Rose felt once more a great sense of loneliness rolling over her, and a dejection too much like a foreboding to shake off.

She would never make a good companion at this rate, never . . . Not to anyone. And certainly not to Miss Jean Brodie, the poor little creature, who looked as though she needed a great deal of a different kind of support and bolstering up from what she was getting from the hoops and pads and whalebones which held her together at present.

Her gloomy toilet was scarcely completed when Ellie bounced back bearing a tray, flushed with success.

'Oh, Miss Rose! It is all settled! I just caught the Deacon on his way out, and he agreed to my idea and sent me to Miss Jean.' The girl shook her head and smiled. 'Perhaps it was the best time to ask her, too, for of course she was only half awake. But anyway, she said I could carry on!' She flapped a white cloth on to the table and set down a small bowl of porridge and a jug of milk, tea and floury rolls and butter. 'Will this do?' she asked anxiously.

'It is always what we have at home,' Rose said. 'But what was your idea?'

For the first time that morning, Ellie hesitated and looked down at her shoes. She seemed nervous and confused, quite unlike her usual positive self. 'How could you know what was burning in my mind all night, Miss Rose? Och, I remembered what it was like the first night I left home myself. I thought you might be lonely and homesick too, the same as I was.'

'Oh, Ellie! What have you done?'

'I should have asked you first, shouldn't I?' The girl looked away with flushed cheeks, and tears in her eyes. 'You will have to forgive me if I have been too forward. But I have got permission to be your maidservant when my other duties allow, and to sleep in the small room next to yours.'

All at once the sun shone brighter, the street noises assumed a more cheerful sound, and Rose no longer heard the secret hissings of the fire.

'Oh, Ellie!' she said again, and laughed. 'If you had not had your brilliant idea, I swear I should not have had the courage to stay!'

'Well, I saw the way you were looking at that trunk,' Ellie smiled, wiping her eyes.

Rose discovered she was really quite hungry after all. The porridge had just the right amount of salt in it, and the milk was as she liked it, fresh and frothy, and ice cold.

'Who made it?' she asked.

'I did, Miss Rose. I am always the first to rise in the mornings, and I serve the Deacon in the dining-hall. I did not know what you liked to eat, or when you liked to get up, so for your first day here I brought you the tray.'

'In future you will not be put to the trouble, Ellie. I will be expected to have breakfast downstairs with the family, I suppose. What time do they have it?'

'Deacon Brodie—Master Will, as he likes to be called

at home—has his at eight o'clock sharp. Every day'
—and after a little pause she added in a voice heavy with
meaning—'no matter when he gets home after his
"night business".'

'Oh . . . And Miss Jean?'

'Miss Jean never appears before noon, Miss Rose. So
you see, you will not be required to eat breakfast
downstairs at all. I shall always bring it up here to you,
instead.'

Last night Ellie had been very insistent that she should
bolt her door. Now, this morning, she was quite clearly
discouraging her from going downstairs in the early
mornings. Why? Did she mean that it would be im-
proper for her to breakfast alone with the Deacon? Rose
hesitated. There were problems and mysteries in this
beautiful house that so far she did not understand.

'Thank you, Ellie,' she said thoughtfully. 'And Miss
Jean does not appear until noon, did you say?'

'Never,' said Ellie primly, as though she could have
said a great deal more, but thought better of it. 'So you
need be in no hurry this morning, either. It will give us
plenty of time to unpack. I will take out your things if
you will tell me where to put them. Then I can remove
the trunk—and I hope you will not be asking me to pack
it up again for a long time.'

'Oh, Ellie, I am so glad it was you I set eyes on first this
morning, or else I don't know what I might have done!'

'Och, we'll soon get into a little routine,' Ellie smiled
encouragingly. 'And I believe I could become quite
expert with the ringlets!'

But Rose had found plenty to ponder over in that
early morning conversation with her maid. Deacon
Brodie sometimes never got back home, then, until
breakfast-time, and Ellie at least, had her own ideas
about that. But perhaps they were more than just ideas?
She searched the girl's face in the mirror, but the blue
eyes concentrating on the long red-gold curls were calm

and gave nothing further away.

Certainly, it did not seem very likely that the 'night business' could go on until seven or eight in the mornings. So what was he doing? Where did he go? And Miss Jean. She retired so early and she slept so late . . . Why was it that the sister required so much sleep, and the brother none at all?

It took a long time to empty the trunk and dispose of all her belongings, the day-gowns, the evening gowns, the nightgowns and all the fine cambric underwear, new and embroidered, which Aunt Bea had insisted on collecting for her—like a trousseau. Ellie took charge immediately.

'The creases must all be ironed out, Miss Rose. Leave it to me. I'm going to fetch Jessie now, to help carry the trunk away, and when I come back it will be time to go and see Miss Jean.'

The two maids departed, dragging the trunk along the corridor between them, and Rose seized the opportunity to consider her reticule and its contents. There might not be time today to go to the Bank of Scotland with the sovereigns, and they weighed so very heavy. Where could she hide them?

There was a key in the top flap of the writing-desk. When she turned it, she discovered it must be part of a mechanism which opened the five long drawers beneath at the same time, for they jumped open a hair's breadth.

The small drawers inside the flap had been released, too, where the leather-tooled blotter lay open and virgin white with tiny inkwells ranged behind it, red and black and blue and all stoppered with brass tops, and with quills all ready and sharpened in the groove in front of it.

She did not have time to explore the wonders of the writing-desk. Hurriedly she pulled open each long drawer in turn. They were all empty, and into the bottom one she tipped the sovereigns. They glittered up at her—so much gold, so rich, so gleaming. So much of it!

There was too much of it—far more than the hundred pounds George Abercromby had given her in the black velvet bag after the Caledonian Hunt Cup. As she gazed back down at them, Rose became aware that the coins were not all sovereigns, and there were more *louis d'or* than just the one she had bet on Rose Royale. Other foreign coins were there too. She recognised doubloons, twice the value of sovereigns, and remembered that Uncle Herbert had brought home foreign gold.

Aunt Bea and George Abercromby between them must have doubled or even trebled her hundred pounds. But there was not the time to count it. She found a ribbon in her sewing box, and a needle and thread. Then she knotted one end of the ribbon through the filigree handle of the key, and stitched the other end securely to the lining of her reticule. Now it could not possibly fall out. She could not lose it.

Rose closed the bottom drawer of the writing-desk silently and turned the small master key in the top flap. Before Ellie came back, the desk was locked up again, the key tucked safely back in her reticule, and Rose was ready to go, with her white shawl over her arm.

Eleven o'clock was ringing on St Giles.

'She should be awake by now,' Ellie said. 'I'll take you down.'

'I can find the way myself; and besides, you have more than enough to do,' Rose said firmly, laying her hand on the maid's arm. 'And thank you for all you have done for me already, Ellie dear. Tonight will be a different night, with you beside me.'

She did not see Ellie's anxious eyes following her along the passage to the top of the curved staircase. And she could not guess the impact of the restrained and polished appearance the maid had worked so hard to achieve for her, in her pearl grey day-gown with its frosty white collar and cuffs. It set off her brilliant colouring to perfection.

On the contrary, Rose's heart was beating fast when she tapped lightly on Miss Brodie's sitting-room door.

'Come in, then,' said a reedy, querulous voice, and she found herself face to face with old Mattie standing like a dragon between her and the bedroom beyond.

'Yes?' the woman said defiantly. 'What is it you want?'

'Does Miss Jean wish me to attend her now?' Rose asked, feeling chilled and infinitely rebuffed by this reception.

'Wait you there,' growled Mattie, 'and I will see.'

Surely the old woman could not be jealous? What was there to be jealous of?

'Of course, Miss Mattie,' Rose had the presence of mind to reply, according the respect due to old age.

The old woman's eyes blinked rapidly while she considered this new approach. Plainly, it had thrown her off course.

'I'll see,' she repeated grumpily and disappeared into the bedchamber, slamming the door in Rose's face.

There were undercurrents in this house, she decided with a prick of interest. Of course, there were undercurrents in every house. Even in Longcakes Lane, for example. She loved Aunt Bea. She was in no doubt that Aunt Bea loved her. Yet she had been sent away. Even if it was for her own good in the end, it still hurt.

And not because of George Abercromby, either, although he had played his part. Nobody wished her better than George Abercromby, dear Uncle George. But now Rose realised how much they had both given up for her sake, how Aunt Bea had tried so hard to be loyal to them both. It must have been very difficult.

It seemed that life became more difficult than it already was, over the question of loyalties, and especially where children were concerned. Children accepted sacrifices as a matter of course, because they knew no better. She had been one of them, and not very long ago. But one night here had changed all that. Now she was grown up.

At the same time as she was working all this out, Rose was sniffing the stale air in Miss Brodie's sitting-room. A strange odour overlay all the others, a fusty, fruity smell that she could not identify. The bedroom door opened again suddenly.

'My mistress will see you now,' old Mattie said.

The emphasis on the first two words of this statement was not lost on Rose.

'Thank you, Miss Mattie,' she smiled, and went in through the door held open so grudgingly, and past the averted old eyes. In here the heavy odour was even stronger, with a sharper note, like vinegar.

'Good morning, Miss Jean. You are well, I hope?'

'Perfectly well, my dear. It takes me a little time to come to myself in the mornings, that is all. Did I see that child Ellie in here earlier?'

'You gave her permission to sleep in the room next to mine, Miss Jean. It was very thoughtful of you.'

'So I did, dear. So I did. I had forgotten. My mind has been concentrating on gloves instead, you see.'

'Gloves?'

'Yes, dear, it is gloves today. Every day, rain or shine, I make a point of going to the shops and the Luckenbooths on some small errand. Today it is a white ruffled shirt for the Deacon, and gloves to match my new gown. Did I show you my new gown?'

'No, I don't think you did, Miss Jean.'

Rose would not have believed that Miss Brodie's day-gowns could be even worse than her evening gowns. But perhaps it was the startling effect of the colours in the strong daylight which made them seem worse. Today she was attired in dashing, clashing shades of red and orange, which only served to emphasise the unbecoming flush on the lady's cheeks. Rose had thought her to be of a sallow complexion, but she was far from sallow this morning.

'How do you like it, Rose?'

Well, at least the new one was all one colour, Rose thought. It was a drab gown, made of a drab brown material.

'It will be a useful day-gown when it is trimmed, Miss Jean,' she answered as tactfully as she could.

'Oh, what did I tell you? I am never wrong with the fashions!' Miss Brodie cried happily. 'And the *trimmings*! They are so exciting, are they not? How shall we arrange them?'

'Perhaps it would be a good idea, as you thought, to start with the gloves. A pretty shade of bright blue?'

'That is what I thought myself, dear. How they will suit this pale grey!'

Rose stared at her. But the dress was brown . . .

'Yes, we will go out and find some blue gloves. Are you ready, Rose? Will you be warm enough with just that little shawl round your shoulders?'

Miss Brodie did not wait for an answer, but led the way to the front door, where to Rose's horror she grasped a long walking-cane, silver-topped and betasselled, from the box of canes which stood in the corner.

'Now let us be off,' Miss Brodie said. 'It is such a lovely day.'

They walked out under the carved stone of the arch-way to Brodie's Close and into the uproar of the milling Lawnmarket, Miss Brodie taking up most of the pave-ment with her wide-hooped skirts and the even wider angle of her walking-cane, scattering the oncomers to right and to left.

The people looked behind them at her with their smiles behind their hands. It seemed that Miss Jean Brodie was not so much a character as a figure of fun,

and to Rose's own surprise she began to feel angry and
then very protective of her small eccentric mistress. She
made up her mind then and there that she would try to
make some changes that would help her, and as soon as
she had done so, the vision of Mistress Scott swam into
the back of her mind. Was that the reason why Mistress
Scott had chosen to send her to the Brodies in the first
place?

'But first for the Meridian,' Miss Brodie said, sweeping into one of the coffee-houses which seemed as
numerous as the taverns in the Royal Mile. 'Everybody
who is anybody takes the Meridian, in Edinburgh.'

'You must excuse me, Miss Jean—the Meridian?'

'You do not know, dear? At twelve noon the gentlemen of the Town repair to the inns for "a cauld cock and
a feather", which means a glass of brandy and a bunch of
raisins. We ladies do not indulge in strong drink during
the day, so we take a cup of coffee.'

Rose could not help noticing that Miss Brodie's coffee
had quite a different aroma from her own, in the little
clouds of steam which hovered over the cups. Miss
Brodie had not needed to order it. It was brought to the
table as soon as they came in. The aroma reminded Rose
of the Turf Inn, and Cameron Kyle's coffee laced with
brandy.

It was having a very beneficial effect on the lady,
anyway, dispersing the mottling in her cheeks and
putting a sparkle in her eye. The coffee was finally
squaring up Miss Brodie. She was alert now, and anxious
to be off to the Luckenbooths.

'Here is the stall I want you to see, Rose. Look at all
the gloves! Leather and lace, and even silk!'

Eagerly she picked out a pair, and paid what seemed
to Rose to be an exorbitant price for them, and
handed them over to her for inspection as they walked
away.

'But you wanted blue, Miss Jean. And one is green

and the other grey. It is an odd pair.'

'Oh, is it, dear?' Miss Brodie said vaguely. 'Does it matter?'

'Yes, it matters.'

'Well, go back and change them for me, if you will. I must go down to Mr McCreadie's shop in the High Street to look out a shirt for my brother.'

Miss Brodie darted off, and Rose was left with the gloves in her hand. She made her way back to the glove stall.

'Well?' demanded the woman in charge, when Rose showed her the odd pair. 'What of it? She wouldn't know the difference, anyway.'

So that was it. Then everybody knew that Miss Brodie was colour blind. And everybody quite blatantly took advantage of her disability.

'Perhaps she would not,' Rose replied quietly, looking at the stall-holder with steady brown eyes. 'But I do.'

The woman sniffed, preparing to be awkward.

'And so do I,' said a man's deep voice behind Rose's back. She hardly needed to turn round to recognise its owner. The shiver which ran clean through her at the sound of it left her almost limp.

Cameron Kyle's face was a hard mask. Only a little muscle tight in his cheek betrayed his anger. But his voice was quiet and controlled when he spoke again.

'So do I, Molly Simpson. I know the difference, too. And what are you going to do about that?'

'Oh, Mr Kyle, sir,' the woman said. 'I did not see you.'

'No?' he smiled grimly. 'I will tell you what you are going to do about it. You will kindly permit Miss Barbour to choose the gloves she requires.'

'Please do, miss. And if you will forget my mistake, I will forget the price—seeing it's you, sir.'

Rose selected a pair of blue gloves, and Cameron tossed down a coin contemptuously on the stall.

'I will forget nothing, Mollie Simpson. Least of all that this stall is banned in future for the ladies of my family and close acquaintance.'

Still angry, he marched Rose away, leaving Mistress Simpson shrilly protesting her innocence behind them.

'Why isn't one of the maidservants here with you?' he demanded sternly.

'Oh, Miss Brodie is not far away. I was changing the gloves for her while she went on to Mr McCreadie's shop.'

'Then you will permit me to escort you back to her there.' His hand under her arm sent waves of shock through Rose. 'You should not be out here alone. Do you understand me, Rose? Ladies do not go abroad alone.'

Her heart sank. His expression had not changed since they left the stall in the Luckenbooths. It remained cold and uncompromising.

'If I had not been running over by the Swifts alone one morning, you would never have met me in the first place,' she replied indignantly.

'I did not approve of that either, as I think you gathered.'

Rose's eyes fell. She wished she had not brought it up again. But now that she had, she was forced to continue her own argument. 'I showed you I could look after myself then. I can look after myself now. You are not my keeper.'

'I am for the moment, at least,' he assured her calmly. 'And it could have been some ruffian you met on the Swifts that morning. As it is, that woman in the Luckenbooths had no intention of giving you new gloves, or your money back. Edinburgh is not the quiet friendly place Newhaven is, Rose. There are all kinds of wickedness here.'

All that was true, she was forced to admit. He was only trying to look after her again.

'It is very kind of you to go to all this bother,' she sighed.

They had progressed down the High Street almost to John Knox's house by this time.

'It is no bother,' he smiled down at her with his sudden rare grin. 'I keep trying very hard to prove to you it is nothing but a pleasure, for me. The tide will turn when it is just as much a pleasure for you. And in the meantime, while you are making up your mind about it, there is a little shop here I would like you to see.'

He took her into the dark interior of what appeared to be a cellar, and for a moment she could see nothing at all. She hoped devoutly that neither could he, for his words had brought a swift flush to her cheeks. If he only knew, it *was* a pleasure to be with him, a very great pleasure, but that was where it must stop between a gentleman such as Cameron Kyle and an unknown such as she.

While her eyes became accustomed to the darkness, the most glorious scents assailed her nostrils, and in an instant she was captivated. She detected rose and carnation, lemon and lavender in a heady pot-pourri of perfumes.

'Oh, it is wonderful,' she cried.

'It is scent for a very small pomander that we have come for, James,' Cameron informed the dim figure behind the counter. 'One to fit into the lady's gold bauble.'

Tiny pellets of wax were thrust under Rose's eyes and nose, a whole tray of them. Their scent was overpowering.

'My gold bauble?' she asked.

'That little birdcage you always wear around your neck was designed to hold a perfumed pellet. It is a little pomander, a great fashion with the ladies of Paris, although I have to admit I have not seen one in Edinburgh before. Have you, James?'

'Rarely nowadays,' a rusty voice growled out of the darkness.

'It was my mother's,' Rose said, and could have bitten out her tongue. She did not want anyone to know about her mother or her past. Especially not Cameron Kyle. But after a moment of silence, the moment passed over.

'Choose a pellet for it, Rose.'

'I cannot. Each scent is more beautiful than the other.'

'Then let us have the perfume of a rose,' Cameron said. 'The rose is the most beautiful of them all, is it not? A red rose, the most passionate, to suit the lady who will wear it.'

She glanced up at his face in the dim light and his eyes burned right through her. But that was nothing compared to the touch of his hand on her breast as he gently unlocked the little cage and placed the little block inside it.

It was as though his fingers were scalding her skin, and Rose was still trembling from head to toe when they came out into the bright sunlight again.

'How did you know about the birdcage?' she asked, to cover her confusion.

'I am often in France on business, and I saw them there.'

'France? And you go there often?'

'As often as I can, at every opportunity, and with the very slightest excuse,' he said.

'Oh . . . You have found friends there?'

'I have found nothing there, Rose. But I am still looking for someone—and something—I have lost. The trouble is,' he sighed, 'I do not know where to begin.'

Rose was still trying to puzzle this out when Miss Brodie appeared in the narrow doorway of Mr McCreadie's shop in extreme difficulties. She could not bend her hoops and hold her parcel at the same time, and so she was wedged in. When her walking-cane clattered to the street in the middle of all her wriggling manoeuvres, Cameron Kyle sized up the situation at a glance.

'Allow me to take charge of your parcel, madam,' he said, picking up the cane, while Rose rushed to help her with her skirts.

'Oh, thank you, sir. Rose, dear, what is the answer to this?'

'We must have narrower, lighter hoops put in your dresses, Miss Jean. These are far too big for you.'

'And you, sir. I did not catch your name?'

'This is Mr Cameron Kyle, Miss Brodie,' Rose introduced them hurriedly.

'You must have thought I was my dear Mama, Mr Kyle, when you called me madam.'

'I beg your pardon,' he said gently. 'But, you see, it was your cane which confused me. It is the older ladies who generally walk with them, is it not? But now I see that you are young—and pretty, too,' he added gallantly —making another conquest, Rose smiled to herself. 'Shall I carry it up to the Lawnmarket for you, and escort both of you home again?'

Once again Cameron Kyle had scored, very neatly. But, somehow, Rose did not think Miss Brodie would be taking her walking-cane out again, and for that she heaved a sigh of relief.

Their journey up to Brodie's Close was pleasant, and made in great good humour.

'I believe Mistress Scott is to have tea with you on Saturday afternoon, Miss Brodie?' Cameron asked.

'Oh, yes,' she fluttered. 'Such a very nice lady! But how could you know, sir?'

'My sister, Alison, is a friend of hers, and would be deeply honoured if she may accompany Mistress Scott. She has met Rose once, and would like to see her again.'

'You must tell Miss Kyle that the honour will be entirely mine,' Miss Brodie replied, as they stood before the turnpike stair in the Close. 'Of course I shall be delighted to receive any of Rose's friends. And,' her little cat's face glowed up at him, 'shall you accompany the ladies here yourself?'

'But perhaps you ladies would consider that a masculine intrusion?' he laughed. 'Unless, of course, other gentlemen are to attend also?'

What was he trying to find out in such a roundabout way, Rose wondered?

'Oh, no, Mr Kyle, not even my dear brother the Deacon. Not at that hour of the day! But we ladies will look forward to the pleasure of your company.'

'My coachman will deliver them here, then, and I shall try to arrange to take them back myself.'

'I shall delay tea until half-past four, in that case, with a cup laid out for you, Mr Kyle.'

It was amazing, Rose thought, as she followed her mistress into the house, how Cameron Kyle could inveigle his way in anywhere and everywhere, and all with the lightest touch, a mere suggestion, a chance remark dropped here and there . . . He seemed to appear wherever she went, and all by the seemingly sheerest coincidence. How, for instance, did he manage to be right behind her at Molly Simpson's stall, just in the nick of time? Was it Deacon Brodie he particularly wished to avoid on Saturday afternoon? It was too late to find out now. Cameron Kyle was long gone.

'I have sent for the two dressmakers, Rose,' Miss Brodie said a day or two later, 'with a message to bring narrower hoops. Much narrower.'

'I am sure they will suit you much better, Miss Jean.'

'I have been thinking so much about what your friend Mr Kyle said, and he is quite right. I have been living and dressing too much in the old style, the style of my Mama.'

'Yes, Miss Jean?'

'And I have been taking special notice lately, when we

have been out. The ladies are not wearing their hair so high, nor have I seen it powdered.'

'No,' Rose answered warily. She had a feeling that here was thin ice. All this was of supreme importance to Miss Brodie. 'But is that because of the new powder tax, perhaps?'

'Perhaps. And I see very few ladies with canes, it is true.'

'No.'

'I have been thinking it is time for a change. But I am afraid I cannot make the change myself.'

'Is there any way I can help you?'

'You see, dear, I have been wondering, for a few years now, if I see the colours properly? I do not think I do. I do not think I see them as other people do, although my eyesight is very good otherwise.'

'Then there is nothing to worry about, nothing at all, so long as you have your sight,' Rose reassured her. 'And I will help you with your colours. But is that all that is worrying you? Is there something else?'

Miss Brodie flushed, and looked away from Rose's candid brown eyes.

'I feel that none of my gowns is quite right, dear.'

Rose could hardly believe her ears. Miss Brodie had always been proud, even boastful, of her fashion sense. Then there *was* something else. The gowns were not the heart of the matter. But whatever it was, she was not prepared to speak of it now.

'Then let us take all your gowns out and lay them on your bed. When the dressmakers arrive, we shall see what can be done to alter them to your satisfaction. What a shock for them when they see all this, Miss Jean!' Rose laughed.

'Oh dear, Rose! You will stay with me, will you not?'

'Of course I will stay with you, dear Miss Jean. You are not frightened of them, are you?'

'I am, a bit,' Miss Brodie admitted.

Poor little thing, Rose thought, gazing at her mistress. To tell the truth, she herself was not much looking forward to the impending interview with the two sewing-ladies. They were sisters, which was quite obvious any time she had seen Mattie conducting them into Miss Brodie's sitting-room. The younger seemed quite agreeable, but the older one a very determined, stern sort of person. She was just the sort to make mincemeat of Miss Jean.

It did not take the seamstresses long to realise that their days of palming just anything off on Miss Brodie were numbered, half an hour later. As Rose had predicted, they stood rooted to the spot at the sight of the garments piled up on the bed.

'You are going somewhere? You require another gown?' the older one asked, when she recovered herself.

'No. Miss Brodie feels there is something wrong with every gown you see there,' Rose said quietly. 'You know it, and I know it, and now she knows it, too. She has difficulty in distinguishing certain colours, which is not an uncommon thing, although more so in a woman. It is a pity that you did not realise that at the time.'

'Oh, but we . . .'

The younger sister stopped short at the warning look from the other.

'But you did,' Rose finished for her. 'Well, we must try to put it right.'

She kept very calm as she delivered these criticisms in a firm but pleasant tone. It was a little trick she had learned from Aunt Bea, who simply did not entertain difficult patients.

'People turn nasty only when they are frightened, Rose,' she had said. 'When there is an unpleasant job which must be done, say so as directly and as kindly as you can, and smile when you say it. A smile and a gentle word works wonders, whatever happens, wherever you go.'

The older woman shuffled her feet uneasily, still scowling. 'I don't know,' she said.

'The workmanship is so good,' Rose said, holding up two of the gowns. 'It is such a pity, for you are such beautiful needlewomen. Would it not be possible to join one bodice to another skirt which would suit it better?'

The sisters exchanged glances.

'Well, out of all the blues, I dare say we could make a blue gown,' the older one said slowly.

'Oh yes! How pretty that would be!' Rose said. Her job was done. 'Wouldn't it, Miss Jean?'

'We could manage to do that with most of them.' The younger sister was becoming quite enthusiastic.

'Could you really?' said Miss Jean. 'And put in smaller hoops as well?'

'And perhaps take the waists in just a little bit?' Rose asked.

'We will be back on Friday with two or three re-modelled,' they told Miss Brodie, preparing to depart.

'How old do you think I am, Rose?' Miss Brodie asked suddenly when they had gone.

'Not old at all, Miss Jean. You must be the baby of the family. Perhaps not much older than I am myself?'

'Now then, you must not flatter me,' Miss Brodie smiled sadly. 'But it is true that I am not yet thirty . . . I always wanted to look older than I really was.'

'But why?' Rose asked, wondering if the truth was coming out now, at last.

'To be like Mama. She was so kind, and yet so strict, you know. She would not have allowed any recklessness, or loose talk, or wild ideas. Although it is in the nature of men—a little gambling, a little gaming, of course. She would have said we women must expect such things. Yes, Rose, this was a happy home as long as my dear Mama was alive. After that our Father seemed to lose all heart.'

To whom was she referring? It could not be the

Deacon, one of the most respected men of the Town. Was there some other man she had known? Rose decided to postpone diagnosing this snippet of self-revelation until later.

'But I am not made of the same stuff as she was, so much is the pity, my dear, so there is no use in trying to take her place any longer. And now I wish to be myself again, and to look my own age.'

'We could start tomorrow by washing·your hair, Miss Jean, to get all the powder out of it. Then it must be brushed until it is dry so that it shines again. Could Mattie dress it in the new style?'

'I doubt it. She has been doing my hair in the same way as she did Mama's. Will you show her?'

'Ellie is the expert with the hair, Miss Jean. And perhaps Mattie would take advice more kindly from her.'

Thursday saw the transformation of Miss Brodie's hairstyle. It took all the afternoon and part of the evening to achieve it, and many basins of hot water before Ellie was satisfied that it was truly clean to begin with. By that time, old Mattie was exhausted and had started to grumble.

'Awa' ye go, and ha'e a nap!' Rose heard Ellie cutting her short in the passage in a broad Edinburgh accent. 'And dinna fash yoursel' getting up ower early to cook the dinner. I'll dress both the ladies, for you'll ha'e a lang night ahead of you before you see your bed again, nae doot.'

'Ay,' old Mattie sighed. 'Like enough, if she's in her usual.'

What on earth had the old woman to do, to keep her up so late out of her bed? It could not be that she was attending Miss Brodie, for she went so early to bed. Surely she did not have to wait up for the Deacon coming home from his 'night business'?

By seven o'clock that evening Miss Brodie's excitement had transmitted itself to the whole household. It ran like tongues of quick-fire through the corridors and passages, and stayed to quiver in the air.

'Stay with Miss Jean, Ellie,' Rose directed her maid-servant. 'It's a great pity one of her new gowns has not arrived to match her new hair-style.'

Ellie smiled a secret smile.

'One of them *has* arrived! Oh, Ellie, which one?'

'It's a secret, Miss Rose. Wait and see. In the meantime, which gown shall I lay out for you?'

'Oh, this evening I shall dress myself. It does not matter much in what. It is much more important that she should look her best.'

Rose selected one of her second-best gowns, pale green with rose velvet ribbons slotted out and in the ruffles about the neck and elbows, and a rose velvet band round the waist. Aunt Bea had not wanted her to take it with her, even if it had been her favourite dress of all time. She had said it would be too small for her now. Once she had put it on, Rose had an uncomfortable feeling that Aunt Bea had been quite right, as usual. It *did* seem a little too low-cut. But it was too late to change it now.

Deacon Brodie was waiting in front of the log fire when she went downstairs. He stood up when she entered, in his coat and trousers of light grey, the coat lined with white silk, his cuffs and ruffles of cream-coloured lace. His eyes glittered when he saw her, and he smiled the Brodie cat's smile.

'A glass of wine, my dear?'

'I have never tasted wine, sir. It is lemonade we drink at home.'

'This wine is very light. A small glass will do you no more harm than lemonade. And call me "Will", Rose. "Sir" and "Deacon" are terms for outsiders.'

'I shall call you Master Will, I think.'

She sipped the wine. It had a pleasant, fruity taste. She could not imagine why Aunt Bea had been so against it. But after she had swallowed it, its fumes rose to her head to give her a strange, happy sensation, one almost of unreality.

It was at that moment that Miss Brodie chose to make her entrance. The door to her sitting-room opened noisily and they heard her feet as she swept through to the dining-hall. She, too, seemed part of the unreality. Now she did not look like Miss Brodie. She was so dainty, so young, so changed.

Rose glanced at Deacon Brodie. His face registered amazement, disbelief and a shocked dismay, all at the same time. Then she looked again at his sister, to admire her gown.

The sisters had taken the pale blue bodice from one gown and attached it to the darker blue skirt and sleeves of another. The trimmings of silver brocade round the neck, the waist, the cuffs and the hem they had kept discreetly to a mere edging.

Her front hair was piled up in a shining brown knot on the crown of her head and tied with narrow ribbons of blue and silver cascading down over her shoulder-length curls at the back.

The gown fitted her to perfection, outlining her tiny waist, revealing her delicate shoulders, while at the same time displaying the unfortunate shortness of her neck. Nevertheless, she looked more elegant than Rose would have believed possible, as she smiled at them delightedly out of her little triangular face.

'Oh, Miss Jean!' Rose said. 'How very pretty you look!'

'Thank you, dear. Do you like it, Will?'

But Deacon Brodie's face was sweating, and his voice like a whiplash when he spoke. 'These dressmaking bills will be the ruination of me. How much did *that* cost, next? Where is the money to come from?'

Miss Brodie looked as though she might crumple.

'It did not cost a penny, Master Will,' Rose said swiftly. 'The dressmakers are having to alter all Miss Jean's gowns because of the terrible mistakes they have made with them. This one was made from two others which were wasted because they could not have been worn the way they were. Since the fault lies with the dressmakers, Miss Jean will not have to pay.'

'Oh, well . . . Well, then, Jeannie, that's a different story,' he said, wiping his face with his handkerchief. 'It is delightful. Whose idea was all this?'

'It was Rose's idea. She carried it out. I am sure I could not.'

'She has brains, then, as well as beauty.' The Deacon was trying desperately to recover the ground he had lost. 'I must say, it makes you look ten years younger.'

But as they sat down to dine, Rose felt a shiver of unease. It was the thought of the money spent which had enraged him. And yet he was so rich and dressed like a dandy himself. 'The Little Macaroni' was his nickname.

But if he had made a mistake, he seemed determined to erase it from their minds. He was laughing, gently teasing his sister now, and she was happy again, dimpling up at him, so very relieved.

A few minutes ago, Rose reminded herself, he had been white-faced, shaking with anger. He had looked as though he could be violent. She had never seen him thus before. But then she had seen very little of him at all, come to that—only at the evening meals he occasionally ate at home.

She concluded that she did not know Deacon Brodie any better now than she had a week ago, and that it would take a long time to get to the bottom of a complex character such as his.

But now he was joking and flirting with them both, and enjoying himself enormously, and his mood was infectious. Rose's doubts evaporated. She did not know if the heady feelings she was experiencing sprang from the wine, or from the daring compliments he was paying her now, for as soon as he had smoothed his sister's hurt feelings he turned to her young companion in the pale green gown with that wickedly low neckline. He could not keep his eyes off it, or her.

Rose found his attentions wildly flattering and exciting. He had been shaved and his hair was newly powdered, and sitting at table he had the build of a tall and powerful man, with his broad shoulders and heavily muscled arms. She supposed he was so well developed because of the work he did.

'And now that I have paid my sister all the compliments she is going to get from me this evening, the time has come to admire you, Rose. Is she not beautiful, Jeannie?'

'She is very pretty, Will.' Miss Brodie smiled down from the cloud she was floating on, and helped herself to another glass of wine, while he carved the leg of mutton.

Rose blushed again, and confined her gaze to the Deacon's hands occupied so skilfully with the carving knife and fork. They were so strong, with the short black hairs on the backs of them; and the fragile cream lace at his wrists only made them seem stronger and more masculine still. Rose watched them, and shivered.

Ellie was in attendance as usual, and took the plates from him, serving the first to Miss Jean and the next one to Rose. Then the Deacon helped himself.

'It is very tender'—he directed his remark and his smile at Rose—'and we have hearty appetites in this house. And you, my dear, even with your slender waist, I am sure you have a healthy appetite, too?'

The sly mischief in his voice alerted her. He was not referring to the dining table, not at all. She decided to ignore it.

'So far as I am aware, it is average, sir. But my aunt complained a great deal about it.'

'But then, perhaps, your palate has not yet been stimulated?' His eyes remained fascinated by her neck-line.

Rose shivered again, and tried to shrink a little inside her gown. 'That is very true, Master Will.'

'Well, we must see what we can do about that in Brodie's Close.'

Ellie removed the oval plates in stony silence, Rose's hardly touched. There was something in the air—something so exciting that it made it impossible for her to eat.

'And now for the spiced peaches, my favourite dessert. Mattie knows what I like!' Deacon Brodie smiled.

Ellie set down Rose's plate before her with the very tiniest thump.

'A peach for a peach,' he laughed easily into Rose's eyes.

The candle-flames bent sideways in the speed of Ellie's agitated speed around the table. As they guttered momentarily and cast pools of darkness before they straightened up again to burn brighter than before, Rose saw Deacon Brodie's eyes glowing, an imp dancing in each one.

They found a response in her, at last. He was so droll and amusing, Deacon Brodie with his teasing! In spite of herself, Rose laughed and gave him back all he wanted, as good as she got.

'Oh, you are clever, Rose, and quick! If only all the ladies in Edinburgh had half your wit! My sister,' he nodded in Miss Jean's direction, 'has happened on a jewel, a treasure.'

Miss Brodie was smiling foolishly and a little vacantly. She was far removed from the conversation, in a world of her own, with her wine glass filled up once more.

And Ellie, muttering about Mattie and the night candles, had retreated with a flounce.

Deacon Brodie's hand suddenly covered Rose's, on the white tablecloth. For a moment she stared, uncomprehending, at her own, enveloped so completely by a man's. And then, under its powerful might, she began to feel infinitely delicate, yet infinitely strong, and from his burning heat she felt for the first time in her life the powerful danger it was to be a woman.

CHAPTER
FIVE

She could have sat there all night listening to his silver tongue. At first she kept reminding herself that same silver tongue could fork like a snake's and hiss out venom. But he had such a way with words, such a way of telling a story, that she was fascinated, and before long Deacon Brodie was telling her the story of his life.

He had never wanted to be a cabinetmaker, but his father had forced him to follow in his footsteps. All he had ever wished to do was to go to sea. When he was only seventeen he could remember Thurot the Frenchman from Dunkirk lurking with his frigates in the mouth of the Forth, and terrifying the merchants of Leith. He had been desperate to join in their defence.

And then when he was eighteen in 1759, the year of Quebec and Quiberon Bay, he had pleaded with his father again to find him a midshipman's berth, pleaded with him to bring pressure on the Secretary to the Admiralty, which he could easily have done through his landed connections in the north-east of Scotland. But his father had obdurately refused. And for that, he had hated his father.

So, said the Deacon, his life had become a dismal twilight, shackled to a carpenter's bench. It was the coming of the Theatre Royal in Shakespeare Square at the other end of the newly built North Bridge almost twenty years later which had made his life worth living again. Especially when his favourite piece was performed—*The Beggar's Opera*.

'Do you know it, Rose?'

She shook her head. 'What is the story of it?'

'It is not so much its story of Polly Peachum, a girl of

the London underworld, and Macheath the arch-criminal, as it is the wonderful topsy-turvy world it opens up, where every value is reversed, every man has his price—every woman, too—and prisons and all authority are for escaping from. Oh, the excitement, Rose! Oh, the contrast to humdrum Edinburgh, where you are too well known and too little appreciated!'

'And the music?'

Deacon Brodie laughed, and began to sing, his eyes gazing into hers all the while.

> 'Tis woman that seduces all mankind,
> By her we first were taught the wheedling arts,
> Her very eyes can cheat; when she's most kind,
> She tricks us of our money with our hearts.

'Oh, it is magic, the purest magic, is it not, Rose?'

So captivated was she by his pleasant baritone, his charm, his humour and his warmth, if a little doubtful of the message behind John Gay's sprightly words, that Rose was forced to agree.

It came as a douche of icy water over her, therefore, when Ellie reappeared with the night candles and with Mattie trailing in her wake to attend to Miss Jean, who seemed half asleep already, for she staggered a little when between them they supported her through to her rooms.

The Deacon laughed when she went, and if Rose had not been so perfectly attuned to him by this time, she might have said it was a wicked laugh, even a little cruel.

'And now, my dear, I must leave you too, for it is time for my night business to begin.'

It was not so much the fact that he was leaving, although that was disappointment enough, as it was the hot, elated glow in his eyes when he said it, which disturbed her so much.

It was not the look of a man going soberly to work. It

was more the look of a man who was going out to some illicit but infinitely pleasurable rendezvous. Who was it with, Rose wondered?

She did not see Deacon Brodie on Friday, and could not understand her own desolation, or Ellie's coldness. The dressmakers arrived in the afternoon with two more gowns for Miss Brodie.

Rose smiled at her employer's wild excitement when she saw them. How did she see them, Rose wondered? One was in shades of damson blending into pale pink, and the other was mauve and purple, and each in Miss Brodie's eyes, however they appeared to her, an instant success.

There was the trying on, the little tucks to be taken here and there, the seamstresses making the immediate modifications then and there, their needles flying in and out of the delicate fabrics at top speed. Nothing but happiness reigned in the house of Deacon Brodie that night, except in Rose's bedchamber.

And then on Saturday, Mistress Scott arrived with Miss Alison Kyle at four o'clock. But of Cameron Kyle there was no sign. Rose did not connect this with the unexpected appearance of the Deacon. She was too delighted, and somehow a little shy, to see him again.

He came into the sitting-room like a merry March wind, dry and cool and sweeping all before him, even the redoubtable Mistress Scott.

'So it is our little companion you have come to see! And I cannot blame you! In fact I have to thank you for such an inspiration, Mistress Scott!'

Mistress Scott inclined her head graciously, but there was a tiny frown between her eyebrows. She had never seen or heard such levity from a Town Councillor before. Rose began to wish that he would abandon this rather wild line of conversation.

Miss Kyle had settled her tall slender frame into the

corner of one of the elegant silk tapestry settees, a little pale of face but perfectly, if quietly, turned out. She wore blue, which brought out the colour of her grave, very blue eyes.

'Yes, we are very happy to have Rose here with us,' Miss Brodie agreed. 'And so glad that you have come to see her—and me, too, of course! You must excuse my brother. He does *so* love to tease. Behave yourself, Will! This is woman's talk, at the woman's hour.'

'I am amazed at how well you look, Jean,' Mistress Scott swept into action with the look of a woman determined to keep the party polite. 'So young! I declare you look ten years younger with that hair-style. So different!'

'A few little changes, Mistress Scott,' Miss Brodie said airily. 'We must move with the times.'

'Indeed,' Deacon Brodie put in with his twisted secret smile. 'And they are wicked, wicked times, are they not?'

He looked directly at Rose when he said this, and she could not help smiling back at him. It was such a pity that Mistress Scott and Miss Kyle did not know him well enough to understand his brand of humour—dry, jaunty, and just a little sly.

Mistress Scott certainly did not understand it. She took his words at their face value and immediately launched into her favourite topic, the disgrace and the shocking decadence of the day. They all sat a little more upright, nodding their heads sadly as she gave vent to her feelings. All except Deacon Brodie, who could hardly contain himself at some private joke. Rose wished he would share it with her. She would have understood it.

'Mark my words,' Mistress Scott finished. 'It is not over yet, not by a long chalk! We are due for another of these scandalous burglaries any minute now! And, in fact, if I did not disapprove so much of my son Walter's fantasies, I would be inclined to agree with him that there is a master mind behind each and every one of them!'

The Deacon choked suddenly, and coughed and laughed at the same time.

'Please excuse me, ladies,' he begged breathlessly, wiping his eyes with his fine lace-edged handkerchief.

'Oh, dear, Will, have you caught a cold?' Miss Brodie asked anxiously.

'Not at all, my dear. If we had been dining, I should have said that something just went down the wrong way. I choked, that's all.' A look of sincerity flooded his face. 'It has been so interesting to talk to you, ladies. Indeed it has. But I must ask you to forgive me now. Business is pressing!'

'It was an unexpected pleasure to see you in the sitting-room at this time of day, Will. But must you go?'

'Yes, Jeannie. The Town Council will not wait.'

'And what is on the agenda today, Deacon?' Mistress Scott asked with interest.

'As a matter of fact, it is a little invention of my own to be considered,' he admitted modestly, 'but too indelicate to mention at a ladies' tea-party.'

'Nonsense,' Mistress Scott said with her usual forthrightness. 'We are all women here, not flowers.'

'Then, much as it grieves me to mention such a thing, it is the new gallows, madam, with a trap on the floor, so that the terrible and ultimate penalty our criminals must pay may be a more swift, more certain and more humane affair.'

An eerie silence fell in the sitting-room. Rose did not dare look up. The subject was one which haunted everyone day and night, all week long. And on Sundays the ministers constantly thundered from the pulpits reminders of the wages of sin. It was their favourite theme.

'Ay, well, you're a good man, Deacon Brodie,' Mistress Scott said soberly at last. 'And Edinburgh has long been fortunate in its Town Council, the good men chosen to look after our interests. But that was one aspect of crime which I must confess I had not thought deeply enough about, to have the proper compassion for the wrong-doers.'

Deacon Brodie bowed over Mistress Scott's hand, and then turned to Miss Kyle, who so far had not uttered one word.

'So glad to meet you, Miss Kyle. A real pleasure.'

Miss Alison Kyle smiled her slow, sweet smile. Rose was shocked to see from it that she was a little amused.

'Yes, I have heard so much about you, Deacon Brodie.'

'All to the good, I hope?' he said, smiling so much into Miss Kyle's eyes that Rose felt the strangest pangs.

But Miss Kyle did not answer, and Rose could not help noticing that her hand extended to the Deacon was quite deliberately limp.

'And now, my dears, to the purpose of our call,' Mistress Scott said when the sitting-room door closed behind him, 'I wonder if you would both care to join my little party at the Theatre Royal on the twenty-second?'

It was so unexpected that Miss Brodie sat with her mouth open, and even Rose could scarcely believe her ears. That Mistress Scott should even contemplate such a place of wickedness, as the Kirk condemned it so bitterly!

'As you will know, I am a Christian woman,' Mistress Scott went on. 'But it does not follow from that that I agree with every opinion our ministers of the gospel try to impose on us. It is true that I do not usually have any truck with any of the less theatrical productions, but on the occasion I speak of it is quite another matter. It is to see Mrs Sarah Siddons herself, no less! The best and the most famous actress of our land! I expect the whole of Edinburgh to come to a standstill when she arrives.'

'Oh, how wonderful!' Rose could not help exclaiming, with shining eyes.

'Mistress Sarah Siddons?' Miss Brodie repeated. 'I believe I have heard of her. Where is it she comes from, again?'

'*Mrs* Sarah Siddons is coming from London,' Mistress Scott told her, 'and the play she will perform is *Venice Preserv'd*, by Thomas Otway.'

'The twenty-second, did you say?' Miss Brodie took up her engagement book from the table at her side and frowned into it, crying, 'But this cannot be the second day of November already! Time passes so fast!'

Mistress Scott and Miss Kyle exchanged glances, and Rose waited on tenterhooks.

'Yes,' Miss Brodie said at last, 'I believe I could manage on the twenty-second. And Rose is included in your invitation?' She made a great show of marking the date.

'She is included,' Mistress Scott smiled.

'And she is included in another invitation, this time one from me,' Miss Kyle said in her gentle voice. 'One which I hope she will accept.' She turned her very blue gaze on Rose.

It reminded her vividly of Cameron Kyle. He was the last person she wished to be reminded of in the new excitement of her life, especially when it was accompanied by these strange prickles, these nasty little feelings of guilt. She had absolutely nothing to feel guilty about, she thought indignantly.

'My brother is also hoping that you will come, Rose,' Miss Kyle was saying. 'It is to our house in Queen Street next Wednesday morning for coffee, and to watch Mr Vincent Lunardi making another attempt to ascend in his hot-air balloon over the Town.'

'Oh, I never accept morning invitations,' Miss Brodie said immediately.

'That is a great disappointment,' Miss Kyle said. 'I am so sorry, Miss Brodie.'

She looked so sad and so regretful that even Miss Brodie was touched. She looked down thoughtfully at her two blue slippers, matching for once, while they all waited for the result.

'But I never require Rose's services until twelve o'clock in the mornings,' she said.

'Oh, if you will permit her to come, we shall see to it that she is back by then,' Miss Kyle assured her.

'Then I cannot see any reason why she should not go without me. Would you like to go, Rose?'

'I should be very interested to see Mr Lunardi, of course. I have heard so much about him with his hot-air balloon, although I have never had the good fortune to see him on any of his earlier flights. Thank you, Miss Kyle. And thank you, Mistress Scott, for your invitation, also.'

'Then that is settled, my dear,' Mistress Scott said. 'Of course, you will not have heard from your Aunt Beattie yet?'

'No, not yet,' Rose was saying, 'but then I could hardly expect to. It is too soon,' when Ellie and Jessie arrived with the tea-trays. Rose noticed that there were five cups set out.

'I am afraid that Cameron will not be able to come and fetch us today,' Miss Kyle said. 'But he will send the coach for us at five o'clock.'

'I am sorry to hear that,' Miss Brodie said, 'for I was looking forward to seeing him again. I was greatly taken with your brother.'

The little cakes seemed tasteless to Rose, as she joined in the polite conversation. She could not understand it. They were the same cakes that she enjoyed every afternoon, light and airy, and baked by Mattie, whose heavy hand turned miraculously fairylike when she was in the kitchen.

'You are enjoying your stay in Edinburgh, Rose?' Miss Kyle came over with her teacup and sat beside her.

'Oh, very much . . . now, Miss Kyle.'

'Now? Does that mean that you did not, to begin with?'

'I missed Newhaven at first,' Rose admitted.

'Edinburgh is very easy to fall in love with. It is such a beautiful town. I have travelled abroad many times with Cameron—which is where I contracted that miserable fever, which laid me so low for so long—but always when I come back I think it must be the most beautiful town in the world. In fact, it soon will be, when all the new squares are laid out, and all the elegant new houses built in the New Town. But you will see what I mean next Wednesday.'

'Could any other street be so majestic as the Royal Mile, Miss Kyle?'

'No, indeed. We are very fortunate to have the best of two worlds here. But please call me Alison, my dear. I have a feeling that we are going to be great friends. And Cameron is truly sorry that he could not be here today. He asked me to give you his apologies. I believe he had to go out of Town.'

'Oh,' said Rose. 'And when will he be back?'

'On Monday, perhaps. Tuesday at the latest,' Alison said vaguely. 'But in time for our coffee-party, at any rate.'

There was a little tap at the door.

'The coach has arrived, Miss Jean,' said Ellie.

'We will accompany you down to it,' Miss Brodie said, ushering the ladies out.

'The fine weather still holds.' Mistress Scott stood for a moment in the sunshine. 'Quite remarkable for the time of year. Now, we shall see you on the twenty-second.'

'Our coffee-party starts at half-past nine next Wednesday, Rose,' Alison said. 'I know that is a little early, but Mr Lunardi makes his attempt at ten. Could you be ready if I had the coach sent for you at nine, dear?'

'I shall be ready and waiting, Alison, and looking forward to the occasion very much.'

And then she wondered if she had spoken too soon, as they stood there waving at the receding carriage. Further down the Royal Mile, beside the Tron Kirk, she had caught a glimpse of a tall, broad figure. Even from the back, she was hardly likely to mistake Cameron Kyle, who was supposed to be out of Town on business.

Why had he not come to the Brodies' house? And why had he made up such an elaborate lie with his sister? From their pressing invitation, it was quite clear that neither of them wished to avoid her. But they wished to avoid *somebody*, or at least, he did. Who was it, and why?

Back up in Miss Brodie's sitting-room Rose was still thoughtful when Miss Brodie went back over the little tea-party anxiously.

'Did they enjoy it, Rose? And what shall I wear to the Theatre Royal?'

'We shall have plenty of time to decide that, Miss Jean. Shall we set about it tomorrow?'

'Yes. I am a little tired after the strain of it all. Perhaps you would read to me? It is laziness, I know, but you have such a pleasant voice to listen to.'

Rose picked up the *Edinburgh Evening Courant*, which was lying on Miss Brodie's table over by the window, and began to read some little items of news which she thought would interest her mistress.

'There is a notice here,' she said, and read it out loud.

By the Right Hon: The
LORD PROVOST, MAGISTRATES, AND COUNCIL of the City of Edinburgh
Whereas, on the night between Monday and Tuesday

the 29th and 30th current, some wicked persons did feloniously break open the doors of the Library of the University of this City, and steal the UNIVERSITY MACE, a reward of TEN GUINEAS, to be paid by the City Chamberlain, is hereby offered for the discovery of all or any of the persons above mentioned, or of any person in whose possession the said Mace shall be found.

Edinburgh, Oct. 31. 1787.

But there was no comment, as there usually was when Rose paused for breath. She glanced up, a little surprised, and then it was as though an icy hand had clutched her heart.

Miss Brodie's face was a study of horror. It was entirely drained of colour, and her eyes so darkly shadowed beneath that they seemed twice their normal size—enormous, stricken and utterly terrified.

'Miss Jean, dear! What is it?' Rose jumped up, scattering the newspaper in all directions in her concern.

But Miss Brodie could not speak. She gasped for breath and turned a little blue. Rose searched frantically on the table beside her, under the engagement book and the pencils and the collection of handkerchiefs until she found the little bottle she knew was there somewhere.

She waved the smelling-salts under her employer's nose, and Miss Brodie gasped and choked, and the tears poured from her eyes. But her colour was returning. Rose gave her a few minutes to recover.

'Can you speak now? Is that better? Can you tell me what is wrong?' she asked anxiously.

Miss Brodie groaned and shook her head, and leaned back in her chair with her eyes closed. After what seemed to Rose an eternity, she opened them again at last.

'Never, never speak to me again of these terrible burglaries, Rose,' she gasped.

'Of course I shall not speak of them again, Miss Jean. I would not have upset you like this for the world.'

The tears began to flow down Miss Brodie's face.

'It was enough to have to listen to Mistress Scott again this afternooon. She does not speak of anything else these days.'

'She does seem to dwell on them, it is true.'

'Well, I do not want to know about them!' Miss Brodie cried passionately. 'They are nothing to do with us, nothing! It is always to us she keeps speaking about them.'

'I have heard her before, when you were not even there. I am afraid she speaks about the burglaries to everyone,' Rose said in a soothing voice. 'None of it was directed at you, Miss Jean.'

Miss Brodie's sobs subsided a little. 'Is that true, Rose?'

'Yes. And as for the newspapers, they have to report everything, so that the people will buy them. But I shall know better in future.'

'It is not your fault, Rose. You were not to know how much it upsets me,' Miss Brodie said in a tired voice.

'I shall go to the kitchen and fetch you another cup of tea, shall I? It will make you feel much better.'

'No. Tell Mattie to come here. She will know what to bring.'

Rose fled, trying to gather her scattered wits as she ran. She had not thought Miss Brodie to be capable of such passion as she had just witnessed. It all went to show how little she really knew about people and about life in general. In her endeavours to understand the new people she had been thrown up against so suddenly, she had been presumptuous to dismiss Miss Brodie so lightly. She would not underestimate anyone like that again.

Mattie nodded, her lips tight, when Rose delivered the message.

'Ay, I'll come right away,' she said, wiping her hands, which were covered in dough on a wet rag.

Rose was at a loss as to what to do next. Perhaps she should go back to the sitting-room in the meantime, and sit with Miss Brodie until Mattie came, to try to keep her calm. She flew back noiselessly towards the door she had left open in her haste.

But on the threshold she stopped short. Miss Brodie was standing at the window with her back to her, and she was reading the *Edinburgh Evening Courant* for herself. The page was opened at the notice about the burglary, and the hands that held it up to the light trembled pitifully in agitation.

Somewhere in the back of the house a door slammed shut, and Rose retreated silently. Old Mattie was coming in the opposite direction when they met in the dining-hall, apparently carrying nothing, although one hand was concealed in the folds of her apron skirt.

'And now what have you done?' she hissed in passing. 'I knew you meant trouble here, right from the start.'

It took a few moments of stunned disbelief—Rose could not believe her ears—before she fled up to her bedchamber and flung herself face down on her bed.

What *had* she done?

She had not known she had done anything wrong, and yet when she considered those closest to her, they were all in disarray. Miss Brodie was hysterical. Mattie blamed her squarely for that. Ellie, too, was angry with her for some reason, and had turned cold. Alison Kyle had told her a downright lie. And as for Cameron Kyle, his behaviour was even worse, for he must have persuaded his sister into such a thing. Rose was sure that Alison would never normally tell lies.

The only one who remained constant, both in character and towards her, with his love of fun and his entertaining ways, was Deacon Brodie himself. But then, Rose consoled herself that night, she had always been drawn to older men. They had the maturity, the stability and the sophistication which proved them to be completely trustworthy.

She had never been wrong in *that* assessment.

Next day the storms of yesterday proved to have been only storms in a teacup. Miss Brodie was fully recovered by twelve o'clock, and after the Meridian which they took in a coffee-house in the High Street, she and Rose walked back up to the Lawnmarket and the Luckenbooths past Mr Creech's shop, where the distinguished men of Edinburgh had foregathered as usual.

'They are the "literati",' Miss Brodie whispered. 'There is Adam Smith. Mr Creech is about to publish his book, called *The Wealth of Nations*. I believe it is a very important book. And that old man is David Hume, who wrote the *History of England*.

'They are all writers who come here every morning?' Rose asked.

'They have literary breakfasts, so I believe. The people of Edinburgh call them "Creech's Levees". Robert Burns was here a few months ago, so I dare say we will be seeing a new book of poems from him, shortly.'

'And there is Walter Scott,' Rose said.

'Where?'

'The young fresh-faced boy in blue coat and breeches going up to speak to Mr Creech now.'

Rose forgot that Miss Brodie could not see the colours. But she would see Mr Creech, dressed all in black and with his hair snow-white with powder.

Back home Ellie had thawed. She was back in her usual sunny, talkative mood. Rose made up her mind to ignore the events of the last few days. She did not want to stir up another hornets' nest. But she could not forget any of the temperament she had seen. She became wary, and for the next few days trod delicately in the house of Deacon Brodie, as if she walked on egg-shells.

At nine o'clock on Wednesday morning, the risp tirled on the front door.

'Is my bonnet on straight, Ellie?' Rose asked for the tenth time.

'I have told you so a hundred times, Miss Rose. Did I not set it on your head? And have I not told you a thousand times how well that lavender gown becomes you? Now we will put on the shoulder cape that goes with it. You may have to go out to see the hot-air balloon, and every day grows colder now.'

When Cameron Kyle handed her into the carriage, Rose had never felt as nervous as this at any other time in his company. He was the same. But now that her life seemed to be taking a different direction in Brodie's Close, it changed everything else as well. She was not the same girl as he had known before, and there was a constraint in the air as the carriage moved off. She flashed a swift glance at his face, and then lowered her eyes again uncomfortably.

She had not been able to assess his mood in that quick look. His brows were drawn down, but then they often were. The lines on his face seemed carved out of stone and his mouth was set hard. Yet she did not believe he was angry, although perhaps that was because the corners of his wide mouth never turned down. They always turned up, instead.

'And what have you been up to this time, Rose?'

It was so unexpected and so accurate a blow that for a moment it took her breath away. She was helpless to stem the wild scarlet which rushed to her cheeks.

'Nothing!'

Cameron smiled grimly, and in the quivering silence when he said no more, Rose felt her temper rising.

'No, that is not true,' she said. 'I have been busy

becoming acquainted with my employers.'

'It was my understanding that you had only one employer. Miss Jean Brodie.'

'Oh, Deacon Brodie comes into it, too.'

'I thought he would, sooner or later,' Cameron smiled.

Rose was infuriated. 'I have spoken to him only once at any length,' she defended herself. 'At dinner. And,' she added defiantly, 'I found him very entertaining.'

'He can be a merry little fellow, that is true.'

Big men could be very superior, very sure of themselves. Rose glared at him. How could she have been so stupid as to blurt out all she was thinking—and more than she even realised herself she was thinking—to this man? Something about him made her do it, there was no doubt of that. She cast around miserably for something witty to say in the Deacon's defence.

'Good gear comes in little bulk,' she quoted.

'Life is made up of little things,' he agreed. 'Such as little sticks to kindle the fire. Great ones put it out.'

'Great strokes make not sweet music, Cameron Kyle.'

'And there is no rose without a thorn.' His laughter roared through the carriage and dispelled the tension, but Rose wondered for how long.

'We are crossing the North Bridge,' he said. 'When we get to the other side, we will be in the New Town of Edinburgh.'

Rose saw that the North Bridge was like the short bar crossing the letter H. One of the long uprights was the ridge of the Royal Mile behind them. The other was the long raised street running parallel to it that they were turning into now.

'Princes Street,' he said briefly. 'The main street in "The Athens of the North", as they call it already, because of the classical way it is laid out, all in wide squares.'

They drove slowly along the very wide, very straight street, and the hairs rose up on the back of Rose's neck at the sight of the Castle perched high on its rock like a crouching lion looking down on its subjects. She had never seen the Castle from this angle before, straddling the two Towns, the Old and the New.

'It is magnificent, and cold, and very austere.'

'For once, I agree with you, Rose.'

'Then why have you chosen to live here in the New Town, now?'

'I did not choose it. Alison chose it. No. 29 Queen Street is Alison's house. I do not have a home of my own—Not yet.'

These last two words were spoken with a world of meaning, while the carriage turned off Princes Street and bowled along another one further back. It was very grand, this terrace of houses, all so uniformly and graciously proportioned, standing side by side looking into the long green ornamental garden on the other side of the road.

It was very different from the tall buildings of the Royal Mile, the great 'lands' some of them twelve stories high, their common stairs as dirty as they were steep and high, and so grossly overcrowded.

'Does all this house belong to Alison?' she asked.

'Yes. There are no flats here. One house for one family.'

Rose was deeply impressed.

In fact, she was quite awe-struck when they stepped up the three wide shallow steps to the very important door, with its brass accoutrements glittering, its iron boot-jacks at either side black-polished, and the fan-shaped window above it the most elegant design she had ever seen.

Afterwards, she had no clear recollection of how she actually crossed its threshold, or who admitted her, and of Cameron, only that he was at her side in the bright square entrance hall, with its floor tiled in a glorious mosaic.

The first thing that met her gaze was a sedan chair tucked into one corner, its long carrying-poles leaning on the wall behind it. So Alison had her very own sedan, and it was beautiful, dark green and gilt, with its own little door and a window with a screen.

The next thing she saw brought her heart almost to a standstill, for there, coming down the square stone staircase with the hem of her honey-coloured gown in her hand, was Miss Cornelia Forbes, her smile sweet, and her eyes quite deadly.

'Oh!' she said. 'It is the little . . .'

'The little Miss Rose Barbour, here as my guest,' Cameron spoke sharply. 'Allow me to present her to you formally. Miss Cornelia Forbes, Miss Rose Barbour.'

His words carried such a warning and such a threat that Miss Cornelia's eyes wavered before she returned Rose's curtsy, and the hand she held out was quickly withdrawn.

'It is true that half the fun of a party is that you never know who you may meet at it.'

'Then this party is sure to be a success, for you, Cornelia. You have had the honour of having Rose presented to you first. I imagine there will be many others here today who will follow you,' Cameron stated positively, and drew Rose away into the drawing-room, its long windows overlooking the other side of the street.

If she had truly had some identity of her own, Cameron would not have had to protest so much, Rose thought sadly.

But Miss Cornelia was not to be so lightly dismissed.

'Alison asked me to send you to her immediately you arrived,' she pouted up at him. 'There is some trouble upstairs.'

'Damn,' Cameron swore under his breath. 'Very well,

Cornelia. Go on ahead and tell her I will be with her in a few minutes.'

He led Rose over to a settee occupied by one old gentleman.

'Lord Braxfield,' he addressed him, 'would you be so kind as to look after Miss Rose Barbour for me? I should not be long.'

Lord Braxfield? The very name alarmed her. Everyone knew of Lord Braxfield, Scotland's chief criminal judge!

'Stay as lang as ye like, Kyle. Dinna hurry back,' the old man smiled. 'And who are you, my lassie?'

'The niece of Mistress Beattie Barbour, sir, from Newhaven.'

'Ah-ha! Beattie Barbour, is it? Ye wouldna' find a better nurse than Beattie Barbour in a' Edinburgh.'

'No, sir.'

'I aye heard she took a wee bit bairn in tae live wi' her when her ain mither died. Would that be you, Rose Barbour?'

'It would, sir.'

'And ye never kent wha was your mither?'

'No,' Rose admitted, her lip quivering. 'I never did find out who she was, although I can remember her quite clearly.'

'Aweel, lassie, dinna fret, noo.' Lord Braxfield patted her hand. 'It's plain tae be seen she must have been a lady, onyway, to ha'e sic a bonny wee lass as yoursel'. I'm pleased tae meet ye, Rose Barbour.'

It was so kindly meant and so kindly said by one of the most important men in all Scotland that Rose managed to control herself. She smiled the smile that had captivated other hearts before the great judge's.

'Thank you, Lord Braxfield. I am honoured to meet you, too.'

'Ay, Beattie Barbour made a guid job o' you. She did

that. And ye've come tae see this Lunardi chiel fly in his contraption?'

Rose had to laugh. 'Oh, I hope he does fly, sir.'

'My, but ye're a bonnie wee lassie! Kyle never was a fool, just awfu' unfortunate.'

'Unfortunate? Why?'

'Dae ye no' ken? He's heir to a fortune, and more than that, dearie. But he canna prove it in a Court o' Law. Ay, the Law's the thing, and ye canna dispute it. It's a grand thing, the law o' this land, Rose.'

'But from what I have heard since coming to Edinburgh, the law is being most seriously flouted, Lord Braxfield.'

'Ay, wi' the burglaries. That's verra true, lassie. But the mills o' God grind slow, and they grind exceedin' sma', ye ken. The evil-doers will be up before me yet.'

Rose looked at the old man. His was not a handsome face. Lord Braxfield's nose dominated it, long and at the same time bulbous, but the two large brown eyes above it were the sharpest she had ever seen. Now they had changed to coal-black, fathomless, implacable.

'I know you already for a man with a heart no less than your head, Lord Braxfield, and therefore the scales are evenly balanced,' Rose said. 'Scotland can trust you to be absolutely just.'

He made no pretence of modesty. 'It can that, lassie,' he agreed. 'I am famed for it . . . Weel, here's Kyle back again. Ye ha'e your problems sorted oot, Cameron, laddie?'

'May God preserve me from hysterical women.'

'I hope ye're no' referrin' to my wee Alison?'

'No, no, not Alison. It was Mistress Ballantyne taking the vapours on account of Mr Lunardi's impending death.'

'She aye was a silly auld besom,' Lord Braxfield observed, laughing wheezily.

'Will you have another little dram?' Cameron asked him, pouring brandy liberally into the old man's glass. 'Lunardi should have set off by now from the Gardens of Heriot's. Shall we all go out and watch for him?'

'Weel, *you* may, laddie, an' tak' this bonny wee lassie wi' ye. I'll just sit here, if I may, an' see him oot o' your windows.'

Cameron tucked Rose's hand under his arm and led the way to the door.

'He's as sharp as a fox, that old man,' he said. 'And thrawn, and as determinedly Scottish as a thistle. He speaks like that in Court, you know, scorning English. But his mind is like a rapier, for all that. What was he saying to you?'

They went down the steps at the front door and across the street into the Gardens. They were a long oval, with a path round the perimeter of it, trees and bushes overhanging all the way. The whole company followed them, some in one direction, some in the other, looking upwards into the sky.

Today Cameron Kyle wore a severe shade of dark royal blue. Rose had felt overwhelmed by it the minute he escorted her out of Brodie's Close and into the carriage. In fact, the sight of him in that colour, so vividly the colour of his eyes, had influenced her reaction to him from the very beginning of the morning. It was so crisp, so clean, so definite, so . . . She struggled to define it. Perhaps the word she was looking for was masculine. In any case, it had given him an unfair advantage.

At first she had been completely bowled over by the sheer impact of the colour, and him, and if she were completely honest, even a little frightened. But now she had relaxed again so far as to remember dear Deacon Brodie, and all the excitement of a very different man. One who was smaller, granted. But one who although so upright, was not so stern. He had another, more entertaining, side to his coin. With this secret knowledge

Rose grew more confident, even bold—in fact, quite pitying.

'Lord Braxfield said that you should have inherited a vast fortune,' she said. 'But you are unfortunate.'

Cameron smiled. 'He laughs best who laughs last, Rose. Do you know that one?'

'Of course I know it, although I should have said, "He who laughs last laughs longest."'

'That does not surprise me,' he observed mildly.

'In what way have you been unfortunate?' she persisted, with a stab of resentment.

'Do you really want to know? Do you really care, Rose?'

He sounded so sad, for Cameron Kyle, that her conscience smote her.

'Of course. You have been very kind to me. One day I may be able to do something for you, if I knew what it was.'

'I hope so,' he said, bending down so that his cheek brushed hers for the merest second. 'That will be a happy day for me.'

The dizzying effect this gesture had on Rose made her hand cling to his arm to steady her. 'Then tell me.'

'Shortly after moving into 29, Queen Street we were burgled, you see. Some of Alison's jewels were stolen, along with a fair amount of money. At the same time the thief stole some of my papers, one of which is more precious to me, by far, than gold could ever be.'

'Lord Braxfield said it was your inheritance.'

'My grandmother's Will, in which she left a property to me. It is the only one I should wish to spend my life in.'

'Then you have seen it?'

'I have lived in it, most of my life, along with my sister and our grandmother. But when the old lady died, we were forced to move out.'

'Why, if she left a Will?'

'Because in it she named a joint inheritor. Someone in

France. And until I find him and try to buy him out, I can never go back.'

'So the house sits empty?'

'Yes, empty, and going to waste.'

Just then the shout went up. 'Lunardi! Lunardi!'

An apparition like a huge grotesque bird floated above them. Rose saw a huge balloon of some light material, criss-crossed with ropes tying it on to a ridiculous basket beneath, and in the basket stood a man.

Was it a man? She shaded her eyes and gazed upwards. Of course it was a man, dressed in a red jacket and red and blue striped trousers, but from down here he looked so silly, so dwarfish, like a tiny mannikin. They could see him waving and hear his faint shouts.

In an instant Rose was back with Grandmam Maddy. The sky was blue, yet she was in a jet-black cloud. Mr Lunardi was actually flying. She could see him with her own eyes, but she could see more than that, the things to come now that he was leading the way, the air peopled with other balloons, other machines, and a terrible doom.

'Rose! Rose!' She heard Cameron's voice from a great distance, and felt his arms round her holding her steady.

She looked at him, white-faced. She tried to concentrate, but the sick feeling persisted; it would not go away, and he held her tighter than ever.

His face swam back into focus above her. 'You are terrified, Rose. But not at the hot-air balloon. Just stand still for a moment and hold on to me.'

She laid her head thankfully on his shoulder until the unhappy feelings, the black wings flapping over her head, all went away, and she came back to herself again.

'Oh,' she said. 'It was wonderful, and terrible at the same time. I do not think I really liked it. I wish he had stayed on the ground. Men flying are men dying. That's what I saw.'

'Perhaps you did, Rose. It was a premonition of

death, certainly. Has this happened to you before?'

'Not to me. To someone—someone I was very close to, once.'

She had nearly given herself away. She came sharply back to reality. She should not be in this position, holding on to a man who had his arms so tight about her, whose cheek leaned so comfortably on hers, who made her feel that here was her real haven at last, the one she had been looking for all her life, although until now she had never recognised it.

She stirred in his arms and turned her face up to his. She could scarcely bear the look in his eyes, so blue, so burning.

'Rose . . . Rose . . .'

'So here you are, Cameron darling! I can just see your head through the trees,' came a familiar tinkling voice, and they sprang apart.

'Cornelia.' Cameron's voice was flat.

'I love parties that are *different*. And this one has been very different—such a success! Was it not amusing, that little man in his hot-air balloon? Where will he be, by this time?'

She completely ignored Rose, as completely as Cameron ignored her question.

'Yes,' he said. 'And now it is late. I have promised to see that Miss Barbour gets back to the Lawnmarket by twelve. Will you excuse us, Cornelia?'

'No,' she said, and Rose saw with a sinking heart that her eyes had narrowed to slits. 'I shall not excuse you, Cameron. Not unless you take my arm, too.'

How much had she seen, Rose wondered, as they walked back in a tense trio to the house in Queen Street? Cameron's carriage was drawn up ready outside it.

'It wants a quarter of twelve,' he said, handing her into it. 'You will just be in time.'

'Rose!' Alison called, running down the steps. 'I wanted to speak to you. I wanted to ask you if you would

come to the French lessons with me? They start on
Monday, down in the Canongate, and they last from
nine to eleven every day. Oh, say you will come!'

'I will ask,' Rose smiled, and waved as the carriage
pulled away.

She smiled and waved at Cameron and Alison Kyle,
and at Cornelia Forbes who stood behind them, her face
a mask of the purest hatred. So she *had* seen them, Rose
deduced, and subsided into a corner of the swaying
carriage.

But it had only reached the North Bridge on its way
back to the Old Town of Edinburgh again when her
thoughts crystallised into a bright, hard diamond of
reason. Cameron Kyle should have escorted her back
himself in his carriage. But he had chosen to remain with
his sister and that poisonous woman instead.

Deacon Brodie would have known better. He was so
upright. He was a Gentleman of Honour. She could trust
him, absolutely. *He* had no other women, no Cornelia
Forbes. Deacon Brodie worked hard, day and night, at
his business. Everybody knew it. That was why he had
been made a Deacon of Trades in the first place, why he
had been elected to the Town Council, why he was so
well respected. She was glad to be going home to the
house of Deacon Brodie, thankful for the way the dice
had rolled for her in 1787 in the Royal Burgh of
Edinburgh.

'How did you enjoy it?' Ellie asked anxiously as she
descended the little steps of the carriage.

'It was wonderful,' Rose replied tranquilly. 'It was so
nice to go to the New Town and to see it. But it is even
nicer, oh, so nice, to come back!'

CHAPTER
SIX

FROM NINE to eleven every morning Miss Jean Brodie lived in the land of uneasy dreams and nightmares that Rose could not even have imagined, of pitch-black wynds and back streets where murder and rape and every evil-stinking foulness were commonplace, the order of the night, if not the day. She had not recovered from her latest sojourn there when Rose went to see her.

'Yes, go to your French classes,' she said, sinking back grey-faced and drawn into her high brocaded chair. 'You will be in plenty of time to attend me each midday.'

Was she ill? Miss Brodie was no longer the scarecrow she had been, but Rose was still alarmed for her. Her employer was an attractive woman who could forget her slight disability now, she had a beautiful home as her background, and she had money enough to buy anything she ever desired, but still there was something wrong. Rose could not understand her lethargy or the unhappiness which was quite obviously eating her away.

On her bad days there was no diversion Rose tried which could lift her depression. On her good days she would recover a little, although never until after the Meridian. Saturday turned out to be one of her good days, and together she and Rose came in smiling from their daily visit to the Luckenbooths, carrying their small parcels.

'It is still only four o'clock,' Miss Brodie said. 'Just in time for tea.'

But before she had time to summon her, Ellie was knocking on the sitting-room door.

'There is someone to see you, Miss Jean.'

'But I did not expect anyone, and my sister and her

husband will not come until tomorrow. Have they mistaken the day?'

'It is not Mr Sheriffs and Mistress Jacobina. It is a young man, asking for you, Miss Jean. He would not give his name. He says it is to be a surprise.'

'Oh? Oh, well then'—she patted her hair a little frivolously, as though young men came calling on her every afternoon, and it was a thing of very little consequence—'you had better show him in.'

'Here he is, miss.' Ellie ushered in her visitor a minute later.

'Oh!' Miss Brodie shrieked with delight. 'Oh, it is you, Jamie! I never thought we would ever see you again! Rose, this is a dear friend of ours, Mr James Leslie.'

Tall of frame and narrow, with a heavy black beard and gangling legs, Mr Leslie shook Rose's hand and stood smiling shyly at them both.

'I have finished the job in Aberdeen,' he said, 'and come back to work with Matthew Sheriffs again.'

'Bring three cups instead of two, then,' Miss Brodie directed the hovering Ellie. 'You will have some tea with us, Jamie?'

'I had hoped to arrive in time for tea, Jean. There were no delays in the Aberdeen coach.'

'Ah . . . So this is your first port of call?'

'After six months, one week and four days? You knew it would be.' He looked directly at his hostess, and Miss Brodie blushed, very attractively. 'For apart from being cold as charity, it was—very lonely, up north.'

'Miss Rose Barbour came to be a companion to me, since then.'

'Ah, I see.'

'I cannot bear to be alone. Not now,' Miss Brodie added, pouring the tea from the little silver teapot, and then filling it up again from the jug of hot water, which Ellie had fetched, all eyes and ears.

Rose took the cup from her trembling hand and gave it to Mr Leslie.

The trembling spread to Miss Brodie's voice. 'When you left, I did not have a friend in the world to speak to, although Rose has helped these last few weeks. But I suppose you will be going away soon on another job?'

Rose offered Mr Leslie one of Mattie's fresh-baked fairy cakes.

'You cannot imagine how I have looked forward to this moment, Jean,' he said. 'No, I will not have to go away again, not in the immediate future, at least. My aunt Mistress Scott has asked me to join you all at the theatre on the twenty-second, and I was able to accept her invitation without any hesitation.'

'Oh, indeed. So you went to her house first,' Miss Brodie sounded quite put out.

'No,' he smiled calmly. 'I had the good fortune to meet her out here in the Lawnmarket on my way up from the coach.' He set down his cup carefully on the table. 'But what is the matter, Jeannie? You were never touchy, like this? Yes, I am back now, and you can talk to me, dear.'

Rose set down her teacup beside his and got to her feet.

'May I be excused, Miss Jean? I shall tell Ellie to leave the tea-things until you ring for her, shall I?'

'Very well, dear,' Miss Brodie said distractedly.

Mr Leslie stood up and bowed when Rose curtsied her farewell. She thought he was too polite to show his relief when she went.

'He is coming to dinner with the Sheriffs tomorrow evening,' Ellie told her later that night.

'Who is Mr Leslie, Ellie?'

'I had never seen him before, either. I have only been here six months myself. He is supposed to be the best upholsterer in Scotland, better even than Mr Sheriffs.

He has to go to all the best houses in the country to attend to the furniture.'

'And Mr Sheriffs is the Brodies' brother-in-law?'

'Yes. He is Jacobina Brodie's husband. They live in St James's Square in the New Town, Miss Rose. They come once a month for dinner, but the master and Miss Jean never return their visits. They say it is because the Brodies do not like the New Town, except for the business it provides.'

And between the cabinetmaking of the Brodies, and the upholstering of the Sheriffs, the family must be even richer than she had supposed, Rose thought. Business must be booming with all the fine houses of the New Town waiting to be finished and furnished.

Promptly at a quarter to nine on Monday morning Rose was ready, waiting for the Kyles' carriage.

She wore a businesslike grey and white checked gown under her white fur cape to go to the French lessons. To her dismay, Cameron Kyle himself was driving the carriage when it arrived.

He leapt down from the coachman's seat in one lithe movement to hand her in. He did not have to flash about like that, she thought sourly, in his tight fawn breeches under the immaculate coat she had first seen him attired in on the Swifts. She knew perfectly well how long and how strong his legs were, how well proportioned. She knew them off by heart.

She landed inside, in an indignant bounce at Alison's side.

'You have a notebook and pencils, Rose dear?'

'No,' Rose replied, with the wind quite out of her sails already, one way and another.

'I took the precaution of bringing them for you,' Alison smiled.

They alighted half-way down the Canongate, with Cameron's help.

'I shall be back at eleven,' he said cheerfully.

Two hours! It seemed an eternity.

'Yes,' Rose said, as the enormity of what she was undertaking dawned on her. 'Alison may last so long. I do not think I shall.'

'Oh, you are made of much sterner stuff than Alison,' Cameron Kyle laughed. '*You* will last it out.'

With a flick of his whip he was gone, the horses galvanised into action, back up the High Street. He was heartless, Rose decided. Worse still, gone back in such a hurry to dally with Miss Cornelia, no doubt. She tried not to think of it, but she was thoroughly dismal when she entered the establishment of Madame Buzonnière behind Alison.

It was a high room, with high windows, and it was cold—almost insufferably cold. Alison drew her cloak more tightly about her and sat down with a shiver. Rose bitterly regretted that she had not accepted Aunt Bea's offer of her full-length grey fur cloak, and drawing her little cape together, sat down beside her.

The other students filed in one by one in a continuous stream, old, young and middle-aged, ladies and gentlemen, until every seat was occupied in a buzz of expectancy and conversation. It quickly ceased when a tiny lady appeared suddenly on the platform. Rose had never seen such elegance before—unless, of course her own Mama, long ago.

Madame Buzonnière wore black, but black with such style that she outshone every other lady there. To crown it all, a minute black hat sat on her very blonde head, and from it a black lace veil fell in a wisp to cover her face. She took off her long black gloves slowly and deliberately, one by one, and then in a gesture that was almost theatrical, she lifted the little black veil.

She had captivated her audience long before they saw her exquisitely painted face.

'*Bonjour, mes enfants*,' she smiled.

'*Bonjour, madame,*' Rose said mechanically, thanking her stars that at least they were to be treated as children, who could know nothing.

'I did not know you spoke French already,' Alison whispered.

'I cannot,' Rose answered. Of course she could not.

'I hope she is not going to speak in French all the time,' Alison said. 'I do not understand it at all.'

But Madame further delighted her class by telling them in a charming broken English that today she would give them lists of vocabulary to write down and to learn, and she demonstrated how to pronounce in French every word she introduced.

By this time the room had heated up dramatically. Rose and Alison took off their furs and draped them over the backs of their chairs, before they opened their notebooks.

The two hours passed like a flash, like a dream, for Rose. She could not believe it when they were over, and they were putting their furs back on.

'Oh, wasn't it wonderful, Alison?' she asked, out in the Canongate again.

'Your cheeks are flushed and your eyes are shining,' Cameron Kyle said at her side suddenly in the crowd. 'It makes you more of a rose than ever. You must have enjoyed the French lessons.'

'Oh, yes!' Rose said, Miss Cornelia Forbes the furthest from her memory in her enthusiasm.

'Yes, we did,' Alison smiled, and lifted her eyebrows in her glance at her brother. 'Then you will continue to come with me, Rose? You will come back tomorrow?'

Rose nodded. 'I am going to try to learn all those words before then,' she said, and wondered why Cameron and Alison laughed so much.

She could not wait to get into bed that night with her notebook, and by the light of her candle she read all the words again and said them out loud to herself. None of

them seemed foreign. As she went over them again and
again, she found she was not having to learn them. She
was merely being reminded of them, and after the candle
guttered out she lay in the darkness and went over them
once more in her head.

She kept sticking at two of them. Not because they
were difficult—they were easy, the words a child might
use, or hear every day.

At that, Rose sat bolt upright, her heart beating fast.
'*La poupée*' for 'the doll'. And '*chéri*' for 'darling'. Poo
Pay for her own doll, broken at the start of all this, and
cherry, the endearment *Maman* had always used.
'*Maman*'? Even that word came naturally to her, and she
was back in the big house again, the house of her earliest
memories, the house with the curtains bordered with
flowers which had three feathery petals.

They were the fleurs de lys, of course, which Madame
had said were the emblem of France. And outside the
long windows she could hear the clip-clop of the horses
pulling the elegant carriages along La Place . . . La Place
de la . . . La Place de la what? She could not remember.

And then '*en bâteau*', with *Maman*, and the heaving
up and down, to merge into the jolts and the shuddering
of a coach. It was the journey from France, from Paris,
she was sure of it. It was the first clue she had ever had of
her origin, and it put paid to sleep for Rose that night in a
surging excitement—and hard on the heels of that, the
tremendous worry of such a discovery.

By the end of the week, Rose could follow every word
of a story Madame Buzonnière read to them, which, she
said, was to accustom their ears to the French language.
And then, on Sunday, Aunt Bea came to visit.

Rose took her up to her bedchamber, and Ellie
brought them tea.

'I thought you were *never* coming, darling Aunt
Bea!'

'After the confinement there was an epidemic of

chickenpox in Newhaven,' Mistress Barbour smiled tiredly. 'But now I think the worst is over. I am so glad to see you have a fire, dear.' She shivered violently. 'The weather is so much colder now, and all of a sudden.'

'You *look* cold. And tired. Are you all right, Aunt Bea?'

'Of course I am, my dear. But it has worried me that I could not get to you sooner.'

'And Uncle George?'

'The same as ever. The same old apple pies on Sundays. When I leave, which I am afraid I must do quite soon, I shall take the coach to Leith. It will be nearer to the Turf Inn. Uncle George is making the supper this evening.'

'Then it will be the apple pie, as usual?'

'Oh dear, I suppose so . . .'

They laughed together and turned their faces to the fire.

'Aunt Bea, I have been going to the French classes with Miss Alison Kyle.'

'Ah. The sister of Mr Cameron Kyle?'

'Yes. They are very easy lessons. I have found out now why I called my doll Poo Pay. It was really "*poupée*", the French for doll.'

'Is that so, dear? And Mr Kyle, do you see much of him?'

'Oh, he is there every day,' Rose said carelessly. 'Can you remember if my Mama was a French lady?'

Mistress Barbour wrinkled her brows. 'Rose, I do not know. French?' She looked puzzled and unhappy. 'She may have been foreign,' she said uncertainly. 'Perhaps that was why I did not understand her very well.'

'Did she tell you her name was Madame somebody?'

'Perhaps she did, dear.'

Rose saw that tears were not far away from Aunt Bea's eyes, and her face was very white.

'It does not matter, darling. We won't talk about it any

more. Let me tell you about the Deacon and Miss Jean
Brodie instead.'

'Yes, tell me, Rose. And be quick about it. I see by
your clock that I may stay only half an hour longer.'

When she left, Rose felt sad and upset. She had never
seen her aunt so ill-looking before, ill and exhausted,
shivering even before the fire, although she had gone in a
flurry of the anxious little commands which reassured
her that Aunt Bea had not changed a bit, either.

'Now, dear, you will never go out upon the streets of
Edinburgh alone, especially at night.'

'No, Aunt Bea.'

'And they are attending to your baths here, and your
hair?'

'Yes, Aunt Bea.'

'And, of course, you have long ago attended to the
money.'

Rose's heart lurched, then sank like a stone. She had
entirely forgotten about the sovereigns. But they were
still safe in the writing-desk.

'Yes,' she said. 'The money is quite safe, Aunt Bea.'

Now that she was alone, she rushed to make sure. It all
still lay there in the bottom drawer, glinting up at her.
She knew it was all there, by the weight of the drawer,
and she heaved a quivering sigh. She *must* get to the
Bank of Scotland very soon.

But the disappointment of her aunt being unable to
answer her questions overrode even that. It blotted out
everything else, and all the next week Rose pondered
over her problem until by the end of it she found she was
even thinking in French.

Madame Buzonnière interviewed each one of her
students in turn, midway through her short one-month
course, speaking in French and hoping for some response in the same language. It came as a great relief to
Rose to have the opportunity to reply fluently.

'But I have had an unfair advantage, Madame,' Rose

explained to her astonished teacher, 'because I believe I was born French although adopted later by a lady here in Edinburgh. All trace has been lost of my parents, although I know now I must have lived in France and spoken French as my native tongue for the first few years of my life. Perhaps I came from Paris. I believe I did.'

'I am Parisienne,' Madame Buzonnière said. 'If only you could tell me what street you lived in, or give me some name, I might be able to help you.'

Rose shook her head sadly. 'I cannot remember, Madame. I was too young.'

The house of Deacon Brodie seethed with excitement on the twenty-second of November. Mr James Leslie arrived far too early at six o'clock to escort Miss Jean and Rose to the theatre, and was unceremoniously dumped in the sitting-room by a distracted Ellie.

'Wait here, if you please, sir,' she said and thrust the *Courant* into his hand. 'As you will see from the advertisements, the play does not begin until half-past seven, and the ladies have not even started to dress.'

Mr Leslie subsided onto a settee with a quiet smile, and the preparations continued.

'Will Mattie be able to dress Miss Jean?' Rose asked anxiously.

'I have laid out her gown. Mattie can at least begin to dress her,' Ellie answered grimly, and fastened Rose into her peach silk dress with all the little bows down the back from shoulder to hem.

'Now I am going to weave these peach silk ribbons in and out of your ringlets, Miss Rose. Sit still, if you please.'

'Do you know what you are turning into, Ellie? It is a dragon.'

'And much need, around here,' Ellie said, quite unmoved.

'You came here polished and shining,' she went on,

lifting the brush in a purposeful manner, 'and you will not leave my hands any other way. I would not have it said. So, are you ready?'

'I am ready,' Rose laughed, and the brushing and the combing and the weaving began, until at last it was over and Rose was ready to go.

'I'll just run down and finish off Miss Jean,' Ellie said, carefully adjusting Rose's evening cloak. 'Lift up your skirts, Miss Rose, and do not trip on the staircase behind me.'

Deacon Brodie was in the dining-hall when Rose made her careful entrance, and went to take her hand. She noticed that when they were standing together side by side like this, he was much shorter than she was. He did not have long legs. It was as though his top half belonged to a man, and his bottom half to a boy.

But the hand holding hers was that of a man. It was clinging, and slightly damp, and his fingers rubbed her palm in a most suggestive way, to send tingles through her of hot embarrassment.

'I wish I could come with you tonight, Rose,' he said thickly.

'Why are you not coming, Master Will?'

'Oh, you know me, Rose! It is *The Beggar's Opera*, the wickedness, the excitement—or not at all! But I wish I could be with you, tonight.'

His eyes seemed to hypnotise her, and his fingers were working feverishly now. They aroused feelings in her she did not know she possessed. She swayed towards him, and he drew her on, his lips wet and smiling, and somehow very shocking. She could not help herself, as his left arm went round her waist and his right hand left her palm to rest hotly under her cloak on her breast. It burned through the thin fabric of her dress.

'Perhaps later?' he whispered.

It was only the sound of footsteps in the passage from Miss Jean's rooms which stopped what might have

happened next, and from the other direction, from the
front door, Ellie appeared. Rose knew she had taken in
the situation at a glance.

'The carriage is waiting,' she announced, and her eyes
were grim and hard, a dark, hard blue.

'For the love of God, Miss Rose,' she said under her
breath as they all went down the turnpike staircase into
the Close. 'For the love of God, stay away from Deacon
Brodie. And if it is the last thing you ever do, bolt your
door tonight.'

She would have to speak to her maidservant, Rose
decided, when they got to the Theatre Royal, her senses
still stirred. Ellie was getting to be altogether quite
above herself—quite above herself.

And then, she forgot even that in the rowdy, perfumed, heady atmosphere. Now she understood perfectly what Master Will had meant. The people were not
in their seats, but laughing and moving about among
their friends, and there was shouting and throwing
orange-skins at each other, and bursts of laughter again.
Anything was possible, in the theatre.

She found herself seated next to Alison on one side
and young Walter Scott on the other. For a fleeting
moment she knew a slight disappointment. She had
expected Cameron Kyle to be there as well. She looked
along the row of seats, but he was nowhere to be seen.

'Your brother, Alison. He is not here?'

'He could not come, dear,' Alison raised her voice a
little to be heard above the uproar of the audience. 'He
has had to go away again.'

'To go away again', the words rang loud and clear
as the speaking stopped suddenly, the house lights
dimmed, and the curtain rose. Well, at least he was not
with Miss Cornelia Forbes, Rose thought. Although it
was strange that she was not here either.

And then the play began. For the next hour all
Edinburgh was enthralled and enchanted by Mrs Sarah

Siddons. Her voice carried to the very rafters, each word
as clear and distinct as though she spoke to each one of
them in joy, in despair, and in every other facet of
human emotion.

'Oh, she is magnificent!' Rose said, when the curtain
came down half-way through for the long interval.
Alison did not reply. She was talking to Mistress Scott on
her right.

'She *is* magnificent!' Walter Scott agreed, on her left,
'for she has breathed fire into a story that is decidedly
weak.'

'Weak?'

'We all know what will happen, do we not, right from
the start? But her acting is so supreme that it does not
matter. She makes the story unimportant. What is
important is her interpretation. I suppose that is why
she has been called back here for a demand repeat
performance.'

'You have seen *Venice Preserv'd* before?'

'Oh, yes! I saw it two years ago,' Walter Scott replied.
'I thought it such a poor story then, that it made me more
determined than ever to write my own stories some day,
much better than that.' He finished on a lower note. 'I
dare not let my Mama hear me. She does not approve of
writing stories.'

Rose could believe him. She turned round in her seat
to face him.

'No one can hear us now,' she said. 'Tell me one of
them. Have you made it up already?'

'This one will be called "Guy Mannering",' he said,
and quickly outlined his plot.

Rose was not so interested in the plot as she was
fascinated by one of the characters.

'Meg Merrilies,' she asked him. 'Did you base her on a
real person? Did you know a gipsy woman like her? Oh,
I knew a gipsy woman so very like her, once, Master
Walter!'

'If you do not call me Walter, I shall not call you Rose. It is agreed? Then tell me about your gipsy woman, Rose. It is people who interest me, too, first and last.'

Before the curtain went up again, Rose and Walter Scott were firm friends. They had found a common bond. He insisted on sitting next to her again when Mistress Scott and her party boarded their coaches after the play, to go to Fortune's in the High Street for one of their famous oyster suppers.

They all walked into the darkness of the Stamp-Office Close and entered the Tavern suitably impressed, when Mistress Scott told them this was the meeting-place of the Poker Club, a most remarkably brilliant set of men, consisting of Hume, Robertson, Blair, Fergusson, to name but a few.

And so it was all the more surprising to Rose, after such an introduction, to find the Oyster Cellar of Fortune's was a dark cavern of a room, dimly lit by cheap tallow candles, whose only furniture was one large rough table round which were seated other ladies and gentlemen. It was covered with dishes of oysters and pots of porter, and from what she could see, the other guests were well dressed too.

The Scott party managed to squeeze in, and immediately, as if by some signal the fun began, the vivacious conversation, the repartee, the laughter and the applause. The strangeness of the Cellar and the dim light added to the atmosphere, and Rose realised that the entertainment could never have been, in any other place. It was so dull and mean and crude that it was the perfect foil for so much brilliance.

The fiddlers who had come in unnoticed and sat in one corner seemed to sense when the company were tiring of conversation, and struck up a reel.

'Will you dance with me, Rose?' Walter stood up and offered her his hand. 'My game leg does not prevent me from dancing.'

'Aunt Bea nursed you through your illness, did she not?'

'Thanks to her I recovered, and after that I was sent to my grandfather's farm in the Borders to convalesce. That was where I met the gipsies.'

Dance followed dance, and maidservants cleared the table of the oysters and the porter, and brought in the brandy and the rum-punch.

'It is time to go,' Mistress Scott said when she saw it. 'And besides, it is very late now. Jean, you and Rose and Jamie will ride in our coach, and we will drop you off at the Lawnmarket. I could not permit you to walk, or to go in sedans at this time of night, not even that short distance.'

They were walking back down the Stamp-Office Close to the coach out on the High Street, when Rose remembered her reticule, still lying under the chair she had been sitting on, and before anyone noticed she ran back for it. All the others were waiting in the coach when she ran out of the Tavern for the second time, and into the darkness towards it.

She fixed her gaze on the lighted square which was the entrance of the Close, and tried not to feel frightened. But the blood froze in her veins when one of the shadows moved in front of her, and became the shape of a tall, broad man, dressed all in black and with his face muffled. He turned it aside swiftly and moved back to merge again into the blackness, and Rose fled for her life.

'You are trembling, dear,' Miss Brodie said when she sat down breathlessly beside her. 'Did you find your reticule?'

'I found it,' Rose said, her mind whirling all the way up the High Street and back to the Lawnmarket.

She knew every inch of him too well, his height in relation to hers, the square set of his shoulders, the shape of his lean face, so quickly averted when he saw her, ever to be mistaken. It was Cameron Kyle. There was no doubt it was Cameron Kyle.

And Alison had said that he was away somewhere.

Rose was thankful that Mr Leslie was there to escort them up to the big front door of the house in Brodie's Close, thankful that he waited with them until Ellie opened it, and thankful that Jessie was behind her with the night lantern. She had had enough of the shadows and the mysteries of Edinburgh—handsome, energetic, intellectual Edinburgh in the light, city of fear and treachery in the dark.

The French lessons went on to the end of the first week of December, and every day Cameron Kyle drove them there and drove them back with his cool, amused expression. Rose spoke to him as little as possible. It made no difference to her friendship with Alison, however. On that last day, Madame Buzonnière said Goodbye and pressed a little card into Rose's hand with her address in Paris on it, in case she could ever help her.

'Miss Brodie will not be in when I get back, Alison,' Rose said, and shuddered at the thought of it, for Miss Brodie would be going out with Mr Leslie in one of her latest excesses of fashion, from which Rose had been unable, try as she may, to restrain her.

She had gazed in horror when Miss Brodie brought it home one day.

'Oh, *isn't* it so very up to date, Rose? The latest thing?' she enthused, and posed before her mirror in the ridiculous Lunardi hat, a huge, round wired monstrosity, a balloon of a hat.

'Never mind, Miss Rose,' Ellie had tried to soothe her afterwards. 'Mr Leslie will think it is entirely fetching. He is quite besotted with our Miss Jean. It will not matter to him *what* is upon her head.'

'She will never be able to get in the coach with that thing on,' Rose sighed despairingly.

'So long as she is happy, and he is happy, there are far worse things than that to worry about,' Ellie had said darkly.

But then Ellie had a habit of muttering darkly and mysteriously, as though there were something of terrible importance she should relay, given the least encouragement. Rose had long since accepted it and ignored it. She had other things on her mind.

'Miss Brodie does not need me so much, now that Mr Leslie is here,' she said out loud.

'Thank goodness for that,' Alison said. 'I have been waiting for an opportunity like this to take you back to Queen Street again. There is something I want you to see. I want you to give me your opinion.'

It must be a new piece of furniture, Rose thought when Cameron had gone with the carriage, and Alison pulled her quite excitedly into the drawing-room. A large frame stood in the middle of the carpet, covered with a dust-sheet.

'This is a surprise we have been keeping from you, Rose,' Alison smiled. 'Stand back! There . . . Do you recognise her?'

She had uncovered a half-finished portrait on an easel.

'Oh, Alison!' Rose said, gazing into the grave blue eyes of the lady in the picture, at her gentle expression, at her blue silk dress. 'A great artist has captured you for ever just as we all see you. It is remarkable. Who painted it?'

'A young man called Henry Raeburn, dear. You will meet him one day. So you like it? Then may I leave you with it for a few minutes, while I go and see what stage they are at in the kitchen—of course, you will stay for lunch?'

Rose walked up and down the drawing-room and noticed that wherever she went the blue eyes in the portrait followed her.

'A real artist makes the eyes live,' said a voice behind

her, and sent chills up her spine. 'The eyes are the most important features of anyone's face. They are the windows of the soul.'

'Yet there is one man I know, sir,' she plunged straight in, 'whose blue eyes are as false as they are blue, whatever that signifies.'

'What *are* you saying, Rose?'

'It is quite simple. You are not to be trusted. You sent word in a devious fashion on the twenty-second of November that you had gone away. Yet that very night I saw you with my own eyes in the Stamp-Office Close, disguised in black clothes.'

'And what makes you so sure it was me? I should imagine there are other men dressed in black clothes every night in the Royal Mile. I can think of one in particular.'

Rose looked up at Cameron Kyle scornfully.

'If you are referring to Deacon Brodie, he goes about his genuine "night business" dressed in black, certainly. It is so that he does not soil his white day clothes.''

'That could be one reason, of course,' Cameron smiled maddeningly. 'Another could be that it makes him less easily seen, whatever he is doing.'

'Then that makes two of you, slinking about the High Street at dead of night,' Rose said, her brown eyes glowing copper with indignation. 'And, in any case, it was not Deacon Brodie. I know by your build. I knew it even in the dark.'

'Ah,' Cameron laughed softly. 'Did you, now? So you have studied it?'

'What am I missing?' purred a velvet voice in the doorway. 'It sounds interesting. Is our little . . . lady from Leith angry again, Cameron? Her face is quite crimson, and I thought her voice to be even a little strident just now.'

Rose was furious. With Cameron Kyle. With her pet aversion, Miss Cornelia Forbes. But most of all with herself, for giving herself away like that to him. And she wondered how long they had been overheard, although it was strange that they were interrupted only when Cameron's voice had softened as it did.

'Miss Rose Barbour,' Cameron emphasised each word pointedly, 'was having a little discussion with me—a very interesting discussion. But every time such a thing happens, we are interrupted one way or another. I have complained about it before.'

'Oh, Cornelia!' Alison said. 'I heard all that! Rose's voice could not be strident if it tried. Do try to behave, dear.' She spoke as though to a naughty child. 'Now, shall we go in? It is only a very light lunch today.'

It was a very light lunch, for Rose. She ate almost nothing, while Miss Cornelia Forbes flirted her way through the meal with Cameron Kyle in a sparkling demonstration of feminine wit and feminine wiles. It was quite superb, and quite impossible not to admire her, and to laugh and be thoroughly entertained. She is like a little kitten, Rose thought.

But the claws were there as well. Underlying it all there was a tenseness she could not define. Miss Cornelia said not one word out of place, and yet there was a subtle sting in the tail of every sentence that she uttered.

Rose began to regret she had ever agreed to come to Alison's house in Queen Street, and by the time the lunch was over she felt her old enemy, the temper the colour of her hair, starting to rise. Why were the Kyles so insistent on bringing her here, of seeming to befriend her with one hand, and then constantly thrusting this wretched Miss Cornelia in her face with the other?

Why had Cameron Kyle been lurking in the Royal Mile two weeks ago, all dressed in black? She had never got to the bottom of that, yet. Why did he not want her to see him? And what *was* his business, if any? How did he come to be so rich, and yet do so little? Why did he not just marry his Miss Cornelia Forbes, she wondered, near

to tears? He said he was going to marry, very soon. And
why, oh why, did it all hurt so much?

Rose managed to wait until the meal was over, and
they were walking back to the drawing-room. Then she
knew she could stand no more.

'I am sorry, Alison. I must be like the beggars, and
run. Perhaps Miss Brodie will be back by now, and I
should be there to be with her.'

'Oh, must you go already, Rose?' Alison was genu-
inely regretful. 'You have been so welcome, dear. But if
you really must go, Cameron will take you back.'

At all costs, Rose promised herself, *that* would never
happen. She never wanted to be alone with him again.
She looked from one to the other, from Alison, to
Cornelia Forbes and back again to Cameron Kyle, and
saw nothing but treachery. She made up her mind to
fight back.

'Oh, that would be very kind! But do you know what I
should like even better, Alison? I have never been in a
sedan chair in my life, and yours is so very elegant!'

She saw the scowl on Cameron Kyle's brows as they
drew down sharply, the muscles tightening in his cheeks,
and felt triumphant.

'Cameron, will you call the chair-men? I will come
with you,' Alison said. 'We cannot refuse her.'

There was a little silence after they left, during which
Rose summoned all her forces.

'You did not come to Mrs Siddons' play, Miss Forbes?
I should have thought theatricals would appeal to you.'

'Oh no,' Miss Cornelia Forbes smiled silkily, while her
green eyes glowed with malice. 'I was much more
romantically occupied that evening. With Cameron. I
am going to marry him—did you know?'

Rose stepped into the green and gilt sedan chair,
smiled briefly at Alison, and then drew the little
curtains.

Perhaps it was the curious jogging, swaying motion,

the hard smacks of the chair-mens' shoes as they ran rhythmically on out of the New Town and back to the Old, or the dim stuffiness inside the chair which was making her feel so sick.

Whatever it was, it was making her cry. She sobbed all the way back to the house in Brodie's Close as though her heart would break. She went directly to her room and locked and bolted the door. She did not want to see Ellie. Her eyes were too sharp. She did not want to see the Deacon. He was too demanding. She did not want to see anyone.

She lay down on her bed and did not go down to join the others for the evening meal.

But she was still desolately awake when the first streak of dawn stole across her window like a ghost, and she knew she would not sleep at all now, not that night. She lay and braced herself to meet the new day, and the noises that meant Edinburgh was waking up. Once they began, Rose knew they would not stop. They would only get louder and louder.

And so she was in a sense prepared, and yet totally unprepared, for the sounds that did come so shockingly out of the silence, the screams and the wild sobbings from below. They went on and on, punctuated by a woman's terrified voice, the voice of Miss Jean Brodie.

Rose had her dressing-robe on, the bolts shot back and her door unlocked all in one movement, and arrived out in the corridor at the same time as Ellie.

'What is it? What is it?' she cried, as the screaming went on.

But Ellie shook her head, and with one accord they were running along the passage and down the spiral staircase in their bare feet, and into the dining-hall. There a terrible sight met their shocked eyes. Miss Brodie was bending over Deacon Brodie, and he was lying just inside the door on the honey-coloured floor-boards in a pool of blood.

CHAPTER
SEVEN

THE OTHER Rose took over, the Rose who became as cold as ice and deadly calm. Later, when she looked back upon it, she recalled that Mama's response had been just the same when faced with life and death, in her decision to leave the gipsy camp.

She pulled her hysterical mistress off the body of her brother and saw that he was still alive. His face was hideously grey, and blood poured out of a deep gash under his right eye and dripped off his chin to soak his cravat, waistcoat and coat.

'Hot and cold water, and soft linen, Ellie, at once,' she said.

While she waited, she put Miss Brodie to sit on a chair, and spoke to her calmly and reassuringly, as she would have done to a child.

'It will be all right, dear Miss Jean. It is only a cut below his eye. It is bleeding a lot, but we will soon stop that. Just sit still and Mattie will come and help you in a minute.'

But Mattie did not come. It was a terrified young Jessie, the maidservant of the lantern, who arrived with Ellie, carrying cloths and buckets and kettles.

'Go back to the kitchen, Jessie, and make a pot of tea for Miss Jean. For us all. We have all had a shock. And do try to stop shaking, there's a good girl. It is not nearly as bad as it looks.'

The stench in the room, in spite of its high airy ceiling, was indescribable, and the Deacon's clothes were covered with slime and purpling stains and something even more unspeakable than all of that.

'He is not dead,' Ellie said, disgustedly. 'He is dead

drunk. What a state to get into!'

Rose bathed his eyes with cold water over and over
again and pressed the gash shut. Being on the cheek-
bone, it bled out of all proportion to its size.

'And you have seen him like this, before, Ellie?'

'Drunk, many a time. But never as bad as this.'

'That was why you did not want me to come downstairs in the early mornings, wasn't it?'

'It is enough to put anyone off, Miss Rose. And I
wanted you to stay.'

'How did his sister manage to hear him, and to get up
and let him in?'

'Perhaps her usual sleeping-draught did not work, for
once.'

Rose glanced across at Miss Brodie. She seemed
half-drugged now, anyway.

'He's not going to come to,' Ellie said in a low voice.
'He is too drunk. What shall we do, Miss Rose?'

'We shall have to get him out of these disgusting
clothes, but we must get Miss Jean out of the way first.
Thank God, here is Jessie with the tea. Keep bathing
that wound in cold water, and press the edges together.'

Rose lifted Miss Brodie bodily out of her chair. Her
head rolled back and her eyes were glazed behind the
tears. Rose smelled the same sweet-sour smell as her
rooms had reeked of, that first morning. But there was
no time to worry about that now. She supported her
mistress back to her bed, with Jessie following.

'See that she has a cup of tea with plenty of sugar in it,
Jessie, and have a cup yourself. Then stay with her and
on no account allow her to rise out of that bed. Where is
Mattie, anyway?'

'Asleep, Miss Rose,' Jessie answered, quivering.

'Asleep? In all that din?'

'She never gets to bed until the early hours, Miss
Rose. She must attend the mistress. And she is too old to
get up again so soon.'

Rose gazed at the little maid in perplexity. But there was no time to unravel any of this at present.

'Look after her, dear,' she said, and went back into the dining-hall.

'I have got his top clothes off, at least,' Ellie said, her mouth a grim, hard line, 'except for his breeches.'

Rose looked at the filthy heap Ellie had tossed aside already.

'We will have them off, too.'

Ellie looked at her in horror. 'Not you, Miss Rose! I will do it.'

'It is all right, Ellie. My aunt trained me for all this, dear. Now you will go and burn the whole lot. Nobody can be expected to wash them. And tell me where his room is, and I will get something for him to wear.'

'Up the other stair from ours, and the first door you come to, Miss Rose.'

Rose paused long enough to press another cold cloth on the Deacon's cheek. The blood was congealing at last. But still he did not stir, although his breathing was loud and stertorous.

Daylight was flooding in now, and through the twin skylights in the roof Deacon Brodie's bedchamber was illuminated. Rose paused uncertainly on the doorstep and gazed around. Why had the master of the house chosen this room, and not the beautiful room she herself occupied?

Its size answered her. This was a room made out of two rooms, and filled with the finest furniture she had ever seen. Here there was the space to display it. She saw bookcases filled with gold-tooled leather books, wardrobes inlaid with mother-of-pearl, and rich brocades such as she never knew existed.

She opened drawer after drawer, all cedar-lined, all piled with the finest linen laid over with tissue paper, and could not bring herself to disturb any of it. Then she

discovered a nightshirt tucked away under the pillows of
the massive four-poster bed, and was retreating with it
when her eye fell on something so completely foreign in
a room furnished to such a degreè that she was halted in
her tracks.

It was an old cash register, big and black and ugly.
What was it doing there? Perhaps it was a relic from the
past, from the old family business, of greatest sen-
timental value. If that were so, she discovered, when she
touched one of the buttons and a great deep drawer flew
open, it had been cruelly desecrated, for it contained
diamond rings, plain gold rings, seals, brooches, crosses,
ear-rings, buckles and even teaspoons, all of the finest
silver, and all hidden away so very cleverly, as a thief
might hide them.

Down in the dining-hall the evil smell had nearly
gone, now that Ellie had removed the Deacon's foul
garments.

'How is the wound, Ellie?'

'Stopped bleeding.'

'Shall we try, then?'

Cautiously, they raised him up to a sitting position,
and put his arms round their necks to drag him upright.
He was surprisingly heavy for so small a man. Step by
step they heaved him up the stairs, his feet dangling and
his head lolling until at last they reached the four-poster
bed, and together they lifted him on to it. Lying there,
his broad shoulders and powerful arms were oddly at
variance with his skinny shanks and hollow thighs, clad
only in his under-breeches.

'And now, Miss Rose?'

'Now go back to bed, Ellie, and I shall go back to
mine. We will rise again at nine o'clock. It is all over,
whatever it was.'

'Yes, Miss Rose.'

Ellie departed, and Rose remained, looking down at
the Master of Brodie's Close, the Deacon of Wrights,

Town Councillor and, some said, the future Lord Provost of the Royal Burgh of Edinburgh—perhaps even to be knighted by King George at Windsor.

As she stared, his eyes fluttered open.

'How did I get here?' he demanded.

'In a sedan, I suppose. You were incapable of walking,' she said coldly.

He put his fingers to his cheek. 'How bad is it, Rose?' His voice was trembling.

'Not so bad,' she replied cautiously.

'But will I be marked?' Deacon Brodie's voice was that of a querulous small child. It shocked Rose, more than any of the other events of the night had done. She realised that here was a coward. A bully, as witness the way he had berated his sister about the price of her gowns, but still a coward as all bullies are, and frightened first and last for his own skin. Rose felt nothing but cold contempt.

'I'm afraid you will be marked. I cannot deny it.'

Deacon Brodie heaved, as though he would vomit, and Rose stepped back.

'What can I do now?' he asked her.

'Resolve never to drink again, whatever the reason for it, for it could not have been for pleasure, not to finish up like this. And go back to sleep. The wine is all through your bloodstream. You will never recover until you are rid of it.'

These blunt words had the desired effect, and William Brodie closed his eyes. Still Rose stood there, looking down at him. How could she ever have been even halfways taken in by him? She had even lost sleep over him, this miserable apology for a man.

Cameron Kyle, by contrast, sprang instantly to her mind, as she negotiated one spiral staircase back down to the dining-hall and then dragged herself by the hand-rail back up the other, and so into bed. He would never, never land up in the gutter as Deacon Brodie had, she knew that for certain. Miss Cornelia Forbes was the luckiest lady in Edinburgh.

Rose picked at the breakfast Ellie brought her at nine o'clock.

'I cannot eat it, Ellie.'

'It doesn't matter. You will eat again.'

'I feel so tired.' The hairbrush rasped through her hair. 'What is the news?'

'At home or abroad?'

Rose's eyes flew open, wide awake and alert. 'What do you mean, Ellie?'

'Well, at home Miss Jean sleeps on, and the Deacon is a better colour, although with a blood-encrusted cut under his right eye. And abroad, there is speculation.'

'Speculation? How do you know?'

'Well, John Robertson is an apprentice cabinetmaker, and I am well acquainted with him.'

'And what has he told you?'

'That there were loaded dice down at Clark's Inn and a gentleman had his eye cut because of it.'

Rose looked at Ellie in horror. Not so long ago she would have dismissed such a tale as idle gossip. Ellie was such a prattler. Now, she was not so quick.

'He cannot mean that Deacon Brodie was the gentleman? That he was gambling? And with crooked dice?'

'That is the rumour, Miss Rose.'

'Has Miss Jean heard it?'

'No, and she must not hear it. I am making every excuse I can think of to keep the newspapers out of her reach, but I cannot trust Mattie not to smuggle them in to her.'

'Then the rumour has reached the newspapers? They dare not print such a thing unless there is some truth in it. Miss Jean is almost certain to find out, sooner or later. And she has been so well and happy lately, since Mr

Leslie came back! She has even been getting up most mornings.'

'That is what I mean, Miss Rose. If she finds out, she will go right back to it again.'

'Back to what?'

Ellie's eyes shifted uneasily. 'Back to her trouble . . .'

'You are hiding something from me, Ellie, I can tell. Back to what?'

'Back to the bottle, then,' the maid cried, stung. 'Oh, Miss Rose, I did not want to say it!'

Rose swallowed and took a deep breath. 'The bottle? What do you mean?'

'That is why she sleeps so late in the mornings. She drinks a bottle of claret far into the night, every night.'

'Oh, Ellie!'

'It is the fault of our Master Will. He introduced her to drink a few years ago, Mattie says, to stop her worrying so much about the robberies. She gets very upset about the robberies.'

Rose had a sudden vision of Mattie slinking past with one hand hidden in her apron skirts. But there was something more here, that she was not seeing. Why should Miss Jean become so extraordinarily upset about the robberies? More upset than anyone else? And why had the Deacon gone to such lengths to keep her quiet?

'Oh, Ellie . . . This is dreadful. She gets no less upset now about the burglaries, and he has done this to her into the bargain. No wonder she never came to herself until after the Meridian. Her coffee had brandy in it. That must have been "the hair of the dog" that Uncle George always used to speak about.'

'Well, we must try to keep her on an even keel, Miss Rose, and as much in Mr Leslie's company as possible. We must keep her mind off everything else.'

This proved easier than they could have hoped during the next few weeks, as the Brodie household settled back into its old routine after the night of the Deacon's misadventure.

Miss Brodie did all her shopping and made her small domestic arrangements in the mornings now, and in the afternoons she went out with Mr Leslie in his carriage. Rose wondered how he contrived it, and concluded that he must be mixing business with pleasure, for Miss Brodie chattered sometimes about the large country houses she had visited with him.

And Deacon Brodie himself was very quiet. His wound healed to leave a very nasty scar. It dragged down the corner of his eye. He came and went about his day business, and then his 'night business', very quietly. Rose wondered how long it would last.

'We have received so many invitations, Rose! They are just rolling in, every day!' Miss Brodie exclaimed one morning, opening yet another small envelope and drawing out another little card.

'What are they for, Miss Jean?'

'That is the odd thing. They are all for the same function—the Christmas Ball in the New Assembly Rooms, to be held on Boxing Day. And we are all invited—my brother, and you, and me.'

'What will you do, Miss Jean?'

'I have spoken to Master Will about it already. His instructions are that we may accept only one, and refuse the others. It is the one from Miss Alison Kyle. My brother says she will not stay long in Queen Street.'

Rose did her best to subdue the wild beating of her heart at the very mention of the name of Kyle, and to try to reason out Miss Brodie's latest muddled statement.

'Miss Kyle is leaving Queen Street?'

'Master Will has heard that she is negotiating for another house, one being built in Charlotte Square. The entire square of houses has been designed by no less than that brilliant architect Robert Adam, and they will be the finest houses in Edinburgh, in Scotland, and my brother says, probably in all Britain.'

And your brother wants the business *that* will bring in, Rose thought.

'Besides,' Miss Brodie added, 'Miss Kyle is the only one thoughtful enough to include Mr Leslie in her invitation. That has settled it. So I shall write all my little letters today, Rose, and you shall help me, dear. Your handwriting is so much better than mine. And after that, we must look to our gowns.'

With all the letters written and given to the caddies to deliver, and Miss Brodie's latest gown of pale pink satin with its turban to match in the hands of the seamstresses, the days rolled on calmly in Brodie's Close.

In fact, a great calm descended on the city itself, a frosty, icy calm, as Christmas drew nearer and nearer. It made the street lamps, dim as they were, even dimmer in their haloes of hanging frozen mist.

But the Luckenbooths became even gayer, even gaudier, as the fog froze down, and locked the soot from the tall chimneys in, and drove it down into the Royal Mile. Down on the street it was yellow, and thick, and made everyone cough. Edinburgh deserved its nickname, Auld Reekie.

The countryfolk struggled in over the icy rutted roads from their cottages with their cartloads of bright green holly, its berries red and gay, and at the same time sad, with its reminder of the birth of Jesus Christ, and His death, and the blood that was shed. Rose thought about that every time she saw a holly wreath, that the berries were like drops of blood against the dark green prickly crown of thorns, and felt depressed.

But fowls hung about the stalls, waiting to be somebody's dinner, tinsel ribbons glittered, apples were polished until they shone, and every day Miss Brodie bought some other little trifle for her Boxing Day gifts. She was quite happy, in the meantime.

Rose still had not heard again from Aunt Bea, not even when Christmas Eve came, and they attended the first of the church services at midnight that night, the Watch-night service, when the shepherds first saw the star over Bethlehem, the star that led them to the Infant in the manger.

It was the service Rose had always loved best, but she found no joy in it this time, nor in any of the others all the next day, on Christmas Day itself. Of course, Aunt Bea would be attending the Old Newhaven Kirk all day, she reminded herself. She was *bound* to come tomorrow. Boxing Day had always been so special in Longcakes Lane. Aunt Bea made such a fuss about the Boxes.

'It does not matter how small the gift inside, Rose,' she had brought her up to understand. 'It is the thought that counts, this one day in the year.'

But by six o'clock she still had not come, nor sent any word, and Rose began the long ritual of dressing with a heavy heart.

'It will have to be your very best evening gown, this time, for such an important occasion, Miss Rose. All the lords and ladies and the gentry of the Town will be there.' Ellie laid out the cream satin, trimmed with gold, reverentially on the bed. 'Oh,' she sighed, 'it is beautiful, with all that embroidery, and all the little pearls hanging from it! You will be the Belle of the Ball. What are you going to wear in your hair?'

Rose shook her head. What did it matter? She did not even want to go to the Ball, far less endure all this. She wanted to go back to Longcakes Lane. Desperately, she wanted to see Aunt Bea. She made up her mind there and then that tomorrow she would go, come what may. But, tonight, she could not let Miss Brodie and Alison down.

'There is a little cap which goes with it,' she said aloud, and opened a little box.

'Of course you will enjoy it once you get there,' Ellie

assured her anxiously while she fixed the tiny cap of gold and pearls on the crown of Rose's head.

She smiled wanly. She did not think so, and she did not argue. She was too worried. Aunt Bea had looked so ill the last time she saw her.

The elegant New Assembly Rooms in George Street, one street behind Princes Street, seemed very large and very grand to Rose, when they arrived before its arches and pillars. She ascended its steps behind Miss Brodie into the imposing entrance hall.

'Which party, miss?' asked a footman, resplendent in a red uniform.

'Miss Alison Kyle's.'

He consulted a paper in his hand and then led them along a short corridor. On one of the doors was a notice. It read, 'Miss Alison Kyle's Anteroom', and the name 'Kyle' darted out at Rose as though it were made up of four letters of fire.

Alison was in attendance on her guests when they went in.

'Hang your cloaks up in here,' she told them, 'and Cameron will greet you when you get inside the hall. Your dresses are lovely.'

In other circumstances Rose's heart would have failed her. 'It is this way,' she said, with her hand on Miss Jean's arm, and taking a deep breath. Mr Leslie was waiting just inside the door. He put Miss Jean's arm in his and proudly led her in, and Rose followed behind.

There was a crystal chandelier hanging from the centre of the vast ceiling, reflected and reflected again and again in the glittering mirrors which lined the walls. Rose had never seen so many people all together in one room before, and all the people of fashion, over three hundred of them at least. The ladies were like butterflies in their dresses of silk and satin, and some wore pink Spanish hats which were so pretty, and all the rage.

The music was so loud and so lively that Rose was

soon lost in the crowd of dancers. Miss Jean and Mr Leslie were nowhere to be seen.

'Thank God you have come.' Before she even looked up, she knew the voice in her ear and the hand on her arm belonged to Cameron Kyle. She knew it from the intoxicating thrill his fingers sent through her whole body, and left her weak and dazed. He had always been the most handsome man she had ever seen, and it seemed that the more severe his dress, the more handsome he became. Down to the last detail he was immaculate, his shirt and cravat snow-white under the flawless austerity of his black velvet coat, his fair hair crisp and curling despite the thin black ribbon tightly knotted to hold it in place.

The expression on his face and the soft dark look in his blue eyes startled her out of her misery.

'I told you once that I would tell you what I think of your name, and now is the time. From the beginning you were as beautiful as a rose, but never so lovely as you are tonight. Will you do me the honour to dance with me, Miss Rose Barbour?'

The music started up again and he whirled her on to the floor, empty and gleaming, with so much space, so much room to move. But Cameron held her tightly, far too tightly for decorum. She could not escape from his grasp in the new-fashioned waltz. She did not want to escape, and that was the trouble. She must. Cameron Kyle was going to be married to Miss Cornelia Forbes.

'I have missed you,' he said in her ear. 'It has been a fortnight. I could not think of any other excuse to see you, except to make Miss Brodie an offer she could not refuse. And I had to see you, Rose.'

Every word he spoke was another twist of the dagger in her heart. She should feel so happy, and yet she felt so sad, and so unhappy, because he was saying them to the wrong woman. It all added to the worry she had started out with. She looked up at him and the smile he had hoped for did not materialise. He did not believe she had even heard him, for the tears in her eyes spilled over to run down her cheeks.

'I should not be here,' she said. 'Least of all, with you. If you will excuse me, I think I must go.'

'Go? Go where? Rose, what is the matter?'

He led her off the dance floor, past Miss Cornelia Forbes dancing with a short rather stocky man who was very handsomely dressed in green, with a lot of lace ruffles. She looked ravishing in lemon and emerald green, with feathers in her turban fastened with glittering green stones. Rose would not have been surprised if they were emeralds. But to her surprise, Cameron only smiled at her in the passing.

Out of the hall and back in Alison's deserted anteroom, he repeated his question.

'Where are you going? Wherever it is, you are not going alone.' He spoke so gently that Rose sobbed in real earnest. She had expected him to be grim and stern as usual, or laughing at her. But he was not laughing now. He was not even smiling. He looked as worried as she felt.

'Is it trouble in Brodie's Close?' he asked, with an urgency she could not understand.

'Oh, no. It is nothing like that. It is that I must get to Newhaven. And at once. There is something wrong with Aunt Bea.'

'How do you know that, Rose?'

'I do not know it,' she sobbed. 'That is the trouble. But I feel it. I know.'

He put his arm round her shoulders comfortingly. Rose had never been so glad of a place to put her head as on his shoulder. It helped even more when he bent down and kissed her forehead softly.

'Well, then,' he said. 'It must be true, if you feel it as badly as that. Wait here while I make the arrangements. I will send Alison to you in the meantime.'

Ten minutes later, when Rose had recovered slightly, Alison took down her fur cloak and put it round the cream and gold dress.

'You will need it,' she said, 'if Cameron is making the arrangements I think he will.'

'Yes, you will need it,' he assured her, coming in with a breath of frosty air about him. 'It is freezing out there. Can you ride, Rose?'

'I used to ride when I was a child.'

'In Newhaven?'

Rose bit her quivering lip and knew she should never have admitted she could ride, even if it had only been bareback on a gipsy piebald. Especially on a gipsy piebald.

But after a penetrating look, Cameron continued, 'The quickest way is on horseback, and my horse is outside.'

'What did I tell you?' Alison murmured.

'Shall we go?' Cameron asked.

'But—but—the Ball!'

'What is a Ball, compared with a horse to ride?' Alison laughed. 'Do not concern yourself, Rose. He is delighted at the excuse.'

It was Rose Royale, waiting outside. She had looked small and delicate on the Swifts. Close to, she was taller than Rose had supposed. Cameron swung her up on the saddle and then mounted himself, behind her, with one hand on the reins and the other round her waist.

'But—Rose Royale, Cameron!'

'Who else? A rose for a rose.'

'But she may slip on the ice, and she is so valuable.'

'She will not slip. Trust her. And then,' he bent down so that his lips were hot on her cheek, 'trust me.'

It was another world they entered, as Rose Royale cantered gently down to Leith Walk, and then broke into a gallop when Cameron gave her rein on its high shingly path where she was sure-footed and could not slip. Now, well clear of the Town, the sky was studded with stars, and the moon hung over the Forth like a round yellow lantern.

Cameron's arm held her close, and she put her hand over his one round her waist and leaned back against him. She was enveloped by him and by his warmth, and although they travelled too fast for conversation, he bent his head from time to time and pressed his cheek against hers.

She could not have explained to anyone the comfort these small gestures brought to her. He understood her; there was no need for words. She had never felt so close to anyone before, in body or in soul.

In the Main Street of Newhaven he drew in the reins and dismounted, and then lifted her out of the saddle.

'Where is it, Rose?' His arm was still tight around her.

'It is here,' she said, and led him through the archway into Longcakes Lane.

All the time she had lived there, it had never looked like this. Rose looked round the little courtyard in wonder. In the moonlight the flour and the frost had conspired together to turn it into a fairyland of sparkling sugar icing, still and cold, white and glittering, like a picture in a storybook.

'Oh, Rose,' Cameron said with a break in his voice, and put his hands on her shoulders. 'I will remember this moment all the rest of my life, and how you look like an ice maiden in that pale shining gown, in a garden of white.'

She looked up into his face and in that second when he bent over her and blotted out the moon, and his lips touched hers so gently, she felt a great longing to be still closer to him. Very much closer.

Her arms went round his neck. It seemed so very natural, the most natural thing in the world. She clung to him, and this time when their lips met again it was in a perfect explosion of kisses. She scarcely had time to breathe before the next, more passionate, torrent of feeling began. She became dazed and drugged with his kisses.

She needed all her strength of will to tear herself away. 'Help me, Cameron,' she begged him, and stood apart, her breast heaving and her hair escaping in a mass of tendrils from the little gold cap.

'How can I leave you alone, now?' he demanded roughly, and came towards her again.

'No! No! Look!' she cried, catching sight behind him of the little forestair leading up to what had been her home, and pointing a trembling finger.

He was struck as dumb as she was to see the windows criss-crossed with planks of wood, the door all boarded up, and the forlorn blankness of the house in Longcakes Lane.

'I knew it,' Rose said in despair. 'I knew something had happened to my Aunt Bea.'

'George Abercromby will know. We must go to the Turf Inn.'

Silently they mounted Rose Royale again, clambered up from the dunes to the Swifts, and galloped on towards Leith. They saw the Turf Inn as soon as they came to the top of the incline. They could not help but see it. There was a light in every window.

Rose's heart sank with every yard Rose Royale took them towards it. One light at this time of night in the long-closed Inn might have been normal. Every light proclaimed an emergency. Something was very far wrong. She prayed as she had never prayed before, when Cameron beat his fists on the front door, and held her breath while they waited for some reply.

'So you have come, Rose,' George Abercromby said tiredly, holding up a lantern at the open door. His face was haggard, his eyes far back in their sockets. 'She is still with us, thank God.'

His words struck terror into Rose's heart. She would

have fallen if Cameron's arm had not supported her through the bar-room, through the back sitting-room, and in a nightmare up the narrow wooden staircase to the upstairs of the Inn.

'She is in here,' George Abercromby said, and they went into a low-ceilinged bedroom. A woman in a nurse's apron stood up as they approached the bed. Aunt Bea was lying in it, and Rose saw that she was very near to death.

She gathered strength she did not know she possessed, and took her aunt's hand calmly in hers.

'It is Rose, Aunt Bea, I have come to stay with you, and I will not leave you again until you are better. It is starting now. Can you feel it? You are going to get better.'

'It is the shingles,' George Abercromby said heavily, 'contracted after nursing so much chickenpox. If she ever survives this, I swear upon the Bible she will never nurse again. Never,' and he broke down and cried like a child.

Cameron led him away, their feet heavy on the staircase.

Rose turned to the nurse. 'Why, it is you, Pansy! I did not recognise you standing back there in the shadows.'

'Ay, it's me, Rosie. When George sent out in desperation for a nurse, I was the first one here. Not that I'm a nurse, ye ken, but naebody has a better heart to Beattie Barbour than I ha'e. And it was my bairns she nursed last.'

'Why did nobody send for me sooner?'

'We couldna snatch a minute, dearie. And George has hardly left her side.'

'Well, you can sleep for a few hours now, Pansy. I will stay with her all night.'

'I'll sleep in the room ben from here, if you need me, then,' Pansy Paris said wearily. 'She's had all the medicine she can have for this night.'

The moon had long since set, and the dark, dangerous
hours in the heart of the night come and gone, when the
greyness of another day began. Rose had talked softly to
her aunt all that night, and patted her face with cool
cloths, and grown stiff with kneeling beside the bed.
When the light came up, Mistress Barbour's eyes
flickered and opened, and she smiled at Rose before
she fell at last into a deep sleep.

'It is too soon to say if she is on the turn,' Rose said
when she went downstairs after Pansy Paris came to take
over. 'But she is holding her own, at least. I shall stay
with her, however long it takes. You should go now,
Cameron.' She turned to him and looked into his tired
eyes. He must have been sitting up with George
Abercromby all night, waiting. 'And let the Brodies
know that I will be back, when Aunt Bea recovers.'

It took another week for that, a week during which Rose
worked harder and longer than she had ever done
before. But Aunt Bea lived.

'It is very dangerous, the shingles,' she said one
morning, and opened her eyes wide. 'It can kill.'

'Not this time,' Rose said, handing over to Pansy
Paris, and collapsing into a bed.

She must have slept the clock round, for the delicious
smell of bacon and eggs woke her up. When she went
down to the kitchen of the Turf Inn, George Abercromby had his sleeves rolled up, and he was in charge of the
frying-pan.

'You are feeling better,' he said, glancing at her
shrewdly. 'And you have put on your Newhaven
costume again.'

'It is an old one. There was nothing else to fit me in the
boxes upstairs.'

'No,' he said, with a mild smile. 'You have grown up,
Rose, in the short time you have been in Edinburgh. The
last time you saw your aunt, when she came to see you in

Brodie's Close, is the last time she was on her feet. She came down to the Turf for Sunday supper that evening.'

'Yes,' said Rose, with her face perfectly straight.

'She took ill that night, and never went back to Longcakes Lane. My man and I closed up the house, and everything that was in it is still in the boxes.' He put a strip of bacon and an egg on a plate. 'I am going to try her with this,' he said. 'Help yourself, Rosie, and bring your plate up to her room.'

Aunt Bea was sitting up against the pillows, a thinner, less ebullient Aunt Bea than of old, but living and life-thinking, to judge from the way she welcomed the bacon and egg.

'We are going to be married, Rose,' Uncle George stated positively, 'as soon as she is fit to stand up before a preacher.'

'Yes,' Aunt Bea said happily. 'What do you think of that?'

'You really are a darling old pair, a silly old pair! Why have you not done it years ago?'

'You know why, Rose. But now that we see an end in sight for you, we shall postpone our celebrations until it is your own wedding day, so that we may have one large party together, dear.'

'My wedding day, Aunt Bea?' Rose said sadly. 'I'm afraid there is no wedding day in sight for me.'

'What nonsense you sometimes speak, Rose! You will marry Mr Kyle. Uncle George and I saw it all along.'

'You have got a bet on with Uncle George, you mean! And you have lost it already. He is promised to somebody else,' Rose said.

'I will not believe it,' Aunt Bea retorted, returning almost to her old self again, with the last morsel of bacon on her fork. 'You will be married in the Old Newhaven Kirk which you have attended all your life. I insist upon it. And your wedding party will be held here, in the Turf Inn, with us. I can see it all, now—all the carriages bowling down Leith Walk! All the ladies and gentlemen of fashion! What a wedding it will be!'

'Your aunt is better, thank God for that,' George Abercromby said.

'Thank God for that indeed,' Rose echoed, and then added sadly, 'But it means I must go back to Edinburgh as soon as it can be arranged, Uncle George, and I have no other clothes here. Will you send word to Miss Brodie? She will send Ellie to me with some.'

'Of course I will, child. But there is no hurry. Stay a day or two with us, until Beattie is on her feet again. It will be like the old times.'

And so it was not until the ninth day of January, 1788, that Rose and Ellie went back to Edinburgh in the afternoon coach from Leith.

'I was glad to get out of it all this morning and come with your clothes, Miss Rose. The house in Brodie's Close is like a battlefield. There is to be a big dinner there this evening, but Master Will said nothing about it until he got up this morning, looking as pleased as Punch with himself.'

'Oh dear . . . And Miss Jean?'

'You will see a big change in Miss Jean. And not for the better.'

Rose felt her heart plummet like a lead weight. 'She has not gone back to her old ways?'

'She has, Miss Rose. It is the latest robbery, of course, which has done it.'

'What has happened? I have not seen the newspapers since I went to the Turf Inn.'

'Inglis and Horner, the silk mercers at the Cross, were broken into. There is a reward of £100 for information.'

'Oh, Ellie, I wish someone would only come forward with it, and let us have these burglars caught, and an end to all this!'

'Do you, Miss Rose?' Ellie asked softly, so softly that Rose looked at her again.

'*Now* what is it, Ellie?'

'It is a family affair this evening, connected with the businesses. Mr and Mistress Sheriff will be there, of course, and Mr Leslie and a few others you have not met, with their wives. Will you have to attend?'

'No. Why?'

'Then you will have the whole evening free. And after I have served the meal I will be free, too. Would you like to come out with me, Miss Rose? There is something I think you should see.'

Plunged back into the problems of Brodie's Close again, Rose was surprised at how much she resented them, at how rebellious she felt. Ellie had aroused her curiosity besides.

'We shall have to creep out by the kitchen door in our dark cloaks,' Ellie went on, 'and remember to wear your thickest shoes. Come down the back stairs at ten o'clock. They will be finished by then.'

'Where are we going?' Rose whispered, as they stole out of the kitchen door like two shadows.

'Down into the timber-yard and into the workshops.'

'But they will be all locked up.'

'We are in the home of duplicate keys, Miss Rose. There is no lock that cannot be picked, you know. Master Will is an excellent locksmith. Anyway, I got John Robertson to provide us with a spare key. And please, Miss Rose, do not let us talk any more. Only follow me.'

Rose smiled into the darkness. As usual, Ellie was doing most of the talking herself. But she followed her directions and crept behind her as quietly as she could, close to the walls where the shadows lay blackest.

January was turning out to be a piercingly cold month, when the bitter winds from the Arctic scudded up the

Firth of Forth, swept in over Edinburgh and puffed out of the blow-holes formed by the narrow closes and wynds of the Royal Mile. In every house that could afford one, a coal fire burned night and day to try to combat it, and the result of that, and the fog when the wind paused for breath, was that any washing that was hung out to dry was quickly blacker than it had been to start with.

Darkness fell in the afternoons, and with it the frost froze every drop of moisture in the city, outside and in, to make matters worse. The gutters were frozen from morning to night, and the Newhaven fishwives did not come up on the coaches with their fish. It was too cold to carry the wet creels.

Ellie had to do much of the outside work, Rose knew. She was often in the wood-yard, for it was there she hung out the washing, and many a time her hands were cracked and swollen.

A loud squawk almost in her ear, a rattling of wire and the violent beating of wings froze Rose's blood in her veins, as cold to her heart as the frost at her feet. She died a thousand deaths in the palpitating silence that followed. She was frozen now into a pillar of fear.

'That is the Deacon's fighting-cock in his pen,' Ellie breathed in her ear. 'I should have warned you, and that he is a great cocker as well as a great gambler, our Master Will.'

'But, Ellie . . .'

'Hush,' Ellie said. 'We can talk inside,' and she unlocked the workshop door and opened it a crack.

They edged round it and stepped into blackness. But it was a warmer blackness with the sweet smell of wood shavings, the fishy smell of glue, and the clean vapours of varnish all around.

A light flared in the darkness, and Ellie held up a candle and signalled the way up to the work-benches and the glass-fronted cabinets built in above them. 'Look,' she whispered, and they gazed at the huge bunches of keys hanging on numbered pegs inside them. Each key was labelled with a little ticket dangling from it.

Ellie lifted down some of the bunches. 'Look at the labels,' she said.

'Thomson, tobacconist,' 'Royal Exchange', 'Wemyss, goldsmith', 'Bruce, hardware', 'Carnegie, grocer', 'Library, University', 'Tapp's', 'Inglis and Horner, silks'. Rose read out the names, horrified. 'They have all been burgled!'

'Yes. All these are duplicate keys, some from shops or official premises as you see, and others of private houses all over the Town. It is a dangerous habit they have here, to hang their key on a hook behind the front door.'

But Rose was reading some of the other labels. One name stood out before her flabbergasted eyes. The label said, 'Kyle, 29 Queen St.' What business did Deacon Brodie have with Alison's front door key?

'Come over here, Miss Rose.' Ellie pointed to a japan-black tin, that Rose saw was filled with soft putty when she raised the lid, with a key pressed down in it. She had seen the little black box many times when the Deacon took it out of his pocket. She had always thought it was a snuff-box. 'See, he is taking an impression now.'

'And,' Ellie added, 'here is something for a lock, a lock he has not been able to obtain a key for.'

They looked at the long thin piece of metal, bent and shaped as though someone had been working on it, clamped in a vice.

'What is it?' Rose asked.

'It is a pick-lock, Miss Rose.

'How do you know so much about it, Ellie?'

Ellie smiled secretly in the candle-light. 'I'm awfully friendly with John Robertson,' she admitted.

'And what is this?' Rose was looking at an evil piece of needle-pointed horn set in a steel mounting.

'Ah, that has nothing to do with the keys. That is a

spur for the cock. Its own spur is hacked off, and this one is bound on to its leg instead.'

'It is vicious!'

'Oh, yes, Miss Rose. The birds fight to the death in the cock-pits. And there is a Main tomorrow night in Michael Henderson's. Master Will's cock is to be there.'

'I cannot believe it, Ellie, that a respectable man such as Deacon Brodie would take part in such a depraved sport!'

Ellie sniffed, and locked the workshop door behind them again, and they made their cautious way back into the house once more.

It took Rose all night and all the next day to recover from that adventure. And then there was the shock of Miss Brodie's appearance, just as Ellie had warned, for she was tearful and depressed, and not the happy Miss Jean she had left on the night of the Ball.

But fortunately Mr Leslie arrived late in the afternoon, and Rose was dismissed for the remainder of that day. She met the little maid in the passage outside the sitting-room door.

'Tell Ellie to come to my room right away, Jessie.'

'Yes, Miss Rose,' the girl curtsied and scuttled away.

Rose had been doing a lot of thinking since the night before. Ever since she had come to live in Brodie's Close, Ellie had been dropping hints, making insinuations, being mysterious. Now she could dismiss them no longer. She intended to find out the truth of all the goings-on in the Deacon's house. That there could be more, that there were things even more horrible to uncover, that the uncovering might prove to be dangerous, never entered her head.

'We carried out your plan last night, Ellie,' she said when her maid arrived. 'Tonight we will carry out mine. I am assuming that ladies are not permitted inside the cock-pit?'

'No,' Ellie replied with a dawning horror in her eyes.

'Then we will go as men. Come back when you get a chance with some of Master Will's dark clothes. He will never miss them. They will fit me. But you are bigger, so you must ask your friend, John Robertson, to help you.'

Just before eleven, Ellie came back with an armful of dark clothes and two iron contraptions in her hand. 'These are Miss Jean's pattens,' she said.

'What are they for?' Rose asked, eyeing the strange, clumsy things shaped roughly like a shoe on a platform.

'Your slippers are all made of cloth to match your gowns; too dainty for the sort of place we are going to tonight. It is a stables, you know. You must put your slippers into these pattens, and walk in them.'

'Put them away, Ellie,' Rose said, hauling on a pair of the Deacon's breeches. 'I can do better than that.' She dived into the bottom of her wardrobe and held up a pair of stout leather shoes. 'These are my Newhaven shoes, and sensible. Just like yours.'

'John Robertson is not pleased, Miss Rose. In fact he is very angry. He says what we are doing is extremely risky.'

'We shall be very careful,' Rose said determinedly. 'And when we put on our cloaks, we shall be ready to go.'

'Man or no man,' Ellie fumed as they ran down the steep incline of the West Bow to the Grassmarket. 'You cannot be permitted to breathe in the odours of the night,' and she put her arm round Rose and held up a square of linen dipped in eau-de-Cologne over her mistress's nose and mouth, and every now and then pushed her close to the tenement walls when a shout went up of 'Gardyloo!' and a pail of filthy water—or worse—cascaded into the street beside them.

'The Roses of Edinburgh,' Ellie choked, as they hastened on their way.

At first, when they sidled into the interior of Michael Henderson's old feed-barn they could see nothing in the impenetrable gloom. But the noise was indescribable of hoarse-throated men all yelling at the tops of their voices. Very fortunately, neither Rose nor Ellie could make out one word. They would have fainted clean away otherwise, since the language and the shouts of laughter were nothing short of obscene.

At last their eyes became accustomed to the gloom, and they discovered that they were in the back row of the audience. The stage set for the cock-fight was not raised up, as in the theatre. It was a small square covered with taut canvas down in the middle, as if in a pit.

Two men squatted opposite each other, behind each of them a cloth-covered pen, and one of the men was Deacon Brodie. He was easy to distinguish in his light-coloured clothes.

'Is he going tae win, Will Brodie?'

'Gie us a tip, Macaroni!'

'Is he a killer? Tell us, man!'

The spectators had less respect for the Deacon than for his bird. Rose was appalled.

And then the shouting died down to a murmuring, a low excited tension, during which coins chinked and a man announced the first fight. It was about to begin. There was a great cheer and a roar of laughter when he tripped on his way off the canvas. Deacon Brodie and his opponent signalled to their setters-on, who brought out the first two cocks, their beaks open ready to strike, and their beady little eyes unblinking and full of malice.

Then the din really broke out as bets were shouted between the owners and the onlookers. Rose clutched Ellie's arm when the Deacon leapt to his feet, his eyes flashing, his face burning, all propriety and all decency gone, yelling and cursing with the best of them and dancing in some strange ecstasy with froth on his lips and a bottle in his hand.

Rose watched, numb with horror, when a yell from the crowd turned into a scream, and the released birds hurled themselves at each other, ripping, pecking, lunging with their cruel spurs, and streams of blood spattered on the canvas.

She had seen more than she bargained for; and sickened, she turned her head away. It was then that she caught sight of the tall broad figure in black, the same figure she had seen in the Stamp-Office Close on the night of the Oyster Cellar. He, too, was watching the Deacon. And he was standing between them and the door.

Rose pulled her wide-brimmed hat down more firmly over her piled-up hair, drew her collar close, and dragged Ellie towards the exit with her head well down. They passed the tall man and she was just letting out her pent-up breath when a hand of steel fell on her shoulder.

'For God's sake,' hissed Cameron Kyle. 'What *is* this?'

He pulled them out into the lighter dimness of the Grassmarket, and Rose saw that he was white with fury. She had never seen anyone in such a towering rage.

'What do you think you are doing, Rose Barbour? And as for you, Ellie, how could you allow your mistress to come to such a place as this? Do you not know that at the best of it you both might have been trampled to death? And at the worst of it, and I mean a fate even worse than that—for a *lady*—attacked, even raped, and left for dead in that mob in there? They are like wild animals!'

He ranted and raved as he dragged them all the way up the West Bow, every step of the way from the Grassmarket, until they arrived at the Lawnmarket. He left them in no doubt of his displeasure.

The few times that Rose dared to glance at him during his tirade, his face leaner and grimmer than ever, the lines more deeply etched, she quivered with the sudden discovery she had made. *She loved him!* She had loved him from the first minute she saw him, and now she loved him more than ever. All this display was because she might have been harmed. She longed and longed to be in his arms again. And with this discovery she regained her power of speech.

'So it *was* you, Cameron Kyle, in the Stamp-Office Close!' she accused him. 'And you are just as bad as they are, ever to be in that cock-pit to begin with!'

He pushed them through the archway into Brodie's Close, too angry even to reply.

'We can find our own way from here,' Rose said haughtily.

'You will do nothing of the sort,' Cameron said through clenched teeth, and marched them right to the kitchen door. They did not bang it shut in his face. He pulled it to, and slammed it in theirs.

'Oh dear, Miss Rose,' Ellie said, almost in tears in the reverberating silence afterwards. 'He is very angry . . . What will you do now?'

CHAPTER
EIGHT

IN FEBRUARY the Scottish winter set in with a vengeance. Every day, fresh snow fell on old snow and froze where it lay. Nobody went outside if they could possibly help it. The streets, even the Luckenbooths, were deserted. People stayed at home and crouched over their fires.

Slowly, painfully, Rose set about nursing Miss Brodie back to a happier frame of mind. The news in the *Courant* was all of people and events comfortably far enough away to be more entertaining, and mercifully less wounding, than of late. The American colonies had asserted their independence. At Windsor Castle, George III ruled his large unhappy family. France was about to pitch herself over the cliff of revolution. But here in Edinburgh the nine-day wonder after the latest burglary had died down, and people were beginning to forget.

And besides, was there really a gang of thieves and rogues? With lowered voices they told each other the latest disturbing story of a masked man who could walk through locked doors as if by magic. For a hundred years, some of the tenements had been deserted and left to the rats. Everyone knew they were haunted.

Even Rose began to wonder. Deacon Brodie came and went about his business as usual, and after the evening of the family dinner party, the night after the raid on Inglis and Horner's silk shop when he had been so wildly elated, she had not once heard his unholy laughter. For when he was excited, Master Will brayed, a high-pitched rattle of a laugh, which made everyone look at him twice, and then shudder a little.

Now she knew that he gambled more than was proper,

even in these times when gambling was regarded as one
of life's little diversions. And he frequented taverns too
much. When nobody was looking, he was a hard-
drinking man. And, of course, there were his
fighting-cocks at Michael Henderson's and out in their
wooden-slatted pens in the timber-yard.

But then, that was the way of gentlemen. Ladies were
supposed to look the other way, remember that gentlemen had needs no lady could imagine, and, besides, it
was a woman's burden to keep social life going in spite of
it all.

These conclusions were reinforced and her fears
further allayed the day that the Deacon was chosen by
the trial judge to serve as a juror in a murder trial.

Miss Brodie sparkled in her relief at the news.

'Dearest brother,' she said when he came home for
the evening meal. 'What an honour!'

'Fifteen good men and true in the jury-box, Jeannie!
And all of us substantial!'

In great good humour the Brodies sat down to their
howtowdie, a pullet boiled in rich gravy with eggs and
chestnuts, along with a bottle of claret. Miss Brodie
drank very little of it that evening.

'Where will the trial be held, Will?' she asked him.

'In the High Court within Parliament House. Next
week.'

'And who is charged with murder?'

'Nobody from Edinburgh, thank God,' the Deacon
said piously. 'It is some soldier who discharged his
musket at an angry crowd in the Argyllshire village of
Dunoon.'

'Poor soul,' Rose put in. 'Perhaps he was only doing
his duty as he saw it.'

'An eye for an eye,' Deacon Brodie said primly, even
sternly. 'Crime must not go unpunished.'

Then, Rose reflected, his fellow members of the Town
Council and even the scarlet-robed Judges of the High

Court—they must all trust him. What on earth had been the matter with her? She had been too suspicious, too quick as usual to think the worst, and she allowed the rather frosty smile with which she had been favouring him of late to thaw a little.

Deacon Brodie and Ellie observed it at once. He smiled at her with a promise in his eyes that sent shivers down her spine. It seemed to say, 'Later! After I have behaved myself and shown them once again how good I can be.'

Miss Jean smiled happily and proudly, oblivious of any undercurrent.

But Ellie glowered first at her master and then at Rose, time about, with quite a different promise in the tightening of her lips and the two spots of angry colour in her cheeks.

Rose went to bed that night determined to keep an open mind, and fell fast asleep within minutes. She had long ago become accustomed to the chimes of St Giles. Why should it wake her, now? She sat up, listening as the last stroke of the hour, whatever hour it had struck, quivered away into the silence.

Except that it was scarcely a silence. Men's voices rose and fell somewhere not far away. She tried to distinguish where they were coming from, and as she strained her ears, the nameless terrors of the night—the same ones that had visited her the first night that she was here in this house—flooded back again.

A little tap on her door made her heart jump so that it skipped a beat. In the dark she felt her eyes widen with fear. The little tap was louder next time, and someone was whispering. Rose's hands shook as she pulled on her dressing-robe and tiptoed across the room.

'Miss Rose! Miss Rose! Let me in, but quietly, quietly!'

She unlocked and unbolted the door to see Ellie's face swimming before her in the shaded light of a candle, and the men's voices were louder now. They must be actually in the house. Ellie crept in round the corner of the door and closed it noiselessly.

'Do you hear them, Miss Rose? He has never taken his cronies into the house before. He usually meets them in the workshop. Perhaps it is because it is so cold tonight.'

'Who?'

'Master Will, with three others. Smith, Ainslie and Brown.'

'What are they saying, Ellie? I wish we could hear.'

'So you shall. It is why I woke you up. I had been tapping on your door for a long time before you heard me. Can you follow me, even without a light?'

Rose nodded, her stomach churning.

'We dare go no further than the crook of the stair. Hold my hand, Miss Rose, and remember we dare not make one sound, not one creak.'

They edged along the corridor inch by cautious inch until they reached the top of the twisting staircase. Here there was a faint glow from the light of a candle below. This was the most dangerous part of the expedition, as some of the stairs creaked, but Rose could not remember which ones.

Ellie guided her down the inner side of the treads and suddenly sat down. Rose sat on the step above. They looked down on a scene which not even she, open mind or no open mind, could deny reeked of conspiracy and corruption.

Bottles of 'Black Cork' were scattered carelessly over the beautiful table in the dining-hall, most of them empty, and one of them used as a candlestick for a tallow candle. Its yellow flickering light showed up the faces of the four men hunched round it so that they looked like four skulls, with great black holes where the eyes should be.

'Now that you're finished complaining about the snow

out at Duddingston,' the Deacon said sarcastically, 'I
take it you got the coulter? You managed to get it off the
plough, Ainslie?'

'And a fine noise it made, too, with only a stone for the
job and our hands frozen into blocks of ice, as Brown
here can tell you,' Ainslie whined.

How could Deacon Brodie even associate with the
dirty rat-like creature, Rose wondered? She turned her
attention to the man called Brown, who would have
been tall and elegant had it not been for the hole at the
elbow of his coat, which he constantly tried to disguise
by leaning on it, and so drawing even more attention to
it. All his clothes looked as though they had seen better
days, down to his scuffed shoes. It was his turn to be
sarcastic now.

'Ay, it's a wonder you could not have made one o'
your impressions instead o' all this, seeing that you're so
famous for it.'

'Oh, I did, Mr Brown,' Deacon Brodie said softly, and
in such a sinister way that the hairs stood up on the back
of Rose's neck. 'I made a key for the outer door. The key
to the inner door is kept by a clerk about his waist. That
is why we will have to force it. That is why we need a
strong crow . . . such as a coulter.'

'And you had nothing yersel' that would do the job?'

'My tools are all distinctive, all of tempered steel
which would snap. We need cold iron—in other words,
the coulter.' The Deacon still spoke in a tone of suppressed rage, underlined by his patient explanations.
'But if you're nervous, Mr Brown, then maybe you
should not join us?'

The tall man glared at the Deacon, furious. 'Me?
Afraid?' he snarled, and Rose saw that Brown could be
quite a different creature from the elegant figure he
presented to the world—a wolf in sheep's clothing, as
Aunt Bea would say.

'Gentlemen, gentlemen!' The fourth man called the

meeting to order in a clipped English voice, and what he had to say next produced a silence that chilled the blood of everyone there, men and women.

'What about the reward, then? A hundred and fifty pounds, and now on top of that a free pardon if the informant is an escaped criminal? By God, it's enormous!'

The silence went on and on. Clearly Deacon Brodie had not seen the latest notice in the *Courant* about the Inglis and Horner burglary. After he had dropped this bombshell, Smith the Englishman stared fixedly at Brown. Brown kept a carefully blank face and the hole in his elbow tucked well out of sight. Deacon Brodie's eyes narrowed to menacing slits.

'Ay,' Ainslie coughed suddenly and nervously. 'That's no' bad.'

'And you, Mr Brown?' the Deacon whispered. 'You would fit into the category of an escaped criminal, would you not?'

'What use is money?' Brown cried. 'A pardon would be a different matter for a man like me bound for Botany Bay, until I escaped. And I'm still on the run, you know. But you don't think I would trust them, or their promises? If I went to inform, they would string me up as fast as look at me. And there's no dignity in dancing on the end of a rope. No pardon, no freedom, there.'

'Yes,' Deacon Brodie said. 'That's just what would happen to you, Brown. You'd be a fool to think otherwise. Especially since it would be the new gallows, designed by me. There would be no hope for you on it, and no escape, I promise you.'

The other three stared at him, speechless.

'No,' he went on, 'there would be no escape for any of you, and don't you forget it. Not that the gallows cannot be fixed. I am the best wright in Edinburgh. So you may be sure that when I invented it, I mastered the fixing of it at the same time.'

Smith's face was chalk-white. 'You talk as though you want to try it, Will. For the love of God, say no more about it.'

'Well, then, gentlemen, drink up and let us turn to the business in hand,' the Deacon said quite cheerfully, now that he felt he had the ascendancy. 'The Excise Office should yield anything from five hundred to a thousand pounds. It must be planned right down to the last detail, and we have wasted enough time. Are you all with me?' He looked around, clearly the master. 'Then here is a plan I have made of the building.'

They huddled together over a map which Deacon Brodie spread out amid the litter on the table. The guard of the Excise Office was old, he told them. He would present no problem. They would take a rope to bind him. They would all wear masks.

He, Deacon Brodie, would drop a spur at the scene. Everyone would think it was dropped by a highwayman, especially if men were seen with masks on. Nobody would ever think the theft was committed by the same gang as those who had raided Inglis and Horner.

They arranged for strong chisels, pick-locks and a dark-lantern, and they would carry a brace of pistols apiece. But the detail that impressed the other three most of all was the Deacon's undertaking to provide a whistle for Ainslie, the look-out man. One blast for the watchman, three for trouble, he said. It seemed to them that it was the final prudent contingency scheme in a masterly and meticulously worked out plan of campaign.

They toasted its success and agreed to meet again before long for another discussion, and after that for a quick run through on the night before the event. Rose and Ellie waited as long as they dared to hear what night that would be, but it must have been arranged already among the four, for no date was mentioned. They made their way back silently to their rooms, and locked and bolted their doors.

Rose crept back into bed, her brain so numbed with horror that she could not recall the scene she had just witnessed. Her mind refused. It ran round and round instead on just one theme—trouble.

She had seen plenty of trouble twice already in her life. She had even known it would strike again a third time. But this was the worst she could ever have anticipated. And there was no one she could tell. There was no one who would ever believe her, in Edinburgh. There would be no one this time to help her out of it. Above all, she longed to turn to Cameron Kyle. He would know what to do. But how could she? It was unthinkable to involve him at this time in his life with such trouble, not when he was happily contemplating his marriage with Miss Cornelia Forbes.

Yet she had never before felt so lonely for anyone as she did for Cameron Kyle. It was the perversity of fate. Rose turned her face into her pillow, and wept.

'Are you sure you are quite well, dear?' Miss Brodie asked her a week later. 'You have not seemed yourself for a few days now.'

Rose smiled wanly. She felt dreadful. She had not had a night's sleep since that awful scene in the dining-hall. And to crown it all, this morning Deacon Brodie had had the temerity to sit on a jury that would hang a man.

'I'll get them to put a little dash of something in your coffee,' Miss Brodie said anxiously as they sat down to the Meridian. 'It works wonders for me when I am feeling low.'

Rose felt too weak to protest. The hot coffee and the burning brandy seared its way down her throat. She forced herself to swallow it, and after a few moments she found that it did indeed make her feel a little better.

'Mr Leslie is taking me out again this afternoon.' Miss Brodie tightened her hold on Rose's arm as they walked back up to the Lawnmarket. 'I feel the time is coming, dear, when he will ask me a very important question.'

She smiled up at Rose, her face quite pink with excitement, and Rose felt a giant hand squeeze her heart. Miss Jean must never find out what was going on. Her little face must never crumple up again. She prayed that Deacon Brodie, at least, might never be discovered when the Excise Office was robbed.

'We will look out your prettiest bonnet, Miss Jean,' she said sadly. 'Do you know what your answer will be?'

'Oh, Rose! He makes me so happy, just to be with him! What should I say?'

'Say yes, and name the day,' Rose said seriously.

If only you could be married and well out of it, she thought. But you cannot do it fast enough, I fear, Miss Jean . . .

Ellie came out on the step and waved goodbye when Mr Leslie bore Miss Brodie away through the archway and into his coach.

'A little fresh air would do you good, Miss Rose,' she said, 'There are hours yet before they come back, and the evening meal. It would help you to have a little nap when we came back.'

'Where to, then, Ellie?' she asked, as they walked out into the Royal Mile.

'You have not explored all the wynds and closes of this street, Miss Rose.'

'No.'

'I thought we would look at two of them. They are not far from here, and the one not far from the other.'

Rose looked at her maid sharply. She knew Ellie well enough by this time to know that she never did anything without a very good reason, however much she prattled.

'Oh?' she said, suspiciously.

'This is the first one,' Ellie said, leading the way. 'Cant's Close.'

Cant's Close did not seem very remarkable to Rose. It was long and narrow, no more than three feet wide, and so overhung by the high tenements on either side that it felt like a tunnel. At the very end it opened out into the Cowgate, enough to let a little light and air filter in through the gaps in the grey stone walls. But by the time it got to Cant's Close, it had travelled so far that it was stale and tired.

Rose looked around at the little windows and bottle-glass lights of the dingy Close, and wondered why her maid had brought her there.

'We will go into this lobby,' Ellie said. 'There is the sound of a child's voice. Perhaps she will talk to us.'

A little girl sat on the first step, well dressed, her dark head bent over her top and whip.

'That's a grand top you've got there,' Ellie said, 'and a fine whip. Are they new, Jean?'

'I got them from my father. He gave me a lovely brooch as well. And he gave Cecil a locket.'

'And what did he give Mistress Grant?'

'Mother? He gave her a necklace with a red stone. It is a ruby, I think. It has little pearls all round it. She cried when she got it. But I didn't cry, and neither did Cecil.'

'And what is it they call your father, Jean?'

The child laughed. '*You* know, Ellie! You work for him. It is Deacon Brodie, and Mother says he is very rich and very famous.'

A tall girl aged about eleven came running down the stair. 'You're to come in, Jean,' she said. 'Mother wants you.'

'Och, *no*, Cecil. I'm playing with my top and whip.'

'Come on, now. You'd better,' Cecil said, dragging her little sister upstairs.

Rose stared after them, unable to believe the evidence of her own eyes. The same brown hair, the same little cats' faces. There was no mistaking the children were Brodies.

'And there is little Jamie as well,' Ellie told her as she led her back out into the Royal Mile. 'He is only two.'

'There cannot be more,' Rose moaned. 'Not after that!'

'Only one thing more, Miss Rose, I promise you. We may as well get it all over now we have begun. I am sorry if I seem to be cruel to you, but I must, to be kind.'

Ellie took her next into Libberton's Wynd, darker and more overhung even than Cant's Close had been.

'The ladies of the town live here,' she said.

Rose could well believe it, to judge from the loose women sitting around on their outside steps. There was one coming towards them who must be the Queen of Libberton's Wynd. She was dressed in the finest clothes of her profession, gaudy and tasteless enough to catch any man's eye, and by her side walked a miniature of Deacon Brodie, a boy perhaps ten years old.

'Noo then, Willie Brodie, will ye look at this?' the woman shouted stridently to the boy. 'Here she is in a' her glory, her that has the cheek to be living in yer faither's hoose! And what may *you* want, madam? Have ye come tae see poor Jean Watt wi' her four weans?'

The other women got to their feet and glared at Rose. She felt Ellie's hand under her arm pulling her urgently away. Without any more ado they took to their heels and fled back into the Royal Mile and back up to Brodie's Close.

'Now you know everything I know,' Ellie said grimly. 'And it is better for you that you do.'

'You are a good girl,' Rose said, 'and I know you are doing your best to warn me and protect me. But now I do not think I could take in any more. I shall go and lie down. It has all been more than enough.'

To her surprise she slept like one dead, and was able to get up and attend Miss Brodie in the absence of the Deacon for dinner at eight o'clock. She could eat nothing, but her mistress was too excited and too preoccupied to notice. Miss Brodie bubbled over with joy.

But Mr Leslie still had not proposed. If he had, Rose would have been the first to know. ·

And then, as sometimes happens on the east coast of Scotland in the dead of winter, there came a green spell, a sudden thaw, when the Edinburgh folk actually saw the sun again, if only in brief tantalising glimpses over the next two days.

'This will fill the graveyards,' they said, shaking their heads, and like true Scotsmen believing the worst before it had happened.

Ellie came upstairs to Rose's room the following afternoon, bearing a large flat box.

'A gentleman has come to call,' she said.

'Mr Leslie?'

'Miss Jean went out with Mr Leslie an hour ago, straight after the Meridian. The gentleman has called to see you, Miss Rose.'

'Do stop being so mysterious, Ellie. What gentleman?' Rose asked, hot one minute and cold the next, and knowing the answer already.

'Mr Cameron Kyle presents his compliments, and invites you to go for a drive with him. He asks if you will do him the honour of accepting this gift?'

'Stop teasing, Ellie! If he is really here, what sort of a mood is he in?'

'He is in the sitting-room, and he has stopped being angry, anyway,' Ellie laughed. 'He even smiled at me. And when he smiles he is very handsome, Miss Rose.'

'Hm,' Rose said, and began to open the box. In the sitting-room? Was he not afraid that the Deacon might come in? She lifted the soft paper under the lid. 'Oh, Ellie!'

Ellie took the white fur out of her trembling hands and shook it out before she spread it on the bed. It was a magnificent cloak with a hood, and even a muff to match.

'You cannot refuse them, Miss Rose.'

'Mr Kyle has a habit of making offers he thinks no one can refuse.'

'His real message is, would you like to go to Leith with him and see Mistress Barbour?' Ellie laughed. 'And he said to put on something warm.'

'Oh . . . Oh, well then. That is different. Go back and tell him I shall be down in a few minutes.'

Rose put on the new cloak, and with the muff in one hand and her reticule in the other, went down to Miss Brodie's sitting-room and opened the door.

Cameron Kyle was pacing the carpet, looking much too large for the dainty room usually inhabited by such small people.

'Good,' he said, grasping her arm. 'You are ready, Rose. Then let us go.'

He bustled her out through the dining-hall and down the turnpike stair. So she had been right. He was in such a hurry that it could only have been to avoid meeting other people.

'I left the coach down by the Tron,' he said. 'It does not always do to advertise your movements in this town.'

They hurried down, and he settled her inside before leaning out to shout up his instructions to his driver. Then he pulled the window up with a snap and sat down beside her.

'I knew I was right about that cloak,' he said. 'It makes you look like a Christmas rose.'

'I have to thank you,' she said nervously, 'although I am not at all sure it is proper to accept it—more so, under the circumstances. Ladies are not supposed to accept gifts of clothing from any other gentlemen than those they are married to. I'm sure Aunt Bea said so.'

'It sounds reasonable,' he said calmly. 'We must ask her. If she says it is true, then we shall tell her it is a gift from Alison which I paid for, instead. She came with me to choose it, anyway.'

Rose felt the tears welling up into her eyes. Cameron Kyle always made everything seem right. There was no problem he was incapable of solving. He was wearing his royal blue again, and a shaft of sunlight through the coach window fell on his fair hair and glistened it silver. He sat there so much at ease, so very handsome in his clean-cut austerity, so uncompromising now that his mind was made up, and she saw that it was hopeless. Whatever he wanted would happen. He had given her the cloak, and that was that. Well, at least she knew where she was with him, she thought miserably.

'And now, Rose, you will tell me why you are so bitterly unhappy.' He took her hand in his. It felt warm and strong and infinitely comforting. 'Your face is almost as white as that fur, and there are dark shadows under your eyes which were never there before.'

She turned her face away and longed to tell him about the worst disaster of her life so far, which had nothing to do with the gipsies, or Mama, or Deacon Brodie, or the burglaries, or the fact that she was a nobody with no name she could call her own. Only he was the last one she could ever tell, in the world.

She longed to lean her head against his shoulder again, and tell him that the worst thing that had ever happened to her was Miss Cornelia Forbes. Why did he have to love Cornelia, and not her?

But she could not bear to look into his face. There was none of this she could say. And so instead she blurted out the thing that paled into insignificance by comparison. It was always the same. He made her do it.

'I have heard Deacon Brodie and his accomplices plotting to rob the Excise Office,' she said, and as soon as she said it the tears ran down her face as though they would never stop. It was all so silly. It did not have the least connection with what was really upsetting her.

Cameron expelled a long breath. 'Then you know,' he said. 'Thank God for that. It has been a long anxious time for me, wondering how long you could remain innocent and trusting. As long as you did, it was your protection. Now, everything has changed, and your knowledge places you in great danger. You cannot stay in the house in Brodie's Close another night. It would not be safe.'

Rose pulled her hand away from his grasp. She had stayed every other night in the Brodies' house, so why not this one? Miss Jean Brodie, and Ellie and all the other maids were there with her. What was so suddenly different now? And was this why he had brought her to Leith, to stay with Aunt Bea?

She had still made no sense of it when they arrived at the Turf Inn and he helped her out of the coach, his face set grim and hard. George Abercromby opened the door and ushered them through the empty bar-room to the back-sitting room beyond.

'Come in, come in,' he said, 'and meet Mistress Abercromby!'

Aunt Bea was in one of the armchairs drawn up beside the fire.

'Oh, Aunt Bea! *Why* did you not tell me?'

'We did it very quietly one day last week, Rose dear. I told you there would be no celebrations. We are saving them up for later. And Mr Cameron, dear, how are you? Come and sit down over here beside me.'

Mr Cameron, dear? How did Aunt Bea know Cameron Kyle? the question darted into Rose's mind and stayed to churn round with all the other questions. But just now the shock and the excitement of her aunt's marriage obscured everything else.

George Abercromby got a word in edgeways half an hour later. 'I am going to make some tea,' he said. 'Sit still, Beattie. Rose can come into the kitchen with me instead.'

'I had no idea that Aunt Bea knew Cameron,' Rose said, buttering the tiny scones set out on a cooling-tray.

'And who baked these?'

'Your aunt did. And, if I did not keep a very strict eye on her, she would be attempting to do a great deal more, besides. But she is coming on well, Rose. Do you not think so?'

'She looks almost back to normal. But I agree with you. It is almost—but not quite, Uncle George.'

'She nursed Miss Alison Kyle when they lived in George Square, my dear,' he said, swilling boiling water round in the teapot and emptying it out before he ladled in the tea-leaves. 'Miss Alison was abroad with her brother when she picked up some infection. She was very ill, I remember. But then, she is quite delicate, you know. We will let this tea brew for a minute. And here is some strawberry jam for those scones.'

'Dearest Uncle George,' Rose flung her arms around his neck. 'I hope you will be very happy together for a hundred years!'

'Hardly a hundred,' he laughed. 'But we have been happy, and we shall be happy, Rose. It is just that we would like to see you settled, my dear. Then there would not be one cloud on our horizon. But speaking of clouds, it was when Miss Alison was convalescing that Miss Cornelia Forbes came to stay with the Kyles, to cheer her up—supposedly. She has been there ever since, parked like the sedan chair in their hall. I do not think they can get rid of her.'

'Perhaps they don't want to. Miss Cornelia told me she was going to marry Cameron Kyle.'

George Abercromby threw back his head and roared with laughter. 'I will believe that when I see it, Rose. No, my child, it is just that Miss Alison would not offend anyone by asking them to leave. It is not in her. And Miss Cornelia *is* their cousin, you know.'

'Oh. A first cousin?' Rose asked hopefully.

'No. It is a more distant relationship than that. Now, the tea is ready. Are you ready, my dear? Then let us go in with the trays.'

'And what do you think of her new cloak, Beattie?'
Cameron was saying, with a wicked glance in Rose's
direction.

'I have never seen her in anything that suited her
better.'

'I bought it for her,' he said with that sudden rare grin
which twisted her heart, while she bent her head over the
scones and waited in trepidation for the answer.

'I thought you must have, dear,' Aunt Bea said mildly.
'Only a man could have picked it out for her.'

'Marriage has done your aunt the world of good,'
George Abercromby laughed, seeing Rose's expression.
'She has even become quite tolerant of apple pies on
Sundays.'

The good-natured bantering went on, as it had always
gone on when Aunt Bea and Uncle George were
together, all through the afternoon tea, until Cameron
put down his teacup and rose to his feet.

'We must go now,' he announced, holding up the
white fur cloak, 'for we cannot trust the weather.'

So he *was* taking her back, after all. Rose lay back in
the corner of the coach, her goodbyes said, and confessed to herself that events were happening so fast that
she could scarcely keep up with them.

'We will go back by the Leith Links,' Cameron told his
coachman, and they bowled along by the green flatness,
the short grassy stretches of the Links, with only a patch
of stubborn snow here and there to remind them that
more would follow. A lot of people were gathered on the
Links. They all seemed to be gentry in their fine clothes,
the gentlemen in strangely belted coats, and the ladies in
short cloaks to leave their arms free to swing their long
sticks.

'What *are* they doing?' she asked Cameron as a little
leather ball arched through the air.

'They are playing golf. They have to knock the ball

into little holes in the ground with those long sticks. Whoever does so with the least number of strokes all the way round the Links is the winner. Shall we stop and watch?'

Rose nodded, curious. The game did not make much sense to her. A man and a woman out in front seemed devoted to the pursuit of the little ball. Rose could not understand them. There were so many other things to do, beside chasing a little leather ball.

She was so occupied in the watching of them that it was some time before she recognised any of them, and then she sat up, wary and aware. The lady out in front was Miss Cornelia Forbes, and the gentleman the rather portly man she had been dancing with at the Assembly Rooms, it seemed a hundred years ago.

And Cameron Kyle was watching Miss Cornelia's every movement. He was fascinated. Rose had to admit that she was the most graceful lady there, and she reached a depth of depression she never knew existed. She hardly noticed when the sun dipped and the coach moved on smoothly. She came out of her doldrums when it took the right-hand turn at the Tron Kirk.

'Where are we going?' she asked.

'Over to the New Town, to Queen Street,' Cameron replied. 'I have told you, you will not spend another night in Brodie's Close.'

To Queen Street! To be further tortured by the sight of Cameron and that woman together all day long! Rose sat up straight in her white fur cloak, the hood fallen back and her hair on fire in the last rays of the sun.

'Stop the coach!' she cried, colour in her cheeks at last. 'Stop it! I have to go back! I cannot leave Miss Jean—not now!'

All this she delivered with the genuine passion she felt for poor Miss Brodie, but what she really wanted to say was something quite different.

'You took me in the sparkling sunshine to my beloved

Aunt Bea. You took me to hear her happy news. But you could not resist looking at your Miss Cornelia at the same time. You could not miss the chance.'

She hated Cameron Kyle from the very bottom of her heart.

His eyes were very dark and very blue as they roved over her flaming hair, her blazing eyes and the determined set of her passionate lips.

'There is no rose without a thorn,' he observed coolly. 'That is what makes the challenge . . . Very well, then. If the mountain will not come to Mahomet, Mahomet must go to the mountain. You *shall* not go alone into that house tonight, and that is an end to it. I must come in.'

'You cannot!' Rose stared at him.

'I can, and I will. Go back up to the Tron,' he shouted out to his driver. 'And you, Rose, go and fetch Ellie.'

Rose never knew what transpired between Cameron and her maidservant. But suddenly that night Ellie was in her bedchamber, locking and bolting the door.

'I shall sleep on the settee, Miss Rose,' she announced. 'Mr Kyle is smuggled into my room. He insists that he will sleep there, for however long it takes.'

It took another ten days and nights, days when Rose and Ellie tried to look as though nothing unusual was taking place, and nights when Cameron's bed creaked reassuringly through the wall from them, and the tension in the house rose to snapping-point, before the news they all three waited for was shouted abroad in Edinburgh.

'The Excise Office has been robbed!'

And the notice in the *Courant* reported the details faithfully.

On the night betwixt the 5th and 6th of March, it is reported that some persons did feloniously enter the Excise Office by means of false keys and other implements, including the coulter of a plough, the which has been discovered on the premises. The loss from the Office is not known for sure at this time but seems slight, the criminals having failed to gain access to secret drawers containing, it is reliably reported, more than eight hundred pounds Sterling. Mr James Bonar, Clerk to the Excise Office, discovered the criminals in the very act of theft. Indeed, if he had not fortunately returned to his office, disturbing them, they might yet have found the great sum of money no matter how well it had been hid.

The next day there was even more speculation in the city. Brown had walked into the Sheriff-Clerk's office. Brown had informed. But how much had he given away to get his free pardon? Rumours were rife in the Royal Mile. They ran up and down the street like tongues of flame. Nobody knew for sure. But Deacon Brodie remained calm and impassive. He considered he had weathered the storm, and today he was going to inspect the progress of his fighting-cocks.

Rose and Ellie watched him sauntering down the West Bow, whistling, and held their breaths. It was an hour later that a very different Deacon Brodie dragged himself back up. Ellie called to Rose to come and watch him from the big window in her bedchamber.

'Why is he going into the Tolbooth?' Rose asked.

'John Robertson says the latest rumour is that Smith and Ainslie have been arrested. They are in the Tolbooth. Perhaps he is going to see them.'

But it was only minutes later that the Deacon came back out in a hurry. He made for home, and his expression was haunted.

'They have not let him speak to Smith and Ainslie,' Ellie said. 'Now he does not know where he stands. He does not know what else Brown may have said, or if he said it at all.'

'Where *is* Brown?'

'He has gone free. He will be miles away by this time.'

Ellie went back to her duties, and Rose was left alone upstairs. She finished tidying up in her own room and on an impulse went next door to Ellie's. She had never been in it before.

Her eyes were drawn immediately to the narrow bed drawn up close to the wall where Cameron had been sleeping so many nights now, and she walked over to it and sat down. It was a very small slit of a room, sparsely furnished, and very different from her own. It was not a room for rest and calm repose, it was merely a sleeping quarter, and she wondered how it had felt to him to have to sleep in here. Burying her head in his pillow she breathed in the faint perfume of the pomade he dressed his hair with, and the underlying scent of his masculinity roused every sense in her body.

It was as if he had come into the room in person, and she was looking up at him, into his lean hard face and those blue eyes that never stopped acting on her as sparks to tinder. She was on fire, now, at the mere thought of him. If she closed her eyes she could feel his arms round her again, and his mouth on hers over and over again, as it had been in the tiny courtyard in Longcakes Lane.

There was a little rustle in the room, and her excitement rose to a new peak. Perhaps he was really there. Perhaps he would really be there if she opened her eyes, and she could not help her lips parting a little and curving in a smile. He was bending over her now. She could sense the heat of his body. Her eyes flew open and she looked straight into those of Deacon Brodie.

For a second she lay there paralysed with disbelief and disappointment, and gazed at the puckered scar that dragged down the corner of his right eye so horribly. It fascinated her, and filled her with a repugnance which the Deacon clearly would not have believed, for his eyes were hot and bold, and he was so sure of his welcome.

How she ever got out of the bed and in one swift movement eluded him she did not know then, nor did she ever recall in future nightmares.

'What are you doing in here, Rose? I thought this was the servant's room.'

She crossed to the doorway dumbly and he came after her. She should have remembered that there was another way round, a back way round this upper storey, that half-way there was the staircase down to the kitchen. He must have crept right round from his room to hers. She had even forgotten that he was in the house, that he had come home so unusually early in the day.

'Don't go away, Rose. I have something to say to you.'

'Then it would be better to do so in a more formal room, sir.'

He hesitated, and then answered impatiently. 'Oh, very well, then. Indeed, since it is of such a private nature, you may be right. Some of the maids may well come up here. Let us go down to the sitting-room.'

There was a strange air of desolation in the sitting-room, a hovering black cloud. She searched her memory until she recalled the same feeling, when Mama had not been there any more, and there had been death and terrible grief. Rose was suddenly overcome by a great dread as she seated herself in the chair nearest to the door.

She waited while Deacon Brodie walked up and down, and when at last he spoke, she thought she had heard before, somewhere, every word he said. In fact, she could even foretell what he would say next. It was as if she had lived through it all before. None of it came as any shock to her.

'I have a confession to make, my dear . . . I have been guilty of taking part in the burglary at the Excise Office.'

She could detect no shame or remorse in the eyes of so prominent and respected a figure in Edinburgh when he uttered these words. Instead, only two glowing imps of mischief. The Deacon was delighted with himself.

'Yes,' Rose sighed.

'I was led astray. It was a momentary lapse. I had no intention of actually *stealing*, Rose.'

'No?'

'No. I had been drinking, and always when I drink I am back in *The Beggar's Opera* again, acting the parts. I went along with the others on the crest of the wave, on the spur of the moment, for the sheer excitement of it. You know how I get carried away, Rose! You remember me telling you?'

'I remember.'

'Then you will also remember how I always dreamed of running away to sea. It is strange how things catch up with you in the end. It is the destiny I was born for. Now I can fulfil my ambition at last. I am free, Rose! Free at last!'

'Free, Master Will?'

'Free to go to Holland, and from there to America, to start a wonderful new life.'

He smiled happily, glowingly, the light of adventure burning in his eyes. She saw that he had not the slightest regret. She wondered if he saw life in a series of scenes as on a stage. When the curtain came down, that was the end of that part of the story, and he lived only in expectation of the next. She knew she would ask him the next question. She had asked him before, in some strange dream.

'But why are you telling me all this? What has it got to do with me?'

She saw the spark of fun go out of his eyes, that little spark that was his most redeeming feature, and watched in horror as the little boy coward's look returned, the lost pained look when the whole world had turned against him and would not join in his game.

'But of course you know, my darling! You must not tease your Will like this,' he whined. 'It is because you will be coming with me, Rose! We have an understanding between us that I have never experienced with any other woman.'

Rose sat frozen and appalled, and thought of Mistress Grant and Mistress Watt and the seven Brodie children she already knew about. She did not believe he would have denied them, even if she had confronted him with her knowledge. He was quick to interpret her expression of disbelief.

'Oh,' he said, half giggling like an idiot, 'you mean my affairs with Ann Grant and Jean Watt? Everyone in Edinburgh knows about them, my dear, do they not?' Well, thought Rose, Mistress Scott certainly does not, but she kept silent. 'But I did not marry either of them, did I? You are the only one I have ever asked to be my wife. You are the only one to have had such an honour.'

Rose was completely shocked. Not at his revelations —she knew all about them already—but in her growing conviction that Deacon Brodie was not entirely sane. Now at last she understood why Cameron had been so fearful for her safety. But he could not have dreamed that the attack would come by day. She glanced at the door to the dining-hall, judged the distance between it and her chair, and thought better of it. As long as she was in this house with Deacon Brodie, she must appear to agree and comply with him. Cameron had very shrewdly assessed the situation, to warn her that as long as she appeared innocent, she was safe. She must not appear to be shocked or frightened. The Deacon was a very dangerous man.

'You will give me a little time to consider your proposal, Master Will?' she asked pleasantly, even managing a smile.

'There is not much time left. Twenty-four hours at the most. The game is up.'

'Then I will meet you here again tomorrow at this

same time with my answer. Of course, you have told Miss Jean?'

Rose realised as soon as the words were out of her mouth that if she had schemed and calculated for a week which question would most have deflated him, she could never have hit upon that one, the only one which could distress him. For the first time a look of genuine pain crossed Deacon Brodie's face.

'Yes . . . I am afraid she has collapsed.' He scuttled past her to the door. 'Now, I have many ends to tie up here, Rose, and many preparations to make. Will you go and see to her?'

It had all come and gone like a dream, like a nightmare, and Rose awoke next day, on Sunday morning, with Ellie shaking her urgently.

'Miss Rose! Miss Rose! He has gone!'

For a minute she did not understand, and then as memory flooded back she was on her feet facing her maid.

'How do you know he has gone?'

'He is nowhere to be found, and there is a proclamation out for him. John Robertson tore it down from outside the Sheriff-Clerk's.'

Rose took the proclamation out of Ellie's hand.

TWO HUNDRED POUNDS OF REWARD

Whereas WILLIAM BRODIE, a considerable House Carpenter and Burgess of the City of Edinburgh, has been charged with being concerned in breaking into the General Excise Office for Scotland, and stealing from the Cashier's office there a sum of money—and as the said William Brodie has either made his escape from Edinburgh, or is still concealed about that place —a REWARD OF ONE HUNDRED AND FIFTY POUNDS STERLING is hereby offered to any person who will produce him alive at the Sheriff Clerk's Office, Edinburgh, or will secure him; and FIFTY POUNDS STERLING MORE payable upon his conviction by William Scott, procurator-fiscal for the shire of Edinburgh.

WILLIAM SCOTT.

DESCRIPTION.

There followed a detailed description of the Deacon which brought the little man alive, joking and strutting before their very eyes.

WILLIAM BRODIE is about five feet four inches high— is about forty-eight years of age, but looks rather younger than he is—broad at the shoulders and very small over the loins—has dark brown eyes with large black eyebrows—under the right eye there is the scar of a cut, which is still a little sore at the point of the eye next the nose, and a cast in the eye that gives him somewhat the look of a Jew—a sallow complexion —black hair, twisted, turned up, and tied behind, coming far down upon each cheek, and the whiskers very sandy at the end; high topped in the front, and frizzed at the side—high smooth forehead—has a particular air in his walk, takes long steps, strikes the ground first with his heel, bending both feet inwards before he moves them again—usually wears a stick under hand, and moves in a proud swaggering sort of style—his legs small above the ankle, large ankle bones and feet, small at the knees, which bend as he walks, as if through weakness—Was dressed in a black coat, vest, breeches, and stockings, a striped duffle great coat, and silver shoe-buckles.

'Oh, Ellie . . . Has Miss Jean seen this? How is she?'

'She has not seen it. Mattie will let nobody in. She says Miss Jean is very ill.'

'And Mr Kyle?'

'I have told him the news. He is dressed and waiting to see you. Here is your hot water, Miss Rose. We had better hurry.'

Rose threw on her dressing-robe. 'I will speak to him now, Ellie.'

'But your hair is hanging down your back!'

'I do not think that will disturb Mr Kyle,' Rose smiled sadly. 'He has been here all this time, not for my sake, but on account of Deacon Brodie.'

She went out into the corridor the way she had got out of bed, her robe clutched about her naked shoulders and her hair tumbling down, and did not care, until she saw she was mistaken. Cameron Kyle was visibly disturbed at the sight of her, the spark from his eyes piercing her, penetrating her, so that she gasped for breath. She felt actually dizzy under his gaze. His hands burned through the thin material of her robe as he steadied her, and she noticed that his mouth had softened as though he would kiss her again. She pulled herself out of his grasp. She could not bear it.

'You have seen the proclamation?' she asked.

He nodded. 'The first problem is Miss Brodie. She must be removed at once. The Sheriff's officers will be here next, to search the premises and to look for her brother. She must be gone before then.'

'What shall we do?' Unconsciously she included him.

'We must send for her sister and her husband, Mr and Mistress Sheriffs, to come at once,' he answered, his smile steady. 'I will go out and send a caddie post-haste over to St James's Square, and I shall take that notice with me.' He took the proclamation gently out of her hand. 'It should never have been torn down. You and Ellie pack up all your belongings as fast as you can.'

It did not occur to Rose to do anything else but follow his directions. She dressed hastily while Ellie went for Jessie to help her to bring back her trunk. It lay open on the floor, looking just the same as the day she had arrived, poised in mid-flight, with nowhere particular to go.

'I will start packing it, Ellie,' she said. 'Go and pack up

yourself. Gather all your things together.'

Mr and Mistress Sheriffs arrived in a coach, and Cameron escorted them up the turnpike stair. He had taken command, and nobody seemed to doubt it. Mr Matthew looked distraught and bewildered, with his clothes flung on any old how. Mistress Jacobina was only a little less flustered and upset.

'I shall see the servants first,' she announced. 'Matthew, write out a suitable notice to pin on the workshop door for the men when they come to work tomorrow morning. After all that is attended to, I shall deal with my sister.'

Rose went on packing, and when everything was inside her trunk and she was ready to go, right down to her gloves, she suddenly remembered with a lurch of her heart and a cold sweat on her brow, the sovereigns.

But she somehow knew, before she ever drew the little key on its ribbon out of her reticule, that she was too late. The writing-desk did not need the key. It had been forced already, and the bottom drawer slid open at the touch of her hand, to reveal nothing but emptiness. All her money had gone.

She was still staring at it blankly when Cameron and Ellie came for her.

'What is it?' he asked sharply.

'It is my money. It has gone.'

'How much money?'

'I never counted it. Perhaps two, perhaps three, hundred pounds in gold. I could never remember to put it in the bank.'

'As things were, it might not have been any safer there,' Cameron said bitterly. 'But how did you come to have so much money with you, Rose?'

'It is a long story. A story about Rose Royale. Anyway, now I am penniless.'

'You must not worry,' he said. 'You will get it back.' His eyes were different now, hard and piercing blue.

'Are you ready, Rose?'

'Yes. But you, Ellie? What has happened? Did you have any money in your room?'

'No, Miss Rose.'

'Had you sent it to your mother already?'

'No. I had none to send.'

'What do you mean?' Cameron demanded sternly. 'You had your wages, had you not?'

'I have had no wages, sir, these last six months,' Ellie said. 'My mother thought that I might get them in a lump sum at the end of a year.'

'Oh, my God!' Rose said. 'What did Mistress Jacobina say?'

'Nothing, Miss Rose. She dismissed us all, except Mattie. She told us to go. Mattie is going with Miss Jean to St James's Square. She was their nurse, you know.'

'And what will you do now, Ellie?'

'I do not know,' the maid said, weeping. 'I must go home, I suppose.'

'No,' Cameron said firmly, with a reassuring pat on Ellie's back. 'Not unless you would prefer not to come to Queen Street with your mistress? Miss Rose is coming with me. It is not that I do not like her hair in its natural state'—his eyes smiled into Rose's—'believe me, I do. But to meet the public, that is a different matter, and you make an excellent job.'

'I would rather you came with me, Ellie,' Rose added, and wanted to say, 'I shall need all the help I can get to combat Miss Cornelia.'

'Another thing, you would be paid,' Cameron said.

'It would not be for the money,' Ellie sobbed. 'It would be for Miss Rose.'

'Then you will come with her?'

'Yes, sir, and gladly.'

'I will see that your mother is informed,' Cameron said. 'And there is a young apprentice I have taken on besides, who tells much the same story, to be a handyman.' There was a ghost of a twinkle in his eyes. 'His name is John Robertson.'

Downstairs there was the sound of a coach departing. So Miss Jean has gone to her sister's house. It occurred to Rose that Mistress Jacobina had come and gone and never sent for her, to pay her for her services either, before dismissing her. But then, money had never been mentioned by the Brodies at any time, it occurred to her.

She did not have time to dwell on it. Cameron and Ellie carried her trunk out to the open front door.

'I had better lock up, once I get you both into my coach,' Cameron said, 'and hand over the keys to the authorities. The coach should be here any minute now. I sent a caddie for it.'

They looked at each other and smiled, all three of them, and then in a reaction, they laughed. Perhaps it was because the sun was shining, enough to dispel all the shadows and the desperation of the last few days. As they stood there at the top of the turnpike stair, a man raced in through the archway of Brodie's Close.

'Where is she? Where is Jean?' he demanded. James Leslie was in a state of distraction.

Cameron took charge of him, as he had taken charge of everything else, and led him down and out into the Lawnmarket. In a few minutes he came back.

'Mr Leslie has gone to St James's Square in a chair,' he said. 'And the coach is here.'

Rose and Ellie got in and faced each other on the seats inside while the coachman strapped on the trunk once more, and Cameron went back to lock up the house. It was to be just another coach ride, Rose thought, the bridge between the past and the future. What next?

'You must not worry, Miss Rose,' Ellie said, taking her hand. 'Everything will be all right now. Mr Cameron will see to it.'

As Cameron climbed in beside them, Rose smiled doubtfully. Poor Ellie did not know the half of it.

CHAPTER
NINE

ROSE KNEW perfectly well that she lived through the next few days in a state of shock. How else could she possibly have got the notion that she had changed from a human being into a child's plaything, a ball to be tossed between them? Where Cameron left off, Alison deftly took over, as by some hidden but pre-arranged signal between them. Rose felt that she was passed from one set of their hands to the other.

It began as soon as they arrived at No. 29 Queen Street, when Alison was at her side dismissing Ellie below stairs with one of her own maids.

'Look after the child, Ruby,' she instructed. 'Show her to her room and explain her duties here. She will take a day or two to settle in. In the meantime I shall look after Miss Rose myself. Come, dear,' she turned to Rose. 'We shall go upstairs at once.'

Rose followed Alison obediently up the square stone staircase she had last seen Miss Cornelia Forbes floating down, a vision in honey-coloured silk, and the first little prick of rebellion stabbed her heart. Why had she allowed herself to be manipulated into this house in the first place?

All such doubts were immediately dispelled by the sight of her bedchamber, when Alison flung open the door to let her pass through. It took her breath away.

'I call it the Rose Room,' Alison smiled anxiously. 'It is a new idea, to dress a room predominantly in one colour, but houses and the furnishing of them is one of my dearest hobbies. I thought it would be appropriate for you. I hope you can feel happy and at home in it, my dear.'

Nobody could fail to do so, Rose thought with a sinking heart. It was all white, with delicate flushes of pink and gilt in the hangings and in the upholstery, and here and there a deeper pink cushion or picture or ornament.

'It is utterly charming,' Rose said. 'But how can I stay here, Alison? I cannot impose in your home, like this. Especially not now.'

'Why ever not, child? Besides, how can you think you are imposing? I want you to stay here, Rose. But perhaps this room does not suit you? There are plenty of others.'

'Oh, no, Alison! It is the most beautiful bedchamber I have ever been in.'

'Well, then, Cameron and I are inviting you to stay as long as you like. We have informed your aunt, Mistress Abercromby. She is in complete agreement, and her message is that at any time you will be welcome back at the Turf Inn.'

'Oh,' said Rose, feeling only slightly cheered.

'But you will stay awhile with us, will you not, Rose? We have so much to catch up with, you and I. I have hardly seen you since our French lessons, and there are so few young ladies like you that I can talk to.'

It did not take long to become accustomed to the Rose Room or to any other room in No. 29 Queen Street, and to feel completely at home. As a result, Rose felt her conscience hanging heavy and very guilty, and her nerves were soon on edge. On Tuesday, Ellie came back again, in time to dress her for dinner.

'Oh, Ellie,' Rose said thankfully.

'Here I am at last, Miss Rose. And what is it you will wear this evening?'

'Anything,' Rose said dispiritedly.

'Hm. So you are still upset. Is it about Deacon Brodie?'

'No.'

'Miss Jean?'

'No,' Rose sighed, and shuddered at the thought of it. 'I—I just feel very uncomfortable here, that is all.'

It forced her, now that she had put it into words, to wonder why, again. All through the washing and the dressing she wondered why. The answer did not come to her until Ellie had taken the ribbons out of her hair and was preparing to take up the hairbrush. She felt condescended to—just as she had felt that very first day on the Swifts. Miss Cornelia's presence in the house was enough to do it. Her temper began to rise.

It was time she came out of the doldrums, time she asserted herself. The fact of the matter was that she was in love with Cameron Kyle, whether he was going to marry Miss Cornelia Forbes or not. Therefore she would stay on here for as short a time as possible without hurting Alison's feelings. But now that she had worked it all out, it did not make it any easier.

'You will lose him altogether if you moon about like this much longer,' Ellie said uncannily.

'*And* what do you mean by that, Ellen MacDonald?'

'Just what I say,' Ellie dashed the brush through her mistress's curls, streaming them out in indignant sweeps. 'You know perfectly well.'

Mistress and maid, they glared at each other in the mirror all through the long grooming.

'You are pulling too tight, Ellie.'

'It must be smooth, Miss Rose. Mr Cameron likes it to be smooth when you are dressed.'

'And what has he to do with it?'

'He has everything to do with it,' Ellie said serenely. 'I have been waiting to get my hands on your hair again.'

'So I see.'

Yet she could not but admit that she looked more like her old self at the end of her maid's ministrations. And not only because of the smoothness of her hair. She had come alive again, and vibrant. Something about the girl sparked her off.

'I shall wear the red,' Rose said positively, and as soon as Ellie shook out its gleaming folds she felt an affinity with the colour immediately. 'That is the mood I am in. Thanks to you, dear Ellie—although you are a great bully, you know.'

'So many people depend on you, Miss Rose, although you do not know it. I am only one of them. I do not mean to be rough. I do it because I am concerned for you.'

'I know it, Ellie,' Rose said and went downstairs. She felt an entirely different person, ready and willing to take on all-comers, especially Miss Cornelia Forbes, who would, of course, be present at the dinner table.

But only Cameron and Alison were waiting at one end of the elegant dining-room, in front of the fire. The curtains were drawn across the windows, shutting out the sleet of an Edinburgh winter evening, turning the inhabitants of the house in towards each other. A large coal fire blazed in the hearth and flickered off the blue and white Dutch tiles of the surround, its warmth echoed in the candles glowing all round the room and in the chandelier above the polished table.

Alison was wearing a silver-grey gown trimmed about with small pink and blue flowers, and she looked cool and serene. Cameron also wore grey. He looked immaculate and austere. At the very sight of him, Rose blushed and shivered involuntarily, her pulses racing. But neither of them spoke at the sight of her, and the silence went on and on.

At last Cameron broke it. 'Do you know the works of Robert Burns, Rose? He was here in Edinburgh last year and published this song:'

> O, my love is like a red, red rose
> That's newly sprung in June;
> O, my love is like the melody
> That's sweetly played in tune.

'I do know it,' Rose said. 'You have turned it into a very pretty compliment.'

'Would you sing it for us, Rose?' Alison asked. 'After dinner we shall go through to the drawing-room and sing some of Mr Burns's songs. Cameron is a great admirer of them. You actually met him, did you not, Cameron, one evening recently?'

'In Johnnie Dowie's tavern. I was following the Deacon at the time. He led me into many an interesting hole and corner of this town.' He looked directly at Rose, and she flushed and looked away. His eyes were so piercing, their expression so openly admiring, that she could not bear it. And besides, there had been the cock-pit. 'Yes, Burns has been a very familiar figure in Edinburgh, in his blue coat and buckskin breeches.'

'He is also very handsome. The ladies swooned over him,' Alison put in.

'That night in Jonnie Dowie's he was ranting against the state, the government and women, and the oppression of men by all three with the utmost recklessness and fluency,' Cameron laughed. 'The Deacon was thrilled by every word.'

Yes, Deacon Brodie would have loved that, Rose thought.

'Then it *was* you, the night of the Oyster Cellar, in Stamp-Office Close?' she asked aloud.

'Yes. It will all come out now, so I can tell you. But that is a long story, and our dinner grows cold. We have waited long enough,' Cameron said, leading them over to the table and seating them. Alison rang her little silver bell.

'So what is the news today?' she asked her brother, when the little pots of mussel ragout were set in front of them.

Cameron cut the brown bread on his plate into long fingers and dipped one into the ragout. 'The Englishman, Smith, has made a clean breast of it. He accompanied the Sheriff's men to Brodie's Close this morning, offering to lead them to some concealed evidence.'

'What was it?' Rose asked. 'Where was it?'

'In the bottom of a vent used as a fireplace for melting glue in the workshop, they found a pair of pistols wrapped in a green cloth. And the night-lanterns were with the gamecocks out in the yard. Of course, all the bunches of duplicate keys for premises all over the city were taken away for evidence. They were all labelled, including the one for the door of this house, Alison.'

'And what of the Deacon himself?' she asked.

'Of him there was no trace.'

'Then he has escaped?'

'He could still be in the City,' Cameron smiled grimly. 'They are searching high and low. But, somehow, I do not think so.'

Rose wondered if she should tell them of Deacon Brodie's intention of sailing to America. She was debating it, when the door burst open and Miss Cornelia Forbes came in bringing a gust of frosty air with her.

'Oh, it is so cold out tonight! I am not too late, am I?' she said gaily, and sat down opposite Rose.

'Oh, Cornelia,' Alison smiled reproachfully. 'You will be at one end of your own dining-table soon, and then you shall have to be on time, my dear.'

The devilled lamb turned to dust in Rose's mouth. This was exactly what she had dreaded, this talk about the forthcoming marriage. Cameron showed his displeasure with his forthcoming bride much more openly than his sister.

'Indeed, Cornelia,' he frowned. 'No husband could be expected to put up with it. I trust you will remember that.'

But Miss Cornelia Forbes remained unconcerned and quite irrepressible, as she laughed and sparkled her way through the rest of the meal. Cameron did not laugh with her. He looked merely irritated, and Rose felt the tension in the atmosphere round the table rising every second. Very soon, there would be a lovers' tiff.

'Shall we go through?' Alison asked when they rose from their dinner.

'Please excuse me, Alison,' Rose said. 'I believe I will go up to my room and lie down. My head is thumping.'

'It is all this talk about Deacon Brodie that is upsetting you again,' Alison said, concern showing in her face as she accompanied Rose upstairs.

'No, it is not that. I have put it behind me, Alison.'

'Then what is it, dear? Can you tell me?'

They reached the Rose Room and went in to sit by the fire. Rose looked into Alison's gentle eyes and for a moment was strongly tempted to tell her the truth. But she suspected that would hurt Alison as much as it was hurting her.

'I am worried about being here, Alison,' she said instead. 'I do not think I should impose upon you any longer than it takes to find another position.'

'If that is all, you need look no further. There is a position for you here. When Cornelia goes, I shall be alone for long stretches while Cameron is about his business. She has not been much of a companion to me lately. Will you not try it for a little while, and see? Oh, do say you will, Rose!'

Put like that, it was a request Rose did not have the heart to refuse. She would have to try and keep as far away from Cameron and Cornelia as possible in the meantime. She went to bed fretting. It was all going to be very difficult, and she made up her mind through the long restless night how she would tackle the following day, at least.

'I am not getting up,' she told Ellie in the morning. 'Go downstairs and tell Miss Alison that my headache persists, and I shall not be joining the family for any meals today.'

Fifteen minutes later Alison entered the Rose Room, bearing a tray.

'Are you ill, dear? I am so worried. I shall not leave until you try to eat some breakfast. If you cannot manage it, I feel we must send for a doctor.'

'Alison!' Rose said, aghast at such a complication to her plot. 'Of course I am not ill. And you should not have come here yourself with this tray. Ellie could have fetched it.'

'She did. I have left her outside. I wanted to tell you some news privately. Now, let me see you eating those scrambled eggs while I relate it. You ate no dinner last night, either, I noticed.'

Rose pushed her fork round the plate in a sorry pretence.

'Mistress Scott is very distressed,' Alison said, 'and has sent me a note. She says she feels entirely responsible for your dilemma, and she is coming here at four o'clock to see you.'

'Oh, no, Alison!' It grew worse and worse.

'If you have recovered by then, would you like to see her up here, alone?'

'By four o'clock, I shall be sufficiently recovered to join you in the drawing-room,' Rose said. 'Believe me, Alison.'

She could not possibly face Mistress Scott alone. At least, downstairs, she would have Alison behind her. And with any luck, Cameron would not be there. She sincerely hoped Miss Cornelia Forbes would be with him, wherever he was.

'Then you must rest now,' Alison said. 'Ellie will come up with your lunch. In the meantime, I shall leave you the last few days' *Courants*. I suppose you have not had time to look at them?'

'No,' Rose said. 'But I can guess what news they contain.'

She pushed the newspapers aside when Alison left and

lay down, too tired to think any more. It seemed no matter what she thought or how she tried, the events that were predestined would happen in any case. There was nothing she could do. For too long she had been swimming against the tides of Fate.

She closed her eyes, and the sleep that had eluded her in the night overtook her now. It seemed only minutes later that a cheerful rap sounded on her door. What time was it? She could not guess when Ellie came in with some broth.

'It is twelve o'clock, Miss Rose. And you have a visitor.' Ellie put down the tray on the table beside the bed and plumped up the pillows behind her. 'We will put on this bed-jacket. Let me tie up the ties. Your hair,' she said sorrowfully, 'could do with a brushing out. But it will have to do. Mr Cameron is in a hurry.'

'What do you mean—Mr Cameron?'

'He is outside. You had better drink this broth, if you can. He told Miss Alison he would supervise you himself,' Ellie whispered.

Before Rose had time to think or to argue, Ellie had gone and Cameron Kyle had come in to lounge on the chair beside the bed. He was dressed for riding, his boots gleaming brown and polished as she had first seen him on the Swifts.

'And what is all this?' he demanded.

'What do you mean?' Rose countered, sipping the broth. 'I have a headache.'

'Rubbish! A healthier woman never existed. You do not have headaches, Rose. You are trying to avoid something. Or someone.'

'Of course I am not.' Rose pulled her bed-jacket more tightly up about her neck, and swallowed two more tiny spoonfuls of the broth. Cameron could see right through her. 'Besides, I shall get up soon. There is no one I wish to avoid.'

'Yes, there is. I have been watching you. It is Cornelia.'

Rose wished fervently that Ellie had brought out the pale green bed-jacket. It might have cooled down the tell-tale flush in her cheeks.

'Why should I concern myself with Miss Cornelia?' she flashed.

'Why indeed? That is what I have been wondering.'

Rose gazed across at his dear face, a line of perplexity between his brows. 'I can assure you, Miss Cornelia Forbes is the least of it,' she said.

'Then what is it? Who is it? Is it me?' he repeated, bending over her, and taking away the tray.

Rose gazed up into the blueness of his eyes, completely unaware that her bed-jacket had slipped down over her bare shoulders, conscious only of his nearness. It tortured her unendurably, when all she longed for was that his mouth should close over hers, just once more.

She put out two ineffectual arms to push him away. But somehow, instead, they wound round his neck and he was kissing her again, burningly, passionately, and she was returning every kiss with a hunger she could not control.

'No!' She burst out breathlessly at last. 'How could it be you? Oh, Cameron, not you! Never you!'

'Then what is it?' he asked urgently, straightening up. 'You must tell me, Rose, before I go.'

'Go? Where are you going?'

'I am to ride out now, within the hour, with Mr George Williamson, the King's Messenger for Scotland, as his escort. We are going to search out Deacon Brodie and bring him to justice.'

'Shall I never hear the end of him?' Rose sighed, back on her pillows. 'And why you?'

'Because I have the horses, and I have the interest to find the little man again. He has something that belongs to me. And something that belongs to you.'

'And what does Miss Cornelia say to all this?' she flung at him bitterly, in her disappointment.

'Cornelia? What the devil do I care about Cornelia?'

Rose stared at him, utterly shocked. She was shocked all round. First of all at herself, and how she felt about a man soon to be married to somebody else. Then at him for kissing her at all, in his circumstances. And now, here he was saying he did not care about Cornelia!

'So that is the sort of man you are, Cameron Kyle! Poor Miss Cornelia does not know you as I do, that is obvious.'

'Perhaps you really are ill,' Cameron said worriedly. 'I shall send Alison up to have a look at you again. But now, unfortunately at such a time, I must go. I can delay no longer.'

'Then go!' Rose flung at him. 'I shall not be here when you get back.'

He came back to the bed again, and bent down to kiss her gently.

'I hope not, my darling, for it may be months before I can return. Think of me, Rose.'

Months? Rose gazed at the closed door disbelievingly, and immediately started to cry. Think of him? Who else, what else, did she ever think about? And now he had gone. For months!

And she had not even told him what the Deacon had confided in her. She had not told him where to start looking for him. She dashed out of bed, but it was too late. Horses' hooves clattered out of the mews behind Queen Street. She went to the window and watched as Cameron Kyle rode proudly at the head of a string of four or five horses, mounted on Rose Royale. She had never felt so frightened in her life. Cameron had gone on God alone knew what mission, and into what danger, with nothing save her bitter, bitter words to cheer him on his way. She was sorry! She was sorry, she sobbed into the silence of her room. But it was all too late.

After an hour, she could cry no more. Gasping and shuddering, she picked up the *Courant* in sheer desperation, and read through each day's events in sequence, faithfully, mechanically, right down to the last detail. Through every word of Deacon Brodie's shocking misdemeanours, as though he were a total stranger and not the merry little fellow she had known—through the proclamations for his arrest, through the notices of rewards issued for his apprehension, or even information leading to it.

She scoured the news-sheets feverishly for all the other news tucked away in the corners. Anything to stop her thinking, for there was an hour yet before she must get up and face Mistress Scott. She must be composed by then. And then, at such a strange time, a time when she should have been too distraught even to look for it, she came across the notice she had always known she would find, some day. She could not believe it, now that it was here, and she read it over and over again before the awful news it contained penetrated her understanding.

GIPSIES AT HOLYROOD

The gipsy tribe of SHERIDAN, encamped in the grounds of Holyrood Palace, have been given Special Dispensation by the Town Council to remain there, pending the imminent deaths of their King and Queen, Nathan and Madeleine Sheridan. It is understood that they are fatally ill, and cannot survive the week.

Rose pulled the bell-pull beside her bed. 'I must get up,' she said when her maid arrived.

'Yes, Miss Rose. You are feeling better?'

'I do not feel anything at all, Ellie. But that does not matter. It is how I look that counts now. Please do your best to help me to appear as normal as possible. Mistress Scott has eyes like a hawk's.'

'Then we will start with cold-water compresses on your eyes. Mr Cameron has gone?'

'He has gone to fetch back the Deacon, Ellie. And that may take a very long time.'

Mistress Scott did not come alone. Her son Walter was at her side during the next difficult and emotional half-hour, while she sometimes sobbed at the dreadful fiasco of Rose's first position as a companion—due entirely, she assured them, to her own blinkered misjudgment of the Deacon's character—and was sometimes patted on the hand by Master Walter, and sometimes snatched her hand away to rail against the entirely disgraceful laxity of morals nowadays in Edinburgh.

'If we cannot trust our very own councillors in this City, who *can* we trust?' she demanded tearfully.

'Now then, Mama,' Walter murmured soothingly.

'Shall we have tea?' Alison asked, pulling the bell-rope calmly in an interlude, as Rose had absolutely depended on her to do.

Mistress Scott dabbed at her eyes once again and sat up straight, more familiar with the little formalities of the drawing-room than how to deal with the wickedness of the world.

'Oh, that would be very pleasant,' she said. 'Most welcome, my dear Alison.'

'We will put all that behind us now,' Alison said, pouring balm on wounded feelings at the same time as she poured out the tea, and taking charge of the situation at the same time as she took charge of the tea-things, dismissing the maids with a drop of her eyelids. 'Now that all the burglaries are over, and Rose is safely here with us, it is the weather that remains as ever our most important concern, does it not?'

'Oh, my dear, it affects so many things!' Mistress Scott turned gratefully to Alison. 'Not least our menus. It is

simply impossible to get fish! And my menfolk are so
very fond of fish!'

'Walter,' Rose whispered urgently, now that Alison was
keeping Mistress Scott engrossed on the other side of the
fireplace with a new recipe to try, 'do you read the *Courant*?'

'Every word.'

'Did you read about the gipsies at Holyrood?'

'I did.'

'They are the ones I used to know. I must go to see
them, immediately. How shall I manage it?'

'Indeed, Mistress Scott,' she said aloud, 'my Aunt Bea
always used to say so. As soon as fish became impossible
to buy, the price of meat just soared. It is always the
same in the winter.'

'My last lecture is supposed to finish at ten o'clock
tonight,' Walter Scott hissed in her ear. 'I shall skip it.
But Mama places the coach at my disposal to come and
to go. Can you be ready at eight?'

By a happy coincidence, Alison had arranged the evening meal for the earlier hour of seven o'clock.

'There is no point in delaying it,' she said. 'We shall be
alone, anyway. And it will give the servants an earlier
night to themselves.'

But all the candles were lit, as usual. The servants
attended, and were immediately dismissed with every
course.

'I shall ring when we are ready,' Alison told them.

'And Miss Cornelia?' Rose ventured, over the cream
of chicken soup.

'Oh, I do not expect her at all this evening. Cameron
was very angry with her last night, and let her know it
after we went upstairs. No, her time here will become
less and less as the wedding day approaches.'

Rose stared at her, puzzled. 'But she will be married
from here, you say?'

'Of course. I owe her that much, at least, since she was

good enough to come to me at my time of need. Yes, I shall see her through her marriage. My aunt, a very distant aunt I am thankful to say, is quite a silly woman, and could not be trusted with it, Cameron says. I could have wished that he was at my side, all the same,' Alison sighed.

Rose was mystified. 'But he will come back in time?'

'I hope so. I hope so, indeed.'

'When is it to be?' Rose asked, her head down, and dreading the answer.

'On Wednesday, the twenty-fifth of May.'

Another nine or ten weeks of this agony, then, Rose thought.

'It will all pass by, as everything does,' Alison said. 'It is Cameron who is my first concern, my greatest worry. Where might he be tonight?'

Where indeed, Rose wondered. And of whom was he thinking? 'Miss Cornelia will make a brilliant bride,' she said flatly.

'Between us, Rose—for I am hoping you will help me—she will be the most beautiful bride Edinburgh has ever seen.'

A gigantic knife twisted in Rose's heart. For a moment the breath was knocked out of her. 'Yes, I will help you, Alison,' she said quietly, when she got it back. 'Only tell me what to do.'

'I do not think she has thought of what to wear, for one thing,' Alison said worriedly. 'She is spending all her time either playing golf if the weather allows it, or in that wretched castle.'

'Castle?'

'Oh, it is only a small castle somewhere out by North Berwick. She has lost her wits about it. She hoped for a title, but a castle will do. And Alexander Laing has plenty of money. Yes, I certainly hope Cameron gets back in time.'

'But how can they have the wedding without him?'

'Quite easily, my dear. There are many of our friends who are ready and waiting to step into Cameron's shoes, you know. Jamie Brown, for one. Simon Johnstone for another. There is always someone ready to be the best man at a wedding.'

'Oh . . . Then Cameron is not to be the groom?'

'The bridegroom?' Alison laughed. 'Whatever gave you that idea? Never!'

'Miss Cornelia gave me the idea.'

'She can be quite wicked at times. No, Rose, that was only wishful thinking. I believe she did hope for a long time that Cameron would pay his attentions to her. But he does not like her, I'm afraid.'

'Then who is the bridegroom?' Rose asked, her heart bursting with happiness.

'Alexander Laing. The gentleman with all the money . . . You must have seen him with her at the Caledonian Hunt Ball. I am prejudiced, of course, but I do not think him so handsome as my brother.'

'Oh, indeed he is not! He is not nearly so handsome. Cameron is the most handsome man I have ever seen in my life! Oh, Alison, suddenly I feel quite radiant!'

'You certainly look as though a great cloud had lifted from your shoulders,' Alison smiled. 'But you must be careful. I think you will have an early night again tonight, so that you are fully restored tomorrow. I think I shall retire early myself. It has been a long day, and Mistress Scott made it seem a great deal longer.'

By eight o'clock the house was quiet; the distant noises of the kitchen had died down long ago.

'It is all right, Ellie,' Rose told her maid. 'I am quite well again, and I shall get ready for bed myself. What will you do all evening?'

'Don't worry about me, Miss Rose,' Ellie said with a mischievous smile. 'John Robertson is waiting for me. We are going out for a walk.'

Then that was Ellie safely disposed of! Rose waited only long enough to hear her footsteps on the wide stone staircase, and then dying away below stairs, before she flung on her dark cloak and tiptoed down to the front door. It was dark, now that the maid had taken the candle with her, but she saw that the key was still in the door. Rose turned it effortlessly and noiselessly. It would, she thought with a frown. Deacon Brodie had seen to that when he fitted the locks to the house.

Once outside, she turned the key in the lock again and put it in her pocket. A coach waited on the corner, and Rose took to her heels and ran towards it. The door opened and Walter Scott jumped out.

'Let me help you up, Rose,' he said. 'Now then, Fergie, on to Holyrood!'

He climbed in himself and as soon as he slammed the door behind him, the coach moved off briskly. Rose hoped earnestly that no one had noticed them. She had not wanted to deceive Alison, but she was afraid that she would not have approved of this little expedition at all.

Walter Scott, on the other hand, was delighted. There seemed only one tiny cloud to mar his heaven.

'It is many years since the Sheridans saw you, Rose?'

'Ten, nearly eleven years now.'

'And you are sure that they will recognise you again, after all this time?'

'You must not worry, Walter. I shall recognise *them*,' Rose said confidently.

Walter Scott's slight frown disappeared, and his sunny grin returned. 'That's all right, then.'

The coach was making a fair speed over the North Bridge, and the driver pulled the reins to the left to turn the horses down into the High Street. It looked cold and grey to Rose when she looked out of the windows. The icy grip of an Edinburgh winter was slowly yielding to a chilly, sulky Edinburgh spring, and the road winding round the walls of Holyrood Palace was a sea of mud.

The coach ground to a halt at the far end, where the road vanished altogether, and Rose and Walter descended. They were in the rough grass on the lower slopes of the Salisbury Crags. The fires of the gipsy camp smouldered and smoked in its shadow.

Rose recognised the site as one Granfer Nathan would have chosen. He always liked to be encamped at the foot of a hill or a mountain. He used to say that when the wind blew, it blew off the mountain and clean over the camp. Granfer Nathan was very clever. He had been a good King.

Rose thought these thoughts, and old memories stirred as she and Walter ploughed on over the rough wet grass. The gipsies had seen them coming. The dogs had warned them. Some of the men had come out of the caravans and were advancing towards them. Their leader was tall and black-haired, gross with fat and ugly with menace.

Rose felt her confidence slipping a little. This was not the way she remembered the tribe. When she had lived with them they were a friendly people, more likely to extend a helping hand than a threatening warning-off like this. In the dim light she looked more closely at the leader. It could not be Leon, the magnificent Leon! But it was, gone to seed.

'Uncle Leon!' Rose called. 'I have come to see Granfer Nathan and Grandmam Maddy. And she will know it if you try to stop her Rosie.'

Leon stopped in his tracks uncertainly, his men behind him, and Rose took Walter's hand and led him forward.

'This is a friend,' she said. 'His name is Walter Scott. He has helped me to get here. I saw the news in the Edinburgh newspapers.'

'You had better come on, then,' Leon said grudgingly. 'But you will not be staying long. The old two will sleep soon, and perhaps in the morning they will not wake up.'

He sounded as if he wished the deaths of his father and mother, Rose thought indignantly, as they moved in a group towards the caravans. She clutched Walter's hand tightly, her courage almost deserting her altogether as the gipsies closed in round them. Except for Leon, there was none of them she recognised from the past. These men must have come in from another tribe, and they were no assets.

They reached the steps of the royal *vardo* at last, lack-lustre now after the long, hard winter and badly in need of its spring painting. The top half of the door opened, and a woman's head appeared.

'Albina!' Rose cried in relief. 'It is Rosie!'

A broad smile lit up the tired features of Albina, lined and middle-aged now, but still pleasant, still jolly.

'How did you know, Rosie?' she asked. 'They have asked for you so many times in the last few weeks. It is as if they have something important to say to you. And who is this?'

'My friend, Walter Scott.'

'He can sit on the steps,' Albina said, opening the bottom half of the door, 'but you must come in. They are very low, Rosie. Only hanging on.'

But Leon was not finished yet. He did not intend that he should be ignored like this, and he swaggered up the steps of the *vardo*.

'I shall decide whether she can see them or not. I am the King now, anyway.'

'That you are not,' Albina said, a brush in her hand. She waved it threateningly at Leon. 'Be off with you! You have not cared whether they lived or died all this long time. All you have waited for are the pickings, you and that bunch of *gorgio* desperadoes. You are not the King yet, Leon Sheridan, and it will be a sad day for our tribe when you are!'

To their surprise, Leon retreated. But Albina was a strong woman, more than capable of tackling the

shambling figure that once had been so virile and so
powerful. She stood back and waved Rose inside, and
then stood guard beside Walter.

Rose took one look at the two old gipsies lying in the
grand and spotlessly white double bunk at the far end of
the *vardo*, and knew at once with a sinking heart that the
newspapers had reported the truth. They were so pale,
so grey, and they had shrivelled away to the ghosts of the
King and Queen she remembered.

Nathan, she thought, was the one closest to death. His
eyes were closed and his breathing hardly discernible.
Maddy's eyes were open; they seemed almost to smile as
she tried to speak.

'It is you, Rosie, at last? I knew you would come to say
goodbye. A good girl, a good girl.' Her voice sighed
away.

Rose crouched at the side of the low, wide bunk.
Grandmam Maddy's voice was now only a thread. 'How
is Granfer Nathan?' she asked.

'He is nearly there. Just waiting . . . for me. He will
not cross alone.'

'Oh, Grandmam Maddy,' Rose said, the tears spilling
down her cheeks, 'I could not remember the name of
Sheridan. Perhaps I never knew it. And there was no
one there to help me who knew.'

'You were too young . . . your Mam ran away with
you . . . Leon did her wrong.' The old gipsy's eyes
suddenly flashed fire. She was very angry. 'Nathan!
Nathan!' Her voice rose, thin and reedy. 'It is time!'
she said, and he nodded imperceptibly. 'Albina, fetch
Benny.'

Albina left the *vardo* without a word, tears streaming
down her face.

'Nathan will choose,' Maddy whispered. 'He is the
King. It is his right.'

Then she closed her eyes and lay so still that Rose
thought the effort of speaking had been too great, and

the end had come. She sat still and waited, holding on to Maddy's hand. It was so thin, almost skeletal, but still it felt warm, with the pulse beating feebly.

'Your Mam,' Maddy whispered again. 'Caro—Caroline. Caro to us . . . Was there a child?'

'Yes,' Rose said sadly. 'He did not survive, and Mama died giving him birth. I was brought up by the nurse who attended them, in Newhaven. But she never knew our names. Mama was too ill to tell her. So she called me Rose. Rose Barbour, because I said my name was Rosie. But what is my real name, Grandmam Maddy? Do you know?'

'Rose de Brus,' the old woman struggled to get out. 'Your Mam's name was Caroline de Brus.'

There was no time to do more than store it in her memory. Benjamin Sheridan came in behind his wife Albina.

'Oh, Uncle Benny!' Rose sobbed, and flung herself into his arms. 'I am so sorry!'

'We must lift my father out on to the step,' he said. 'He must make his Will known before all the tribe. That is our law. I have gathered them all outside.'

'Mr Scott will help us,' Albina said. 'He is Rosie's friend.'

And so they lifted the old man as easily as if he had been a bit of paper, and wrapped him in a blanket, and stood him up between them at the door of the *vardo*.

Surprisingly, his eyes were open when he spoke in a loud, clear voice. Rose wondered if he had been saving the last of his life's energy just for this moment. She noticed that Leon and his cronies stood apart from the rest of the tribe with their wives and children. She did not recognise any of them either, except Katina, no longer the beautiful woman Leon had betrayed her Mama with.

'Leon was the prince,' old Nathan said. 'But he will never be the King of the Sheridans. He knows why. We all know why. He broke our laws ten years ago. Now he will go, and take his people with him. My second son, Benjamin, will be your King, and very soon now. I have spoken. It is the gipsy law.'

Leon looked first stunned, then belligerent, and then very dangerous. He took a step forward.

'You will stop there,' Walter Scott said in his educated, authoritive Edinburgh accent. 'You have been given Special Dispensation ever to be here at all, remember. You are within the City limits of Edinburgh, the capital seat of Scotland, and subject to its laws first, and your own laws second.'

Rose could not believe her ears. Her respect for Walter Scott rose to a new pitch at that moment that was never to be lowered all the rest of her life.

'Nathan Sheridan, King of this tribe of Sheridan, has spoken. It is accepted by you all?' his voice rang out over the silent people.

'Yes!' rose the shout from the tribe.

'You heard him say that Leon Sheridan must go?'

'Yes!' rose the shout again.

'I am a representative of the law,' Walter said coolly. 'I shall write out the Will of Nathan Sheridan. You shall all be the witnesses. Rose, fetch me paper and ink.'

Grandmam Maddy's eyes were shining when Rose pulled down the tiny locker and took out paper, a quill and the inkstand. There was everything in the royal *vardo*. She could die proud. Walter wrote rapidly and briefly, held Nathan's hand while he made his cross, and then handed the paper to two elders of the tribe at the foot of the steps.

'Make your marks here, and here,' he instructed. 'Now it is law!' he shouted. 'The Sheriff's men will be called, if necessary. You are evicted, Leon Sheridan, and I will see to it that you will not be back in this City again.'

They all watched while Leon and his people went back

to three of the caravans, harnessed their horses and eventually rumbled away. Then Nathan was laid back down in the bunk again, to his eternal rest this time. They all knew it, and none better than the King himself. He took his wife's hand and then closed his eyes. He looked at peace.

'Rosie,' Queen Madeleine said, 'look in the locker again. There is a paper there, all folded up. Your mother left it behind, and I have looked after it all this time. It belongs to you.' They all looked at her in amazement. She, too, had got that last burst of earthly energy. 'And now it is all over and done with'—she smiled round at their faces—'all the love, and all the travelling, and I have reached the River at Nathan's side. We are ready to cross over. Leave us now,' she waved her hand. 'Leave me with my husband. We want to go together, and alone.'

'Goodbye,' Rose kissed each of the old gipsies in turn, and left the *vardo* with Walter. Benny and Albina were the last to take their leave.

It was a sad farewell all round, as they walked back afterwards to the waiting coach, Walter still with the rolled-up Will in his hand.

'I shall see that this is properly legal in the morning,' he said, shaking Benny's hand, and then Albina's. 'I have never made out a Will before.'

Rose climbed into the coach again, weeping. She had found out that she was Rose de Brus, daughter of Caroline de Brus. But what good had it really done her to find it out at last? Her dear old friends were dying. And Cameron was gone, it seemed for ever. The past stretched out behind her, the future before her, just as much an enigma as ever.

It was not until some days later, when she read in the *Courant* of the deaths within an hour of each other of Nathan and Madeleine Sheridan, that Rose remembered the folded-up paper she had thrust into the pocket of her cloak.

There had been too much to absorb, the pinning-down of Cornelia to make some decisions about her wedding, all the preparations to set in motion, and the bride's total lack of interest in the whole affair.

'I do not understand her,' Alison sighed.

Rose tried to imagine how she would feel herself if she were only weeks away from marrying the man of her dreams—if she were marrying Cameron Kyle,

'Neither do I,' she said sadly.

But now she drew the paper out of her cloak and spread it out on the little table in her room. The left side of the paper was perfectly square and trimmed, as would be the page of a book. But the right side was jagged. It had not even been folded and torn neatly, but done in a hurry, carelessly. Rose read it and could make no sense of it. Nobody could.

I,
James's Court and now of This
of much sounder mind than any I s
the follies and pitfalls of
death, and the expediency
of my estates, do therefore he
Testament, all my other lan
divided in gifts between my gran
grand-daughter, his sister A
son and heir Gregor Sco

the house and the lands, t
with his right to the hered
one condition.

T
thus: that in Paris,
to my marriage with Sir John

extra-marital union between me
Pascal was born to me, and name
Pascal. The aforesaid child hersel
to Henri de Brus in January 1766,
to the best of my knowledge an

And
out that child, and with her
the house, lands and estate
Sig

Quite clearly it was a legal document of some kind,
perhaps one-half of a Will. The word 'Testament'
suggested it. 'Paris' and 'Caroline' made her suspect that
it had been sent to her mother somehow, delivered by
hand perhaps, or sent by post, almost as hazardous an
affair. Had her mother known how the whole document
read? She could not have known, Rose decided. And
yet, had she been on her way to Edinburgh all along, to
James's Court in particular, and Leon had only delayed
her another eighteen months longer?

The more she thought about it, and puzzled over it,
the more convinced Rose became that this might be
the answer. Mama must have known someone in
Edinburgh, and known them well enough to be sure of a
welcome. But then, she had been so weak, especially
where men were concerned. One look from Leon, and
she had deserted her child for his caravan.

She could decipher no more herself, guess no more,
and besides she knew very little of legal terminology.
But at least she knew someone who did, or who would
some day. And she had seen Walter Scott so many times
at Mr Creech's bookshop at the Meridian.

She summoned the first sedan chair she saw at the
corner, and within a quarter of an hour was at the Tron.
Walter Scott was in his accustomed position, among the
men of letters, the 'literati'. It took her some time to
attract his attention.

'What is it, Rose?'

'It is the folded-up paper I got from Grandmam Maddy. Here it is. I cannot make head nor tail of it.'

Walter opened it out and frowned as he studied it. 'Neither can I, at first glance. It seems to be part of a Will. Where is the other half?'

Rose shook her head. 'That is all there was.'

'Leave it with me, Rose, and I will see what I can find out. But you must not expect an answer soon. I could take it to my father first, and then all the rounds, if he cannot help.'

Rose had a sudden inspiration. It was something which had lain in the back of her mind for a long time. How had Lord Braxfield known the terms of the Will that was worrying Cameron to distraction? Not that it meant he would know anything about this other Will, or the part of it in her possession now . . .

'Try Lord Braxfield first,' she said.

'Lord Braxfield? Do you know what you are asking, Rose? It would be a miracle if the great man ever consented to give me five minutes of his time, least of all when he is likely to leave any day, if he has not already gone on the spring circuit. Even now his coach may be lumbering along the road to Stirling, or through the hills to Inverary, or he may even have arrived in Glasgow. And he will not return until June, at least.'

'Please try, Walter? I cannot wait so long!'

They were in the throes of the interminable jaunts to the Luckenbooths and the shops of the Royal Mile choosing materials for the wedding gown, and trying to unravel the arguments of the bridesmaids in the selection of theirs, when Walter Scott eventually came back to see Rose.

'I managed to catch Lord Braxfield,' he said. 'He was on his way out of Edinburgh. But he took the paper. He said it reminded him of something, and he would try to remember what it is by the time he gets back.'

'But that will not be until June at least!'

'Better late than never, Rose. And he told me to tell you that he would not be doing it at all, if it wasn't for the sake of a bonnie wee lassie who also reminded him of someone long ago.'

With that she had to be content. She was struggling to conceal her impatience, when the news came to Edinburgh that Mr George Williamson had come back empty-handed, except for a letter for his escort's sister, Miss Alison Kyle.

Alison opened it with hands that trembled, and her face fell.

'It is from Cameron,' she told Rose despondently. 'They have not found Deacon Brodie, and so Mr Williamson has returned, pending future news of him. Cameron says he has seized this opportunity to go to France, to look once more for the missing heir, without whom he cannot inherit his beloved estate.'

'Oh, no, Alison!' Rose said in despair.

'Somehow we must get through this wedding without him, Rose!' Alison dissolved into tears of disappointment. 'I did not believe this would happen, right up to the last minute. But at least, thank God, he is safe.'

'Yes. Thank God for that,' Rose said grimly, and quietly took over where Alison did not have the strength to continue.

CHAPTER
TEN

QUEEN STREET Gardens were green with high summer, the pinks and the mauves of the rhododendron petals long since withered upon the grass, and blown away like dust in the soft breezes. Now the geraniums had taken over pride of place, masses of scarlet in their neat, round beds, and everywhere the roses sprawled in gay profusion.

The heat was stifling, even although the maids had kept the blinds down all day and the doors ajar upon their stoppers. Up in Rose's room it felt a little cooler, but the light was still strong and disturbing at ten o'clock that night. Her thoughts were even more restless than the atmosphere.

Where was he? After four long months of sheer endurance waiting for him, where was Cameron Kyle? With every day that passed, Rose had grown thinner and more tense, and her eyes were dark and unhappy as she faced her maid.

'I am not going to bed, Ellie. You may fetch me the chair-men, instead.'

'You are not going out, Miss Rose? At this time of night?'

'Yes. And alone, Ellie.'

'Very well, Miss Rose . . . Will you be going far?'

'Three or four miles, perhaps.'

'So far?' Ellie's eyes widened in alarm. 'Will you not let me go with you?'

'No. This I must do alone.'

'Then I must call the very best chair-men, Ned Burke and his partner, if I can get them.'

'When I am gone, you will stand guard, Ellie? All

night, if need be? It is important business I am going about. If Miss Alison calls or asks, I am a little off colour. There is no use in alarming her. Do you understand?'

'Och, I understand, Miss Rose,' Ellie said on her way out, 'and of course I will see to it. But I cannot pretend to like it.'

Rose scrabbled in the bottom of her reticule, but all that was there was the key still on its ribbon for the writing-desk in Deacon Brodie's house. In the pocket of her cloak, the one she had left Newhaven wearing all that time ago, were still the coins Aunt Bea had insisted upon.

'Where to?' the tall, old Highlander asked when Ellie had gone back inside, and she was settled upon the seat of the sedan chair.

'To the Thistle Courts,' she answered, gazing at Ned Burke almost in awe. Everybody in Edinburgh knew about Edward Burke, the bravest Highlander of them all, who might have gained thirty thousand pounds by a word from his mouth about the Prince, but who had returned quietly to his duty as a chair-man on the streets of Edinburgh rather than betray him, after Culloden.

'It will take an hour at least,' he said in perfect English with a lilting Highland accent, his proud black eyes upon her face.

Once, Rose would have been intimidated. But not now.

'However long it takes, however much it costs, Mr Burke,' she said, offering him all the money she had in the world.

'Not yet,' he said proudly, and shut the door.

Rose did not draw the little curtains when she felt the sedan chair lift, and its curious swaying motion begin. She left them open and watched as the street lamps flashed by. Soon there were no more lights or even streets, and the soft dim of the summer night bore in upon her, sad and melancholy with long memories and infinite regrets.

Out here, in this strange little moving world of her own, alone with her own thoughts, Rose looked back over the tapestry of all the threads that had been woven in to the last two months of her life at the Queen Street house. There had been the wedding of Miss Cornelia Forbes and Mr Alexander Laing, its brief flame and its almost unbearable anticlimax, when she and Alison had sat down to dinner that same evening.

'It all fell flat, somehow,' Alison said sadly. 'She was so beautiful, it all went so smoothly. and yet there was something wrong.'

'We all went home immediately afterwards. That was what was wrong. There was no celebration,' Rose said. 'Nothing for the guests to let off the steam of their emotions. There should have been music and dancing.'

'Of course! You are right. And feasting. Cornelia did not consider the guests who had come from far and wide. Let it be a lesson to us for our own weddings, when they come . . . Still, I suppose we should be thankful that she ever turned up at all, and without a golf stick in her hand.'

Rose gazed out of the little windows of the sedan chair at the soft dreaming countryside and wondered how they had lived through it all, and the worry that they had had over that wedding.

But hard on the heels of the wedding had come Mr Henry Raeburn to paint her portrait. All the mornings in June had been taken up with the sittings.

'It is Cameron's idea,' Alison told her. 'And he left instructions that you must wear your red gown.'

'Ah,' said Henry Raeburn. 'A red, red Rose! Then we have found the theme, already. We shall have you surrounded with roses, pastel pinks and creams, with the one red rose glowing in the middle.'

'I do not feel that I am glowing,' Rose sighed.

'No woman does, if she is in love, and separated from

the man in question,' the young artist smiled, his eyes on his canvas, and the charcoal in his hand to make his first rough outlines. 'He has gone away?'

'What makes you think so, Mr Raeburn?'

'Henry, please. We shall be closeted here together for an hour at least every morning, so let us drop the formalities straight away . . . I think so, because he would not have asked me to paint your portrait otherwise. And you seem so sad.'

'Yes.'

'He will not be gone for ever, Rose. He has his business to attend to.'

'I have always meant to ask about that. What *is* his business?'

'Why, Cameron Kyle is one of the Improvers,' Henry Raeburn was sketching swiftly. 'One of the gentlemen who own large estates and lands, who seek to improve the lot of those who live on them by introducing new methods of farming and small industries to keep them employed.'

'Oh, so that is why he is away from home so much! Alison has often complained about it.'

'The more you talk about him, the more you are glowing. We shall talk of nothing else each time I come.'

'Then you will be very bored,' Rose laughed. She liked Mr Raeburn, with his shrewd eyes and his gentle ways.

'Oh, but then you see, I know what it is like. I am in love, too. With my beloved Ann, my dearest wife.'

'And would you not rather speak of her?'

'But it is your expression we want on this canvas,' Henry Raeburn said, 'not mine. Besides, it will be no hardship. I admire Cameron. He is a good man, and a friend of mine.'

And so June was passing, more pleasantly for this diversion in the mornings, and in the afternoons Alison turned her attention to her new house in Charlotte

Square. She took Rose with her to inspect its progress.

'Oh, I have never seen anything so elegant!' Rose exclaimed. 'The Brodies were right when they said there would not be a finer square of houses in all Britain.'

'We must concentrate on the furnishing of it,' Alison said. 'I would like to have some of it ready when the house is finished: the drawing-room, the dining-room and at least two bedrooms, to begin with.'

It had all been an education, for Rose. Alison had remained calm and gentle, but obstinate when shown anything other than what she had set her heart on. No, the green would not do, not even the sea-green, which the furnishing men were trying hard to sell her. It must be blue, and a particular shade of blue, at that. It must be a grey-blue, and the tapestry must be of silk. She would wait, but only a reasonable length of time.

'I think I must speak to Mr James Leslie,' Alison said despairingly to Rose. 'I believe he would know what I am driving at. I wonder if he is still in Town?'

And so Mr Leslie had come to Alison's rescue, bringing news with him of Miss Jean.

'How is she?' Rose asked anxiously.

'She is very upset, of course. And she will not be better until this wretched affair is over, one way or the other. You have heard no further news?'

'They have not found Deacon Brodie,' Alison said.

'Jean is weathering the storm, but only because I have filled her mind with happier things,' Mr Leslie admitted with his shy smile. 'I have decided to go to Glasgow in September and set up on my own in business. She has done me the honour to accept my hand in marriage, and go with me.'

'Oh, that is wonderful!' Rose cried.

'But, you will understand, the wedding will be very small and private, under these sad circumstances. Perhaps the fewer people who know about it the better.'

And so they reached the last few days of June, and Mr Henry Raeburn had gone away, the portrait finished. It had been a busy month all round that year, in Edinburgh. The Town Council had leased the cleansing of the streets to a private contractor for £500 a year, and so now every morning except Sundays, of course, the dreadful smells were washed away before the people got up.

The alarm that had been caused when Smith and Ainslie nearly escaped from the Tolbooth prison through its roof had died down, and with it the renewed speculation about the vanished Deacon.

The General Assembly had come and gone, filling the town with the ministers of the Church of Scotland from far and wide. Every year it was conducted with the utmost ceremony and splash. This year there had been more pomp than ever.

And on the fourth it had been the King's Birthday, an occasion well marked in this most royal of Scottish burghs. The street wells and the lamp brackets were adorned with flowers, but none so colourful as the garlands which adorned the statue of King George in Parliament Close. It had been a holiday. The guns had fired a royal salute from the Castle walls, and at night there had been fireworks.

But even more important than any or all of that, in June the word came to Edinburgh of Deacon Brodie's whereabouts. The city was all agog, rife with rumours.

It had made Rose's heart leap up in a great surge of excitement. It meant that Cameron would also know where he was. He was only waiting over there for Mr George Williamson, the King's Messenger, to arrive again, and then they would all come back to Edinburgh together. It gave her the sparkle Henry Raeburn had nearly despaired of ever seeing, and he had finished the portrait in record time.

'How did they find the Deacon?' she asked Alison.

'You will never believe it, my dear. He sent letters home from Amsterdam, three of them, and they were intercepted.'

'How could he have been so silly and so rash?'

'One to his brother-in-law, Matthew Sheriffs, asking him to look after a lady called Mistress Ann Grant, and her children. One to a Mr Michael Henderson who has stables in the Grassmarket, all about his fighting-cocks, and boasting of his getaway. And a third, also to Mr Henderson, but this time in a more prudent vein. It is all in the *Courant*, dear.'

Then July had come in, hot and wearying, and as one day of waiting followed another, so Rose's excitement had ebbed away cruelly. In vain she searched the news-sheets every day for news of Mr Williamson's imminent departure for the Continent. But it never came.

And then, only yesterday, on the fifteenth, Walter Scott had come back with Rose's paper.

'Lord Braxfield laughed,' he said.

'Laughed?' Rose was almost in tears. 'Why should he laugh?'

'He said it was all so simple, after all, and it is not the first time that he has seen a left hand not knowing what the right one is doing. He also said that Lady Susanna had been a lady after his own heart. She always enjoyed a good laugh.'

'I do not understand any of that, Walter.'

'Neither do I,' he confessed. 'But it does not matter. Lord Braxfield said one last thing. The clue lay in just four letters, "T-h-i-s". He says to try the Thistle Courts.'

'And what is that?'

'A big house, three or four miles to the south of Edinburgh.'

And still the chair-men were jogging along with the sedan chair. It had grown dusk, and now there were wreaths of mist along the hedgerows. And then, sud-

denly, full and startling in its appearance out of nowhere, the moon sailed magnificently into view. It lit
up the roadside, the bracken and the broom and
the tall feathery grasses, and swept the mist away
contemptuously.

The chair-men plunged on round a curve between two
iron gates. Past a lodge, the road opened wide to a long
drive beyond. They must be coming to the big house
now, Rose thought, her heart beating quickly.

At first the road ran straight, and then it began to
snake through an archway of trees. Even the moon in all
her brilliance could not penetrate the thickness of the
leaves above, and only little flickering patches of light
came in waves to dapple the path with silver. It was very
silent, with only the pad-pad of the chair-mens' feet to
break the curious stillness.

The silver path became an enchanted path, winding
like a ribbon into the heart of the forest, here and there
over little bridges, over streams, and on and on. Rose
wondered if it would ever end, and did not care if it never
did.

And then ahead she saw a clearing, a tiny patch of
luminous sky. The trees were thinning and the path
became a broader sweep as they turned the last corner of
all. There, drenched in moonlight, lay the Thistle
Courts, built in a hollow of lawns, a fairy castle.

The sedan chair stopped, and Ned Burke came round
to open the door for her.

'We are here,' he said. 'But there are no lights in the
house. It seems to be deserted.'

Rose looked up at the imposing door, tight shut,
above the wide steps. Two large boulders, one at either
side of the top step, had been chiselled out in the shape
of thistles.

'I must get in, nevertheless,' she said.

Ned Burke took a night-lantern from the back of the
sedan, lit it, and led the way.

'There will be a window broken somewhere,' he said. 'There always is.'

He helped her to climb in through the first one they came to, and then stood back. 'Do you wish me to come with you?' he asked.

'No. Thank you, Mr Burke, but I can manage alone.'

'Then you will take the lantern?'

'I shall not need the lantern, the moon is so bright.'

'We shall wait, then.'

Then once again Rose had that strange feeling that sometimes came to her, that she had been here before, although she knew that was impossible. She turned round and then stood still for a moment, and in that moment felt the old house open its arms to her in a rush of music. Yet no music played, and the silence continued. But it was a gentle silence, and she did not feel afraid as slowly she moved from one room to the next, remembering things she had never known, as though now at last, she had come home after years and years of absence.

It was in the east wing that she came upon the little jewel of a sitting-room, and knew instinctively that this was where the lady of the house had always spent her mornings, writing her letters at the writing-table, making up the meals for her cook, adding up the accounts for her husband's approval. It was a woman's room, furnished with great care.

She could imagine how the sun would warm it in the mornings, how it would look with vases of roses on the mantelpiece, and great bowls of them on the little tables by the sofa. She knew before she went to the window that the scent of roses was not a ghostly thing, it floated in from the bushes massed beneath and climbing all around, so that their heads nodded sleepily against the panes.

She could see it all in her mind's eye, and in reality the moon made it all spring to life as bright as day. Its moving rays slanted suddenly on the portrait above the mantelpiece, and Rose gazed up at it, startled for the first time since she had entered the fairy castle, frozen into a statue, at the face of her mother.

It *was* Mama! There was no doubt of that. Dressed in the style of nearly a hundred years ago, her beautiful hair in jewelled knots, with a little dog upon her lap. Perhaps she had dressed up like that for a fancy dress ball, Rose thought. There was mischief in her eyes, and they were darker and more animated than she remembered them.

'Mama,' she breathed.

'Lady Susanna Kyle, Rose,' said a deep voice behind her, and she whirled round, the moon full in her eyes, to see the ghost of Cameron Kyle. A queer mist grew all round him, and the music of the house changed to a buzzing sound in her ears.

She found herself lying on the sofa in the moonlit sitting-room. Someone's hand held a glass of water to her lips, Cameron's hand. She took a sip and lay back quite still, while the floor, the walls and Cameron's figure took solid shape before her.

'I thought you were a ghost,' she said.

'I am so sorry, Rose. I should not have startled you like that.'

'It wasn't that. I do not usually faint when I am startled. But I had just seen one ghost already.' Rose glanced up at the portrait. 'My mother's.'

'Perhaps it was a trick of the moonlight,' Cameron said gently, holding the glass to her lips again. 'You must not worry. Just lie still. It is not your mother, Rose. It is Lady Susanna Kyle.'

Rose looked again, and now little differences were there in the picture. The lady's eyes really were dark, and Mama's had been pale blue. Her expression was too lively for Mama's, bold and adventurous.

This lady was self-sufficient.

'My grandmother, the eccentric one in older age, that I told you about. The portrait was painted for my grandfather, Sir John, when they were married, and hung for many years in their house in James's Court.'

'Yes . . .' Rose said. 'I see it now. But at first glance the likeness was very striking.'

'And you are like your Mama, Rose? Perhaps that is what attracted me to you from the beginning.'

'Oh.'

Rose felt the colour rushing back to her cheeks again. All the time they had been so matter-of-factly discussing the picture, she had felt the dizziness and the sickness draining away. Now it came to her that perhaps she should not be lying here in this indecorous position, feeling as she did about Cameron Kyle, and least of all in a deserted house in the moonlight. She struggled to sit up.

Cameron put a restraining hand on her shoulder. She trembled violently at his touch.

'Oh, Cameron, is it really you? Have you really come back, at last?'

He put both arms round her comfortingly. 'Yes, it is really me, Rose. I have really come back. And I missed you every minute I was away. But you are not going to sit up yet. I am going to get some logs for a fire in here. It is a beautiful night, but after midnight there is always a chill. And I see you brought no cloak with you.'

He took off his coat and wrapped it round her.

'But I cannot lie here! The chair-men are waiting.'

'No, they are not. I paid them off before I came in. They will be half-way to Edinburgh by this time.'

Rose did not even try to comprehend the enormity and the strangeness of the situation, and when Cameron left the room she closed her eyes and breathed in the scent of him from his coat. Then it was all real, she had not imagined it all, and within minutes she slept the first dreamless sleep for many months.

The glow and the sparks from the burning logs woke her up later, and she saw that Cameron was back in the room again.

'How long have I been sleeping?' she asked him, wide awake now, and sitting up.

'Half an hour, perhaps. How do you feel, Rose?'

'Better. Oh, much better, now. Better than I have felt for such a long time.'

'I see that you are much thinner than when I left,' Cameron said accusingly. 'Have you not been eating? When did you eat anything last?'

Rose considered the matter. She had eaten very little that day, it was true. Just like every other day since he had gone. 'I cannot remember,' she said.

'I thought not. And so, I brought in my saddle-bags.'

He took something out of one of the bags, wrapped in a white cloth. As soon as he untied the knots a wonderful aroma wafted to Rose's nostrils, and suddenly she was ravenously hungry.

'What is it?'

'Chicken rosemary, according to the landlady of the last inn I spent the night in. She roasted it fresh, and baked this loaf to go with it.'

He tore off a wing, and handed it to her. 'How does it taste?'

'Wonderful. How did you know I was here?'

'I saw the sedan chair disappearing up the drive from the road, and followed it in.'

'Do you usually follow sedan chairs?'

'Only when they are on my property late at night. I left George Williamson and the others to carry on northwards to Edinburgh with Deacon Brodie.'

Rose watched him tossing one drumstick into the blazing fire and taking its fellow.

'You are going too fast for me. You are back with the Deacon?'

'Another crust of bread, Rose?' Cameron dived into the other saddle-bag and drew out a slim green bottle. 'Shall we wash it all down with some of this? I found some glasses. Yes, we brought him back. He is in chains.'

She tried to visualise the little dandy in his lace ruffles all marked black with the chains round his wrists, and with more chains round his absurd little ankles, and the tears sprang in her eyes.

'Oh, Cameron! What will happen to him now?'

'He will be put into the Tolbooth to await his trial,' he said calmly. 'You must not be upset, Rose.' He bent down to his saddle-bag again and pulled out a little black velvet bag which looked much the worse for wear and tear. 'Does this belong to you?'

'Oh, Cameron! Yes, it is my bag of sovereigns.'

'He had it with him in his trunk, and many other things he had stolen. A whole bag of sovereigns, Rose? How much money did it come to? Another glass of wine?'

'Perhaps I shall. A little. I don't know exactly how much money there was. It is an old, complicated story. But what if the Deacon is found guilty?'

'There is no chance that he can be found innocent. There is all the damning evidence, and the witnesses. He knows already that he will hang, and on the gallows he himself designed. He is amazingly cheerful about it.'

'Oh, poor Miss Jean!' Rose burst into tears. 'She will never be able to get married now!'

'Perhaps Mr Leslie will have something to say about that.'

Cameron took the glass gently out of Rose's hand and took her in his arms, raining soft little kisses all over her face.

'I am kissing away all those tears, Rose. It does not seem to me to be a time to cry, not with all this talk of weddings. It seems they are very much in the air. And how did Cornelia's go?'

'Oh, it was wonderful . . . No, it was horrible! It was not the sort of wedding I should ever hope to have.'

'Now that is very interesting. What sort of wedding would you have?'

'You are teasing me, Cameron Kyle. One with eating and drinking and music and dancing.'

'A wedding after my own heart, in fact. And when you make the arrangements, will you see that there is Chicken rosemary?'

Rose laughed and cried at the same time, choking a little when she replied, 'There is no use in thinking about it, Cameron, not for me. Everything about me is so mixed up.'

'Then you are in the same boat as I am. After four long weary months of searching, I am very little further forward in my quest for the missing heir.'

'Oh! You did not find your missing document either?'

'I found the most important document, also in his trunk, thank God for that. Although why he did not screw it up and throw it away, I shall never understand. It certainly does not look of any value, and neither it is, as it stands. Are you finished?'

Rose nodded, suddenly shy when he took the remains of their supper away and came back to sit beside her. He had opened one of the windows a little, and the scent of the roses was strong now, in the little sitting-room. She trembled when he took her hands in his. His face was so grave and sad, and she dreaded what he may say next.

'All this,' he said, 'might have been for ever, darling Rose. The moonlight suppers, the roses and the wine, this little room which I have always loved, in the house I never wanted to leave.'

She sat stunned . . . 'This house?' she said at last. 'This is the house you have waited for all this time?'

'Oh, Rose, I had made up my mind I could not ask you until the Thistle Courts was mine to offer you as your home. But now,' he crushed her to him, 'I can wait no longer to tell you how much I love you, and how much I have missed you. Will you marry me, wherever we live?'

'Oh, Cameron,' she said, a long time later, clinging to him. 'I love you too, so much.'

'Are you happy? I know you are happy! It is shining in your eyes. Then give me your answer.'

'How could I feel happier than this? It would not matter to me where we lived, as long as it was with you. But I cannot give you an answer. It would not be fair, until you hear the whole story I have tried so hard to keep from you and everyone else. But especially you. You may change your mind. And,' she sighed, 'it is a long story.'

'It is a long night. And I shall not change my mind, no matter what dreadful things you will tell me. Come and sit close to me, and remember that I love you.'

They sat on the sofa, their arms round each other, while Rose told him her story, starting with her earliest memories of France, and finishing with Lord Braxfield's directions. When she came to the end of it, there was a gleam in Cameron's eyes.

'So he laughed, did he, the old fox? He was more than just a friend of my grandmother's, I am sure of that. They had too many private jokes. And he was her lawyer. Is it not strange, Rose, that we are both sitting here worrying over a Will, even if it is not the same one? The one you have, with the jagged edges—do you have it with you?'

There was a suppressed excitement about him that made her hands tremble again.

'It is here in my reticule, for what it is worth.'

She took out the folded up paper and straightened it out. Cameron took it out of her hand slowly and stared at it incredulously for a long moment. And then he began to laugh. Peal after peal of laughter that echoed around the little room until it tickled Rose too, and together they sat on the sofa and laughed until they were sore.

'What are we laughing at?' Rose gasped, wiping her eyes.

'Oh, what a way to start a marriage!' Cameron laughed again. 'Hide your eyes until I tell you to open them again. I have something in my pocket which you will find as funny as Lord Braxfield and I do.'

'Are you ready?' she said, with her hands over her eyes.

'Nearly.' There was a sound of rustling paper. 'But you are not allowed to look until you give me my answer. I love you, Rose. I shall to my dying day. I want you to be my wife. Now, will you marry me?'

'After all that? You would marry a girl who had been brought up by the gipsies, a girl who has had no place in society, a girl who did not even know her name until so recently?'

'None of that makes any difference, my darling.'

'Then yes, I will marry you, Cameron.'

He kissed the hands over her eyes, and then her eyes, and then her mouth. 'Now you can look,' he said.

By the light of the moon she saw that he had laid her paper down on the carpet, and alongside it another, its jagged edges on the left side of the paper, and its right side as straight and ruled as the page of a book. Joined together like that, they were the two halves which made up the whole. She could not believe what she saw, and he touched the half on the right.

'Does it look familiar, Rose? This is my half. This is the important document I chased the Deacon for. It is as useless by itself as your half is. Together, it is a different matter. It is like you and me, two halves of a whole.'

'I am no use without you, Cameron. I found that out.'

'Do you realise what this means, Rose? Shall I join them together, and read it out to you? No wonder Lord Braxfield said the right hand did not know what the left

hand was doing. He meant that you were the left-hand
side of this page, and I was the right. And I am as useless
without you as you are without me, my darling.'

The light of the moon was fading a little. It was not so
bright as it had been when they came in to the Thistle
Courts. Cameron took the halves of the Will and went to
the window to catch its last rays, and then read it out
slowly to her.

       I, Lady Susanna Kyle, formerly of
James's Court and now of Thistle Courts, Edinburgh,
possessed of much sounder mind than any I see about me,
and considering the follies and pitfalls of this life and the
certainty of death, and the expediency of the disposal of
this, the last of my estates, do therefore hereby execute my
last Will and Testament, all my other lands having already
been equally divided in gifts between my grandson,
Cameron Kyle and my grand-daughter, his sister Alison
Kyle, their father and my son and heir Gregor Scott Kyle,
having predeceased me.

       I leave and bequeath Thistle Courts,
the house and the lands, to the aforesaid Cameron Kyle,
along with his right to the hereditary peerage and the title,
on one condition.

       The explanation of the condition
thus: that in Paris, in the year 1744, the year previous to my
marriage with Sir John Kyle, a daughter, the issue of an
extra-marital union between me and one Jean-Jacques
Christophe Pascal was born to me, and named Caroline
Susanna Jeanne Pascal. The aforesaid child herself married
in Paris, to Henri de Brus in January 1766, with one child
of that union to the best of my knowledge and belief,
surviving.

       And that Cameron Kyle should seek
out that child, and with her or him to be the joint inheritors
of the house, lands and estate of Thistle Courts.

       Signed,
              Lady Susanna Kyle,
              June 1st, 1785.

There was a long silence, and Rose did not laugh. 'Yes, I realise something, now. Caroline Susanna Jeanne Pascal was my mother, and she was born out of wedlock.'

How could Cameron inherit a peerage and this magnificent house, and marry the daughter of an illegitimate? Her dreams collapsed and crumbled at the mere idea.

Cameron put his arms round her and held her tight. 'I know what you are thinking. But it was not your Mama's fault. She was the innocent child. And, knowing my grandmother, she would be entirely unrepentant, I can tell you. Anyway, your mother grew up none the worse, and married well when she married your father. I got so far as to find that out, at least, in Paris. There were bits and pieces of your story that I already knew from your Aunt Bea, you see, and I worked out a lot of it with the help of Madame Buzonnière.'

'You saw Madame Buzonnière?'

'She was intrigued by your story, and by the fact that you thought you had lived in Paris. She made it her business, after she went back, to find out what she could. And when I went to see her, I paid her well for her information. She said that your parents had a fairytale wedding. Your Mama was very beautiful, and your father was tall and as fair-haired as she was, and very, very rich.'

'He was fair?'

'Very fair, it seemed. But there is a sad ending, darling Rose. Your Papa had an accident while out riding, and died. You could only have been a baby at the time, Rosalie de Brus.'

'Rosalie?'

'That is the name you were born with, apparently. Anyway, that is where the trail ended. Madame Buzonnière could find out no more, except for gossip for which there was no proof. Your Mama simply disappeared from society.'

'But not from Paris, Cameron. I was five or six years old anyway, before we left. And the man on the sofa under the rugs I told you about was very dark. He could not have been my Papa. What was the gossip?'

'That your mother took up with a rogue, a man who soon gambled away all her money, and then died of consumption.'

'I believe it. No wonder she was so sad when we left France! And then to have been so cruelly betrayed by Leon! My poor Mama . . .'

'Yes, the poor lady. But at least she did bring you to Edinburgh, Rose. No doubt she was heading for this house, and her own mother. This house of which you are now the joint owner, whether you marry me or not.'

'And you are Sir Cameron Kyle, whether you marry me or not,' she laughed into his eyes. 'So it is only the house you are marrying me for?'

'And you will be Lady Rose Kyle. So it is only the title you are marrying me for?'

'Of course!'

'I wonder if that is true, Rose? How can I find out?'

'I do not want to go the way of your grandmother, which I can see I will if we stay here much longer,' she said some time later, sitting up with great difficulty, and mustering together what dignity she still possessed.

Cameron roared with laughter. 'She was your grandmother, too, Rose.'

'Oh yes . . . So she was! And in any case, my name is Rosalie.'

'Not to me, it isn't. You will always be my beautiful Rose, to me. But I will bear Rosalie in mind. It would be a very pretty and a very suitable name for our first daughter.'

'Our *first* daughter? And what if it is a son?'

'We can have one of each, to begin with, then. After

that, you can choose. But we had better get married first, and we cannot do that in the Thistle Courts. We must go back to Edinburgh.'

'Yes. How did you get in?'

'By the same window you did. And that is how we shall have to get out. I shall send John Robertson out here later today to fix it. By that time I shall have the key to our own front door, at last. And, speaking of John Robertson, you will want Ellie to come out here, to be your maidservant?'

'Are they connected?'

'Not yet. But I suspect they soon will be.'

Rose thought of her maid, sleeping no doubt on the sofa inside the locked Rose Room. 'Yes, I can trust Ellie,' she said.

'And she does your hair so beautifully.'

'A little while ago, you said I must always have it hanging down my back like that.'

'Of course, in the privacy of our own bedchamber, for my eyes only, along with everything else.'

They paused again, inside the broken window, locked together, before he tore himself away.

'Wait inside here, on the window ledge, and I will lift you out, Rose.'

She watched as he swung his long legs easily over the bottom half of the window, and leaned his elbows on the wood to look back at her.

'And now, before I do, tell me why you sent me away for four long months with a flea in my ear? Why were you so angry? I only kissed you.'

'It was because Cornelia said you were going to marry her.'

'Marry *Cornelia*?' Cameron's laugh woke the birds sleeping in the eaves. They fluttered their wings and twittered noisily in protest. 'Not for all the houses and lands and titles in Scotland!'

'*And* I saw the way you looked at her playing golf. So I

believed her,' Rose said, as he swung her on to the gravel path.

'Where?' he asked in genuine astonishment.

'On Leith Links.'

'Was she there? I did not even see her. I was watching the golf. We could lay out a whole golf course here, Rose, do you realise that? It is a game I have been interested in for a long time. We could learn to play together.'

'Shall we?'

'We shall have a lot to learn together,' he said, in a way that made her melt again, and holding her close. 'I shall not be able to part with you, even for a few hours, not now.'

'But you will have to, Cameron, when you go to your other estates.'

'I have made up my mind to sell them. There is enough here to keep one man going for the rest of his life. And at last, I can breed my horses.'

They smiled at each other, aware of the secrets and the promise of the future at the Thistle Courts, with a new intensity of feeling that had grown stronger for their trial by fire and separation, and watched the branches of the trees stirring against the sky in the first faint breeze of dawn.

'Are you going to name the day?' he whispered.

'What is the date today?'

'The seventeenth of July.'

'On the seventeenth of August?'

'A whole month! But so be it. And seventeen shall be for evermore our lucky number. And now,' for they had arrived round at the front of the house, 'here is my wedding present to you, Rose. It is Rose Royale. You shall breed her, and become the owner of a whole succession of racing horses. Just imagine the fun Aunt Bea will have with that!'

Rose smiled at her future husband. He would never

change. He would always be there, strong and straight, proud and determined, persistent as his own emblem, the Scottish thistle.

'It will be the marriage of the thistle and the rose,' he whispered in her ear, for he had read her thoughts as he swung her up to sit before him.

'It might never have happened,' she said, with her hand on the horse's velvety ear when they surged forward, 'if it had not been for Rose Royale.'

The sun came up, throwing a handful of roses across the sky in a promise of another perfect summer day, and a new life together.

'No,' he laughed, holding her close. 'That is true. I must have been inspired the day I named this horse. But then, I have told you before, have I not, I am never wrong about a filly, on two legs or on four, my Rose of the Royal Mile? My Rose Royale.'

DISCOVER LASTING LOVE.

True love is everlasting.

Rather like our Nostalgia Collection.

This delightful set of books gives a fascinating insight into the romances of the 30's, 40's and 50's.

Each decade had its own popular writers and we've chosen 3 of our favourites to take you back in time in their own distinctive style.

We've even re-printed the original covers, to create a real collector's item for lovers of romantic fiction.

We think you'll find that times may change, but true love simply improves as years go by.

Available from April 1986.

Price £4.75.